Across the Narrow
Blue Line

Across the Narrow Blue Line

Faith Martin

ROBERT HALE · LONDON

© Faith Martin 2009
First published in Great Britain 2009

ISBN 978-0-7090-8841-7

Robert Hale Limited
Clerkenwell House
Clerkenwell Green
London EC1R 0HT

www.halebooks.com

2 4 6 8 10 9 7 5 3 1

Typeset in 11/14½pt Palatino
Printed in Great Britain by the MPG Books Group, Bodmin and King's Lynn

CHAPTER ONE

H illary Greene took a deep breath as she turned into the car
park of Kidlington's Thames Valley police headquarters. It
was a rather dull Monday morning at the beginning of October,
and it had been nearly two months since she'd last seen the
place. It did not feel good to be back.

It had been a hot day in August when someone with a rifle
had shot and killed her oldest friend, and her superior officer,
Superintendent Philip 'Mellow' Mallow. Right here, in this very
car park, and right in front of her and her team. They'd just
solved their latest murder case, and the mood had been one of
celebration. Doubly so, since Mel's third wife, her one-time
sergeant, Janine Tyler, had just informed her husband that she
was pregnant.

Now, Hillary parked her car, an ancient Volkswagen Golf,
beside a rather racy-looking Mazda, and climbed slowly out.
She wasn't officially due back to work until tomorrow morning,
but she wanted to say hello to everyone and cast a quick look
over her in-tray before once more going into battle.

A clock somewhere in town struck eleven o'clock as she used
her key-card to gain access into the foyer. As she'd expected, the
desk sergeant called her over the moment he spotted her.

'Inspector, good to see you,' he said, eyeing her carefully. Like
most desk sergeants seemed to be, he was middle aged, cheerful
and totally unshakable, but even so, Hillary sensed his wariness
as she approached. She didn't like it. She understood it, but

5

didn't like it, and the sooner she could dispel any ideas he had that she was made out of bone china, and was sure to break with the least little delicate tap, the better.

'Sarge,' she said amiably. 'What's new?'

The desk sergeant grinned widely. 'Now how would I know? Nobody tells me anything.'

Hillary laughed. It was a well-known fact that desk sergeants were the biggest gossips in the station house, and if you ever wanted to know the latest little dirty secret doing the rounds, you went straight to the front desk to find it out.

'Thought you weren't due in until tomorrow,' the desk sergeant said, leaning his elbows cosily on the desk and bending his back, to get into a more comfortable position.

'I'm not. You haven't seen me,' Hillary said flatly.

The desk sergeant nodded, then looked uncomfortable. 'We're all so sorry about Mellow, ma'am,' he said gruffly. 'Well, you know.'

Hillary did. The whole station house had been in shock at the time, and the fact that his killer had yet to be apprehended hadn't helped the healing process much. Two months later, things were still feeling raw.

'You hear anything from the London mob?' she asked casually. When Superintendent Mallow had been shot, a task force team had been set up, primarily consisting of Oxfordshire officers not assigned to Kidlington, and officers from the Met, headed up by a big shot named DCI Gawain Evans. She'd met him once, during his debriefing of her, nearly two months ago. London born and bred, despite the very Welsh name, she'd sensed both a keen intelligence and enough grit to get the job done. It had reassured her enough to trust him with the job in hand, but ever since then, she'd been out of the loop, surprising a lot of people by taking the compassionate leave she'd been offered.

'Not a bloody peep,' the desk sergeant said grimly. 'You ask me, they can't make up their minds whether it was Myers or a copycat sniper killer.'

6

Hillary sighed heavily. During her last murder case a nutter with a rifle had been busy in the country, shooting and killing police men and women with a single rifle bullet. Just before Mel was shot, a police officer in a nearby town had become the latest victim, but the sniper killer had been caught shortly afterwards. Ironically, everyone at Thames Valley HQ had heaved a sigh of relief, only to see one of their own gunned down barely forty-eight hours later.

Many thought that a man called Clive Myers was the culprit. An ex-army man, he'd seen the rapists of his daughter walk free from court due to a clerical error on the part of the police. His wife had subsequently committed suicide, and his daughter remained in a mental institution to this day. Mel, as nominal head of the investigation, had taken most of the flack.

But, as far as she knew, Clive Myers had been leading a blameless life ever since, and although his premises had been searched thoroughly, and his movements on the day of the shooting meticulously investigated, no charges had been forth-coming. And it didn't look likely that they would be, any time soon.

'Well, can't stand chatting all day,' Hillary said. 'I'd better go and see how my DS is getting on. Any gossip about how she's been doing since being left in charge?' She cocked an eye at him, but the older man grinned and shook his head.

'Nobody'd dare say anything against DS Fordham, ma'am,' he said drily. 'Too scared they'd be wearing their goolies for earrings.'

Hillary was still smiling grimly over that one as she climbed the stairs, and entered the huge, open-plan office on the second floor, where she and her team had their cluster of tables. She was aware of a slight stir rippling throughout the room as her presence was noted. Just inside the door a big man rose and smiled at her. DS Sam Waterstone held out a hand, and she quickly took it. 'Hillary, glad to see you back.'

'Thanks Sam.'

She didn't linger, and he didn't keep her, but it had broken the ice, as he'd intended, and several of her colleagues called out greetings and sympathetic murmurs as she passed. The whole station house knew she and Mel went back for ever, and that her loss, perhaps more than any other's (save for Janine Mallow's, of course) was almost certainly the greatest of them all. For Mel had been both a pal and her boss, a combination guaranteed to cover her back, should she ever have needed it.

And now that she had returned, she was feeling the cold draught of his absence more than ever.

When she halfway across the room she saw that her team was already on the move. At first she thought they were coming to greet her *en masse*, which made her feel distinctly wrong-footed. But as they got closer she realized that she'd mistaken the mood. The tall woman in the lead was wearing her trademark trouser suit, and her bony, striking face was set in stone. Her short blonde hair was as spiky and in-your-face as ever and, as she acknowledged her DI's presence, her eyes flickered with something that looked remarkably like chagrin.

'Guv,' Gemma Fordham said, with a curt nod. Behind her, DS Keith Barrington grinned with genuine happiness, his red hair brighter than she seemed to remember it. Last, as always, was DS Frank Ross, who nodded at her wordlessly and looked at her curiously. He was wearing a nearly clean white shirt and loose grey trousers. As ever, he smelled faintly of beer and cigarette smoke.

'Can't stop, Guv,' Gemma Fordham said, barely breaking stride, and Hillary's eyebrow rose. Keith shrugged meaningfully, and Frank Ross grinned wolfishly. Ever the troublemaker, he was no doubt hoping for fireworks, but Hillary merely nodded and moved a little to one side to let them pass.

Well, she'd hardly expected the welcome wagon and a brass band. For cops, work always came first.

Before she could carry on to her own desk, however, she saw the door to DCI Paul Danvers' cubicle open and he beckoned her in.

'Hillary.'

Paul Danvers, at thirty-eight, was a good seven years her junior, and always looked as if he'd just stepped out of a photograph for a mail order catalogue. His head of thick, perfectly barbered blond hair and expensive suits reminded her of an insurance salesman.

'Sir, I just thought I'd pop in to get a head start on the paperwork,' she said blandly, not wanting to have to stay and chat. The fact that Danvers had always fancied her, and hadn't yet seemed to give up on his very discreet pursuit of her, left her feeling both impatient and wary.

'Word's already got out that you're in the building, I'm afraid,' Danvers said, and Hillary cursed the desk sergeant's grapevine under her breath. 'The chief super wants to see you.'

Hillary sighed slightly and nodded.

Chief Superintendent Marcus Donleavy's office was situated on the next floor up. After knocking on the outer door and being greeted warmly by his secretary Hillary looked across as the door to the inner office opened and she was beckoned in.

Marcus Donleavy wore a silver-grey suit, which perfectly matched his silver-grey hair and silver-grey eyes. He'd always been a calm and crafty boss, and was well respected at HQ. He'd always rated Hillary's detective abilities highly, and his faith in her judgement had never wavered, even all those years ago when her soon-to-be ex-husband had been killed whilst being investigated for corruption.

'Hillary, sorry to nobble you like this. I expect you wanted to get a head start at the grindstone.' Marcus Donleavy smiled briefly as he stood aside to let her enter his office. 'I won't keep you long, but thought we might as well take this opportunity for you and your new super to get acquainted.'

Hillary felt her face tighten. She forced herself to smile slightly and nod. This, more than any other, had been the moment she dreaded. The moment she had to come face to face with the man who was replacing Mel.

Donleavy moved to his desk as a slim, brown-haired man rose to his feet. 'DI Greene, Superintendent Vane.'

Hillary forced her eyes across the few yards that separated them, to meet those of Brian Vane. He hadn't changed much since she'd last seen him, when he'd held the same rank that she held now. He still had the same flat brown eyes and beetling brows. And no doubt he still had the same relentless drive to succeed, as his current rank proved.

He smiled briefly. 'DI Greene.'

Donleavy glanced from one to the other, and in her peripheral vision she could see him begin to frown. 'I believe you two have met before?' he said cautiously.

'Yes sir,' Hillary agreed briskly. 'I was a newly made sergeant, assigned to DI Pullman's team.'

'Pullman and I used to work some cases together,' Brian Vane put in. 'Back in the days when we weren't so stretched for senior officers.'

Hillary nodded and looked blandly at Donleavy, who smiled but cursed silently under his breath. Nevertheless Hillary – who knew him well – could almost hear him doing it. She knew that Donleavy wanted to keep her happy, especially after the trauma of what had happened to Mel, and assigning someone as her new super whom she'd worked with before had probably seemed like a good idea.

Too bad he didn't know as much about Brian Vane as she did. Or perhaps, it was just as well. Depending on how you looked at it. But the truth was, when she'd been informed nearly a month ago just who had taken over Mel's job, she'd sat down and instantly written out her letter of resignation. At least she'd had the good sense not to post it off straight away, and a few sleepless nights thinking about it – and one or two stiff margaritas – had persuaded her to tear it up.

Now, face to face with the man again, and seeing the resentment hidden carefully behind his eyes, she was feeling strangely ambivalent.

Coming back had felt weird from the moment she'd stepped through the door. Her abortive meeting with her team had only served to make her feel even more unsettled. And now, here in Marcus Donleavy's office, she was in two minds about whether to stay or go. Just walk out of the door and never come back.

'Well, I won't keep you,' Donleavy said heavily. 'Hillary, I don't have to tell you, do I, how we all feel about Mel?'

Hillary shook her head. They'd all been through most of this at Mel's funeral. Like all funerals of a 'hero' cop, it had been a bit of a media circus, but afterwards all those in the know had met back at The Boatman, Hillary's local in the small village of Thrupp, where she lived on a canal narrowboat. There they'd toasted Mel, and reminisced, and talked themselves out until exhausted.

Now there was little more to be said, or done.

'If you need to speak to the grief counsellor at any time, DI Greene,' Superintendent Brian Vane said cordially, 'just take all the time you need.'

Hillary's lips twisted wryly, and she saw Marcus Donleavy shoot him a quick, surprised, and not very pleased look. 'Thank you sir,' Hillary said drily. *In his dreams* would she ever speak to the company shrink. She nodded blandly at Donleavy, whose own bland face hid his growing dismay, turned and silently left.

She walked slowly back to the main office. She supposed she should be feeling angry, or hard done by, or upset. But in fact, she felt very little at all. Good, bad, or indifferent, she'd done her grieving for Mel, and the nightmares that had plagued her for weeks after seeing his lifeless body hit the tarmac were now getting less and less frequent. It would take more than Brian Vane's sour, oily presence even to reach her, let alone affect her.

She wondered, uneasily whether this listless indifference was normal, or a bad sign, and then shrugged. It didn't much matter either way. No cop willingly consulted a shrink; even in this day and age of so-called enlightenment, it was still regarded as a sign of weakness. As Superintendent Brian Vane knew only too well.

She had no doubts at all that he wanted her off his team at the earliest opportunity. Knowing that she was around must be a constant thorn in his side, but if that was his opening salvo in getting her promoted sideways or shuffled off into early retirement, she had very little to worry about.

Always supposing that she didn't want to be shuffled off, of course. At the moment the jury was still out on that one.

Financially she was in the perfect position to leave the force. Not only had she put in just about enough years to qualify for her full pension, but since selling off the family house, the small fortune it had netted her had just been sitting in a high-interest bank account accruing yet more money. And living on the *Mollern*, her narrowboat, she could tour the country and simply relax. What was more, she was still young enough to retrain for a second career if she felt like it. Perhaps make use of her literature degree, earned from a non-affiliated Oxford college.

The options were there, if she wanted to take them.

She pushed through the door into the large open plan office again, but was once more waylaid by Danvers.

This time, however, he was all business. 'Hillary, we've got a suspicious death out in the sticks. It was called in barely an hour ago. Little village called Steeple Knott. You know it?'

Hillary did. 'Just off the main Oxford to Banbury Road, on the way to Duns Tew, right?'

Danvers shrugged. 'If you say so.' He was originally from Yorkshire, and had only come down south when he and a fellow officer had been assigned to investigate Hillary Greene's possible involvement with her husband's illegal animal parts smuggling operation. An unfortunate circumstance that he was hoping like mad she didn't still secretly hold against him.

'That's where Gemma and the others were off to in such a hurry, right?' Hillary asked, nodding. No wonder Gemma hadn't been pleased to see her. She'd no doubt been hoping to be left as acting SIO for the day at least. With Hillary due back tomorrow, it was unlikely Danvers would assign another DCI to it for just twenty-four hours. It would have given her the chance to shine, if only briefly.

'Yes,' Danvers agreed. 'Gemma's perfectly capable of doing the preliminaries, of course, but if you want to go out there, it's up to you. If you prefer to ease in gently, that's OK too.'

Hillary wondered whether Danvers, like the desk sergeant, was worried that she was going to crack under the slightest pressure. If only they knew that the appointment of Brian Vane had already piled more pressure upon her than they ever could, they wouldn't be so worried.

She smiled flatly. 'I'm on my way.' She turned, then said over her shoulder, 'You'd better warn Gemma I'm coming.'

Danvers smiled and nodded. 'Right.'

He returned to his desk, but didn't reach for the phone. Instead he stared blankly at his desk. He wasn't sure he'd done the right thing, letting her know about the murder. But instinct had told him that she needed to get back into the thick of things fast. And solving crime was something she was very good at. Perhaps it was just his imagination that she seemed so out of it. There was no doubt that the old sparkle was gone from her eyes, but then, she was still mourning the death of her friend.

He couldn't expect her to just breeze back in like her old self as if nothing had happened. As everyone was always saying: it would take time.

He hoped that that was all it was. And that time was all it would take.

The desk sergeant looked up, surprised, to see her back again so soon.

'That was quick! The powers that be have finally cut down on the amount of paperwork we need to do, have they? The sods didn't tell me.'

'You wish,' Hillary shot back. 'No, I got a call-out.'

The desk sergeant shook his head. 'Glutton for punishment, you are. Met the new super yet?'

Hillary's face instantly closed down. In the old days, when she'd been on her top form, she'd never have let it show. Now though, she felt her lips snap shut and she forced herself to nod.

'Yes.'

The desk sergeant's beady eyes sharpened.

'If anybody wants me, I'll be out at Steeple Knott,' she added, firmly and obviously changing the subject.

'Right, Hill,' the desk sergeant acknowledged. After the door closed behind her, he let out a long, slow whistle.

So DI Greene didn't rate the new super. The desk sergeant racked his brains for what he knew about Brian Vane, but the man had only been working at HQ for a month, and so far the scuttlebutt about him was fairly neutral. He'd come up the ranks, and hadn't obviously stepped on anybody's toes. Consequently, nearly everybody had been prepared to give him the benefit of any doubt. After all stepping into Mel Mallow's shoes wasn't an enviable job for anyone.

But everyone knew that Hillary Greene could spot a wrong 'un at fifty paces. He'd have to have a word with Fred when he took over at five, and see what he thought about it. 'Course, there were bound to be those who said that nobody would suit her, not after Mel. But anybody who knew DI Greene knew that she wasn't like that.

No. He reckoned if Hillary Greene didn't rate her new super, there'd be something solid behind it.

Gleefully, he wondered what it was.

Hillary Greene returned to Puff the Tragic Wagon her ancient Volkswagen Golf, and headed north. She drove carefully but automatically, and didn't even notice that the clouds had cleared off, and that a beautiful autumn sun was shining.

CHAPTER TWO

The small hamlet of Steeple Knott was virtually deserted when Hillary pulled up on to the grassy verge just before the fake white gates set on either side of the road. She ignored their appeal to DRIVE SLOWLY THROUGH OUR VILLAGE and walked towards the set of patrol cars she could see lined up beside an attractive Cotswold stone cottage.

'Ma'am.' The constable on the gate knew her and she signed his log with a nod of acknowledgement. After she stepped through the white-painted gate, set in a white-painted picket fence, she took a moment or two to look around silently.

A large stand of amethyst-coloured Michaelmas daisies just to her right gave way to a bed of glorious multicoloured dahlias and chrysanthemums. Lining the walls of the house were late-flowering honeysuckle, rose and clematis. The lawn was small but immaculately clipped, and a showcase dwarf magnolia tree stood in the centre. The paving was weed-free and pristine. Given the season, the garden was breathtaking, and it was obvious to Hillary that the owner must be a green-fingered enthusiast.

'It's all happening around the back ma'am,' the constable on the gate offered tentatively. Hillary thanked him and followed the path to the side of the house. The cottage had originally been two small buildings which had later been made into one and with today's real estate prices, its original wood-framed windows and old original grey-tiled roof must have made it worth a small fortune. Set in such a rural and picturesque spot, with easy motorway access to both London in the south and Birmingham in the north, the owner was sitting pretty.

Or not, as the case might be. The owner of the cottage, she soon realized after stepping out into the back garden, was not sitting anywhere at all, pretty or otherwise, but was in fact sprawled out face down in an onion patch. And from the state of the back of his head, was most definitely dead.

Hillary, unnoticed as yet by the others at the crime scene, surveyed the area carefully. SOCO were already *in situ*, and white-overalled figures went about their business calmly and methodically. A photographer had evidently just finished photographing the body, and was packing up his equipment. Ross was chatting to a woman SOCO, and Barrington was busy scribbling in his notebook. Gemma Fordham was staring down at the body as if it was going to talk to her at any minute.

The victim looked to Hillary to be an old man, for his hair, where it was visible amongst the blood and brain matter, was white. He was wearing old-looking dark-brown trousers, scuffed and well-worn boots, and a loose-fitting, red, blue and white tartan work-shirt. Obviously, old gardening clothes that he'd felt comfortable in. Beside the body, now being dusted for fingerprints by a boffin, was an old but well-kept garden spade. From the discoloration on the metal, it was almost certainly the murder weapon.

Which suggested that the murder hadn't been particularly premeditated, but rather smacked of someone, perhaps enraged or frustrated beyond endurance, simply reaching for the nearest object available and letting swing with it. Unless, of course, the killer knew his victim well, and had guessed that he or she was likely to find a murder weapon amongst the garden implements available.

The back garden, Hillary saw at once, was devoted to the growing of vegetables and fruit, and she could make out several wigwams of runner beans, still producing the odd specimen, and rows of freshly planted leeks. A stand of rhubarb, now old and too leggy to be of any use, grew amidst a fair forest of gooseberry bushes. The beds were all laid out neatly, but pleasing to the eye. On the far walls she could see pear trees that had been pegged and pruned severely, heavy with delicious fruit. Through a wooden gate set in the wall she guessed there would be a small but well-stocked fruit orchard on the other side. A small greenhouse and a garden shed hogged the two corners and several compost heaps lined the hedgerows.

A veritable gardener's paradise, Hillary mused sadly. And wondered who'd let the serpent in this time.

Just then Gemma Fordham, sensing eyes on her, turned and spotted her. Hillary could see her shoulders stiffen and then sag a little in resignation. She'd probably known, as soon as she'd seen Hillary walk into the office, that she wouldn't be able to resist getting in on the opening act.

'Guv,' she said flatly, warning the others to her arrival.

Hillary nodded and moved forward to join her, following the boards that had been laid down by the SOCO team.

'No footprints worth mentioning Guv,' Gemma said, filling her in without asking. 'The victim is Mr Edward Philpott, aged sixty-five. He lives here with his daughter, Mrs Rachel Warner, and her two children, Mark, ten, and Julie, twelve. Mrs Warner returned from taking her children to school at around 8.50 a.m. and found her father, as you see him, at roughly 10.15 a.m. this morning.'

Hillary nodded. 'He was alive and well at breakfast, I take it?'

'Yes Guv.'

'So we've got a limited time span for the murder. That helps.' She looked around the garden morosely. High hedges matched the high wall at the end of the garden, making it secluded and private. No other house overlooked it, and the back garden couldn't be seen from the country lane outside either. She turned around and looked at the house. The downstairs window was obviously the kitchen window; above was a bedroom window and a clouded glass window that usually indicated the bathroom.

'No obvious witnesses, I take it,' she noted drily. Gemma smiled a grimace in reply. 'Right, well you and Ross had better get started on house-to-house.'

'It's a tiny place, Guv, and nearly everybody's bound to be at work at this time of day,' Gemma pointed out.

Hillary nodded glumly. 'I know. So you'll just have to track most of them down to their workplaces. But there's bound to be the odd little old lady or two in residence. There nearly always are.'

Gemma nodded and glanced across at Frank Ross. Although they both held the rank of sergeant, it was obvious whom everybody believed to be senior, for she jerked her head to call him away from his chat, and he gave her a brief two-fingered salute in reply.

Hillary's eyes narrowed at this latest piece of insolence. Yes, she had plans for Frank Ross. She'd had enough of his idleness and sloppy work, and was no longer in the mood to put up with it. But she'd have to speak to Danvers first.

As Gemma headed towards the house, she stepped aside to let a small, dapper man pass her. He was carrying his bag and had already slipped into white overalls. His dyed black hair gleamed in the autumn sunshine, and he beamed as he spotted Hillary.

'Hill, you're back. You've been missed.'

Doctor Steven Partridge placed his feet carefully as he approached the corpse, and stood beside Hillary looking down at him.

'Well, at first glance it all looks pretty obvious, doesn't it?' he murmured quietly. He hadn't mentioned Mel, and had no intentions of offering her yet more commiseration, rightly guessing that she'd have had enough of that to last her a lifetime.

'Time of death was probably between 8.30 and 10.15 a.m., so that'll save you some effort,' Hillary supplied briefly.

The doctor nodded, sighed, and got down to work. Hillary turned and left him to it. She spotted Barrington, patiently waiting for her by the house, and walked over.

'Guv, glad to have you back.'

Hillary smiled briefly in thanks and leaned somewhat wearily against the wall. 'So, what are your impressions so far?' she surprised him by asking.

He blinked, not sure of what she wanted. Sensing it, she smiled briefly again. 'It's not a trick question, Constable. You were one of the first people on the scene. Just tell me what struck you first and foremost.'

Barrington looked towards the body, then at his boss, opened his mouth, then shut it again.

'Whatever it was,' Hillary prompted wearily.

'Well, to tell the truth, Guv, it wasn't the old man that interested me the most at all, but his daughter.'

'Oh?'

'Only because she looked so ill, Guv,' Barrington hastened to add.

'Shock can do that,' Hillary said, but already the young redhead was shaking his head.

'Don't think it was just that Guv,' he insisted. 'Well, you'll see what I mean when you talk to her.'

Hillary nodded, not willing to push it. 'Anything else?'

'No, Guv. Well, apart from the fact that it all seems so unlikely. I mean, who'd want to hit a retired postie over the head and kill him in his garden?'

So he'd been a postman, Hillary thought. Interesting. And possibly significant, if he'd been inclined towards dishonesty. Postmen were in such a unique position to be naughty. With handling cheques, money or other valuable items sent through the mail the opportunities to steal or read other people's post and pick up blackmail tips had to be numerous.

She pointed this out to Barrington, who bit his lips and looked chagrined not to have thought it out himself.

'Had he been in the job long?' she asked.

'All his life, Guv, from a lad of eighteen, apparently,' Barrington told her.

'Of course, Mr Philpott might have been as honest as the day is long, and his one-time occupation has nothing whatsoever to do with this,' Hillary pointed out, waving a hand over the crime scene. 'But keeping an open mind won't hurt.'

Barrington made a mental note of the saying, hiding a smile as he did so. It was good to have DI Greene back. DS Fordham was very competent and able, but she was not much good at teaching a bloke the ropes.

He followed Hillary in as she opened the door to the kitchen and walked inside.

The interior was an odd mixture of old and new. The big stone sink was probably centuries old, but new chrome taps had been added at some point. An old Aga had been supplemented with a modern microwave. The terracotta floor tiles looked original, as did a battered oak table and chairs, but the cupboards fixed to the walls were new-looking, as was a large fridge/freezer standing pressed up behind the door. The walls were whitewashed and bulged in places. It had a kind of schizophrenic charm, if you were in the mood for that sort of thing.

The trouble was, Hillary had no idea what kind of a mood she was in.

'She have company with her?' Hillary asked, and Barrington shook his head.

'No. We offered to get someone – a friend or relative, or her doctor, but she flat-out declined. Said she'd be all right. She's in the living room, Guv.'

'Right.' She let Barrington lead the way, and a moment later, stepped into a small parlour.

Like most country cottages, the windows weren't huge, and the light was inclined to be a little dim, but the woman who rose from a chair had been sitting by the window itself, and Hillary could see at once what Barrington had meant, when discussing Rachel Warner.

She looked ill. Very ill indeed.

She must have been about five feet ten, just about Hillary's own height, but she seemed much taller. It took Hillary a few seconds to realize why that was, then saw that it was because she was so thin: she gave the impression of being a beanpole. She was wearing a skimpy white cotton top that clearly showed the ridges and nobbles of her shoulder and collarbone, and being sleeveless as well, her stick-thin arms. She was wearing a dark-blue skirt that came to just above her bony knees, revealing shins so sharp they looked as if they could slice bread.

She couldn't have carried a spare ounce of fat anywhere on her frame. She had dark hair, cropped uncompromisingly short, and large blue eyes which stared out of a gaunt face that reminded Hillary uncomfortably of those photographs of holocaust victims. Dark exhausted bags sat under her eyes.

'Mrs Warner? I'm Detective Inspector Hillary Greene. I'm going to be in charge of your father's case.' She introduced herself and held out her hand.

The other woman nodded, shook hands, and indicated the settee behind them. The bones of her hand felt frail, like bird's bones, and Hillary was scared to squeeze them, even a little. She sat down on the settee, but Barrington opted for the plain wooden chair set against the wall on the other side of the window.

'Mrs Warner. I understand you live here with your father?' Hillary began with the easy stuff first, and the younger woman nodded and collapsed back into her chair.

'That's right. For nearly three years now, it must be, ever since my husband died.'

Hillary nodded. 'He must have been young?'

Rachel nodded blankly. 'He was. Farming accident. He cut his hand on some rusty equipment. Silly bugger was always scared of needles, and it turned out he hadn't had a tetanus shot. I bullied him into getting one and it turns out he was allergic to the bloody stuff. Killed him right off.' She managed to give a grim smile, but Hillary could tell the guilt still gnawed at her. 'Of course, now I wish I'd just let him take his chance with the tetanus. At least he'd have been with us a bit longer.'

She turned her head to look out of the window, giving Hillary a clear view of her profile, which looked even more skull-like than ever. 'He was the cowman of the farm just the other side of Steeple Aston, and the farmer needed a new man in, so of course, we had to get out of the cottage that came with the job.' Widowed and homeless at a stroke, Hillary thought grimly. And her kids orphaned to boot. Wonderful.

'Lucky you had your father then,' Hillary said softly, and the other woman nodded, tears welling up in her eyes and her mouth twisting in pain. She reached into the pocket of her skirt and came out with a piece of torn-off kitchen roll. She rubbed her nose, but let the tears slide down her face unchecked.

'I'm very sorry for your loss, Mrs Warner,' Hillary said softly and simply.

Rachel Warner nodded, but said nothing.

'I know you've been over all of this before, but can you tell me what happened this morning? From the time you got up?' Hillary asked gently.

'Sure,' the other woman responded gruffly. 'That would have been half past seven. The alarm clock always goes off then. I got the kids up, washed, and made sure they cleaned their teeth, just like always, then we went downstairs.

'Dad was already up, and had got the tea brewed, and was making porridge. It was what he always did – both Mark and Julie love porridge.

'Me and Dad had toast and marmalade, that's what we both prefer, and listened to the radio. Radio 4, Dad's favourite. Then I got the kids in the car to take them to school – I was scared we were going to be late, but we weren't, as it turned out.' She shrugged her thin shoulders and took a long, shaken breath. 'I took Julie to the primary school in Duns Tew, and then took Mark on to the secondary in Banbury.'

She paused for a moment, then wiped her cheeks with the tissue. 'When I got back, the sun had come out, and I thought I'd take a little walk. I don't often, but today I was feeling better than I usually do, and I decided to take advantage of the feeling. If only I'd come in the house there and then.' She trailed off with another helpless shrug of her shoulders.

'You don't know that that would have made any difference, Mrs Warner,' Hillary said gently. If there was one thing this woman didn't need, it was yet more guilt.

Rachel smiled an acknowledgement, but the aura of defeat and exhaustion that hovered around was almost a visible thing.

'Where did you walk?' Hillary prompted, just to get her talking again.

'Oh, just down to the cow meadow at the end of the village. There's a little footpath to the spinney. I didn't go through the trees but went around them and then came back. I must have got back to the house about ten past ten, or something like that.'

Hillary nodded.

'Did you notice anything odd, or different? Any strange cars parked in the hamlet, or strangers walking about?'

'No. Nothing like that. It was all very quiet.'

'What did you do then?'

Rachel Warner sighed, and two fresh tears rolled down her face unchecked. 'I went into the kitchen and put the kettle on. I saw as I went past that Dad wasn't in the allotments, so I guessed he was out back in the garden.'

'The allotments?' Hillary put in quietly.

'Yes. Just over the road.' She gestured vaguely through the window. 'Nearly everybody in The Knott has one. To start with, when my Dad was young, it was a necessity – to feed the big families they had then and all that. Nobody had the kind of money they have nowadays. But just recently, what with all the gardening programmes on telly, and the fad for organic food and what have you, all the incomers and second-homers wanted allotments too. Dad always had two chains.'

'I see. Sorry to interrupt. Go on, you came home and put the kettle on?'

'Right. Yes. I made the mugs of tea and took them both outside. I was going to sit at the table, and maybe later on, give Dad a hand tying up the strings of shallots he'd got drying in the shed.'

She looked down at her hands and frowned. 'Dad always pickled his own onions. I don't know what I'll do with them all now.'

She shook her head, as if she knew that she was straying from the point, and looked briefly up at Hillary. Her face had a blank, lost look, and Hillary realized that she'd lost the thread of what she'd been saying. Shock was catching up with her. This preliminary interview would have to be finished quickly. And then, no matter what Rachel said, Hillary was going to get Barrington to ask a doctor to come and look at her.

'You often helped your father in the garden?' Hillary asked curiously, thinking of the spade and fingerprints.

'Used to,' Rachel said without expression. 'Not so much nowadays.'

So if we find her prints on the spade, it won't mean a damned thing, Hillary thought. Most killers now knew enough to wear gloves anyway.

'I took the mugs outside and saw him lying there,' Rachel ploughed on, obviously wanting to get this second telling over and done with. 'I thought at first he'd just tripped over. I think I may even have called out something funny to him. You know, something like, "You'll have to take more water with it next time, Dad", or something like that. You know how you do.'

She looked at Hillary helplessly, and Hillary nodded.

'But he didn't move or get up so I went over and … well … saw him. His head like it was. All the blood on the spade. I sort of backed away and came back inside. I don't really know what

I did next, to be honest,' Rachel gave a dry laugh. 'One minute I was outside, the next minute I was in the kitchen, still holding the mugs of tea.'

Rachel took a deep, heaving breath, and looked down at her hands. 'Then I seemed to get my head into gear and came in here to telephone you.' She nodded across at the telephone on a small three-legged table in the corner. 'Then I sat down here and waited. You came. And that's it.'

Hillary nodded. 'Thank you, that's all very clear. Now, what can you tell me about your father?'

'Dad?' She looked surprised, her head lifting once again to the policewoman's face. 'What about him?'

'Was he popular? Did the people in the village like him? Had he lived here long?'

'Oh yes, all his life. He was born in The Knott, as was Granddad before him. He still owns Granddad's cottage – it's the last one on the way out the other side of the village. Granddad left it to him when he died. Dad bought this place for himself when he got married to my mother.'

'You're mother's dead?'

'No. She left when I was thirteen. Married some other bloke up North. She never kept in touch,' Rachel told her impassively.

Hillary noticed her reaction, but didn't want to push it. Not at this stage. The woman was exhausted and flagging fast.

'Your father didn't remarry?'

Rachel Warner gave a bark of laughter. 'Not him. He said once bitten, twice shy. Besides ...' She blinked, then shrugged. 'Dad lived for his garden anyway. That and the annual seven village flower show.'

Again, Hillary didn't miss that tell-tale word: besides. Besides what? She'd been going to say something, then caught herself, and stopped. At some point, Hillary would have to find out what, but not now.

Instead, Hillary looked outside the window and smiled. 'Yes, I could tell at once that a serious gardener lived here.'

'That was Dad all right. I've never had to buy fruit and veg, for all the years I've lived here. It came in handy, that, what with the grocery bills and the cost of food just lately. I'll give him that. I've had to give up work recently, and the cost of raising two young ones …' Again she trailed off, too exhausted to finish the sentence.

Hillary nodded.

'So everybody liked your father?'

'Yes. Well, apart from his rivals,' Rachel said, making Keith Barrington nearly fall off his chair.

Hillary smiled, not quite so taken aback. 'You mean at the flower show?' she asked knowingly. Her own father had been a bit of an aficionado of flower shows, and she knew how sharp the so-called 'friendly' competition could be.

Rachel nodded. 'The competition is always cut-throat. As the name suggests, there's seven villages involved, and every year it's held at one of them, on a rota basis. Last year it was in Little Tew. The marrow's the really hot competition, of course, but the tallest sunflower, the tomatoes, runner beans and asparagus are also war zones. The year before last there was a big scandal over alleged cheating in the gooseberry section. The ructions can still be felt to this day.'

Hillary smiled widely. 'Your father was a regular winner?'

'Oh yes. Flowers too. His dahlias and sweet peas nearly always brought home the silverware.'

'Did your father seem worried this morning, or distracted, anything like that?'

'No. He was just the same as ever.'

'Was he expecting visitors, do you know?'

'No. Well, if he was, he never said.'

'And when you came back to the house after your walk, did you notice anything different? Anything moved or taken?'

'No, nothing's been stolen,' Rachel said. 'Your constable there asked me to check, and I haven't found anything missing. Although Dad's watch and the gold signet ring he wore aren't on his bedside table, so I'm pretty sure he must have been wearing them.'

Hillary caught Barrington's eye. She hadn't inspected the corpse all that thoroughly, but she was fairly sure the victim's wrist and fingers had been bare. Barrington nodded and underlined something in his notebook. He would make sure to check.

'I see. Well, that's all for the moment, Mrs Warner. Are you sure you don't want me to get in touch with anyone to come and be with you?'

'No thanks, I'm better on my own.'

Hillary nodded. 'Well, we'll be around for quite some time to come yet, and I'm afraid that at some point a thorough search of the house will have to be made. Do we have your permission?'

'Of course. Do what you like,' Rachel Warner said listlessly.

Hillary nodded and rose, and Barrington followed her out. Outside, she saw that Steven Partridge had finished his examination of the body and was about to leave.

She beckoned him over. 'Steven, I know this isn't in your remit, but I'd feel better if you'd just run your professional eye over the daughter inside.'

Steven Partridge sighed, but nodded. 'Probably just shock. I don't have anything to give her, but I can recommend hot sweet tea and bed rest.'

Hillary didn't think that that was somehow going to cut it, but she knew better than to argue with a medical man. When he'd gone on inside, she turned to the young redhead and sighed.

'All right, Keith. Find out the name of Mr Philpott's solicitor, and find out the terms of his will. Mrs Warner didn't mention any siblings, so I think we'll find that she'll inherit everything, but it needs to be checked. Then get on to the schools and find out what time Mrs Warner arrived with the two kids, and the time she left the last school.'

'You don't suspect her, do you, Guv?' Barrington asked, surprised.

'Not particularly. But confirmation is everything in this game, Constable,' she informed him flatly. 'Remember that.'

Barrington flushed, and made another mental note. He watched her walk back down the garden towards the victim, his eyes anxious. It was obvious she was still feeling down, and he only hoped that she hadn't come back to work too soon. He felt a chill crawl down his spine at the thought that she might not be up to the job in hand, and he quickly chased the treacherous notion out of his head.

It was a stupid idea anyway.

Straightening his shoulders, he set about tackling his to-do list.

CHAPTER THREE

Hillary Greene saw the mortuary van arrive, and stood by as the body was loaded up and taken away. A blackbird sang in an apple tree laden with burgeoning fruit, and a brilliantly coloured red admiral butterfly flittered past her and landed on a patch of blue speedwell flowering amid the grass on the path in front of her. It didn't seem a day for death, somehow, but death had come nevertheless.

She sighed and turned away. Returning to the lane outside, she saw that Gemma had started her enquiries with the houses furthest north, which meant that she'd probably told Frank to take those to the south. As far as Hillary could see, the entire hamlet consisted of just this one street, and the cottages that lined it. There was no sign of a pub, or a church, or, of course, that rarity of rarities nowadays, a village shop.

With a sigh she decided to take the house next door on the left. This house was built of red brick, which had mellowed to pink over the ages, and had neatly trimmed but uninspired lawns at the front and side. There was no answer to her knocking.

She then tried the neighbour on the other side, and as she was walking up the flagged path, the front door of the house opened even before she reached it. An old lady with a mop of curly white hair stood there anxiously, looking at her out of wide, watery-blue eyes.

'Don't say she's gone already,' the old woman said bluntly.

Hillary blinked. 'I'm sorry.'

'Rachel. She isn't dead is she?'

'No, Mrs … er…?'

'Mobbs. Mabel Mobbs. What's going off next door then?' she asked, just as bluntly. She peered at Hillary's card short-sightedly when Hillary introduced herself.

'Police?' Mabel Mobbs repeated, her voice slightly raised in that scandalized squeak so often found among her generation. 'Trouble?' she asked avidly.

Hillary smiled. 'Mind if I come in?'

''Course not, chick, come on in. I'll put the kettle on. Go on through to the back, there.'

Hillary followed her pointing finger to a small, modern-looking space at the rear of the cottage. She pulled out one of the two chairs set at a small round table and, unasked, took a seat.

'Burglary is it?' Mabel asked chattily, filling the kettle and reaching up for the tea bags. 'Would you prefer coffee?' she added, very much as an afterthought, and sniffed a little when Hillary admitted that she would. She had to stand on tiptoe to reach the back of the cupboard, and her hand came back holding a rather ancient-looking jar of Nescafé. She was barely five feet in height, Hillary guessed, and was wearing comfortable slippers and a floral dress, with a pinafore tied neatly over it.

'Biscuit?'

'No thanks,' Hillary said automatically. She had what men called an hourglass figure, but she was constantly fighting to stop it running to fat.

'Was anything really valuable taken?' Mabel asked, standing by the kettle and watching it impatiently.

Hillary eyed her curiously. She was fairly sure that the old woman must have seen the mortuary van arrive, and the sombre cargo that it had taken away. A woman as inquisitive as this one must have had her nose pressed up against the windowpane for the past hour or more. So she knew that someone was dead, and her first words to Hillary indicated that her immediate thought had been that it was Rachel who had died. But since Hillary had told her that it wasn't, that only left Edward Philpott or one of the children. And since she had probably seen Rachel take the children to school and come back, she must know that it was the old man who was dead.

So why this dogged insistence on pretending that it had been a burglary which had brought the police to her neighbour's doorstep?

Hillary realized there was probably only one likely reason for this, and smiled gently.

'I'm afraid it was more serious than a burglary, Mrs Mobbs,' she said softly. 'Were you very fond of your neighbour, Mr Philpott?'

With a small moan Mabel Mobbs sat down abruptly into the chair facing Hillary, her face collapsing. 'It *is* Eddie then?' she said mournfully, her eyes filling with tears.

'I'm afraid so.'

'Heart attack was it? Or a stroke? It's usually one of them, isn't it, when it comes on sudden like?' She took a gulping breath and seemed to push the tears aside. 'And it must have been sudden, mustn't it, because he was fit as a fiddle and all right this morning?'

Hillary tensed slightly. 'You saw him this morning?'

'Oh ay. About quarter to seven it were.'

Hillary nodded towards the window. 'You saw him in his garden, over the hedge?'

'Oh no, chick. He was sitting where you are now. He'd bought me over some gooseberries. He knows I like my fruit pies.'

Hillary smiled. 'So he was here at a quarter to seven. That's rather early, isn't it?'

Mabel Mobbs snorted. 'Not for us old ones, chick. I'm up by six most mornings – especially in the summer. Don't sleep much at night anyways, and once I'm awake and it's light, I can't lie in bed twiddling my thumbs. Drives me crackers. So I'm always up, and Eddie was the same. 'Course he liked to get an early

31

start in the garden or the allotments, before the sun got really hot. This time of year it's more mellow like, but still, old habits die hard. He was always up much the same time as me.'

Hillary nodded. 'Have you been neighbours for long?'

'Nigh on forty years it'd be, now,' Mabel said with pride. 'Me and Fred moved in here when we got married in 1946.'

'Is your husband in? Did he see Mr Philpott this morning too?'

'Bless you, chick, I've been widowed for nearly thirty-two years now.'

Hillary shook her head. 'I'm sorry. So, tell me about Mr Philpott. He called in to give you some gooseberries, you say?'

'Ah, that was it. He popped in most days with something or other – leeks, sprouts, apples and what not. Really helped out with my pension I can tell you.'

'He sounds like a good neighbour to have,' Hillary agreed with a smile.

'Oh he was. Always got a cheery word, old Eddie. Not a gloomy puss like some in the village. Even when his wife left him, he didn't stay down for long.'

Hillary nodded. 'So he got on well with everyone? He didn't rub anyone up the wrong way, or get on the wrong side of people or anyone in particular – anything like that?'

'No. Well, maybe Tom Cleaves,' Mabel said uncertainly. 'But Tom's a bit of a stick anyway.'

Hillary lifted an eyebrow. 'A stick?'

'You know. A stuffed shirt. A bore, a stickler for petty rules, that sort of thing. Always bossing them around on the parish council, and what have you. I can't stand the man myself either.'

'And he and Mr Philpott didn't get along?'

Mabel Mobbs looked at her sharply and with sudden alarm. 'Here, don't go reading anything into that! I'm not saying they were sworn enemies or had a blood feud going or anything daft like that. They were just rivals, that's all.'

Hillary smiled. 'Let me guess. The flower show?'

Mabel chuckled. 'Started ever since Eddie won the marrow prize back in '82 that Tom thought he had in the bag. They were both growing marrows on their allotments see, and Tom had one bigger than anything Eddie had, come the day of the flower show. But Eddie had been growing some in his back garden all secretive like – fed 'em up on all sorts of manure and compost and what have you, and grew this real whopper. Didn't Tom kick up a fuss! 'Course, there was nothing in the rules about *where* your marrow was grown.'

Hillary frowned just slightly. 'It sounds to me as if Mr Philpott deliberately wound him up.'

Mabel sighed and nodded. 'Yes, I suppose he did, chick. But don't go thinking he was malicious or anything like that. We were all glad that he did – Tom sometimes needs taking down a peg or two. But there's no real harm in Eddie. Or wasn't, I suppose I should say.' She corrected herself heavily. 'That man would have given you the shirt off his back if you needed it.'

Hillary nodded. 'So, to get back to this morning. How did he seem?'

'Well, not ill or anything, or I would have noticed,' Mabel said at once. 'He handed over the gooseberries and sat down and we had our usual cup of tea. I reminded him about the meeting this afternoon, and joshed him about forgetting about it on purpose like, and I asked how his girl was, and he said all the usual things. Nothing out of the ordinary.'

Hillary waited until she'd finished, and then wondered where to start again.

'His daughter?' she asked curiously.

'Rachel. She's ill, isn't she? You've seen her, haven't you? I reckon it must be something serious, but Eddie would never talk about it much. I reckon he was just being a typical man. You know, stick you head in the sand, and the problem will go away.'

Hillary nodded thoughtfully. 'You mentioned a meeting?'

'Yes, the Forget-me-Knott club. The old folks' club. We're meeting this afternoon in Little Tew.'

'Oh, Mr Philpott was a member?'

At this, Mabel Mobbs let rip with a loud guffaw. 'Eddie, a member of the old crones' club? Not on your life. He said the day he went to the seaside on a day trip in a coach with a load of old fogeys was the day he'd have his head tested.' Mabel wiped the mirth from her eyes, then suddenly sobered, as she realized that the man she was talking about would never be going anywhere again.

'No, he was going to give us a talk about growing your own fruit and veg,' she said soberly. 'Well, he was well qualified to, wasn't he, and he had lovely colourful slides and everything. A lot of old folk are trying to make ends meet nowadays, and I put it forward at the general meeting that a talk like that would be more use than how to arrange dried bloody flowers.'

'And Mr Philpott was happy to do this, was he?'

Mabel looked a shade crafty now, as she shrugged. 'Well, I had to twist his arm a bit,' she admitted with a sly grin. 'But I don't think he minded, not really. He laughed anyway when I reminded him about it, and he said he might forget, because when he got in the garden on a nice day, time just flew. I told him he'd better jolly well not forget, or I'd bring the whole club over here to pester him in his garden. That made him blanch, I can tell you! So then he promised he wouldn't forget, and even put his watch on a half an hour while he sat there, so that he'd be sure to be on time.'

Mabel sighed heavily and shook her head. 'I'd better ring up Mrs Colchis and tell her the speaker won't be coming after all. She'll probably do a talk herself on crocheting quilts out of dog hair or some such thing,' Mabel added gloomily, and Hillary hid a quick grin.

'When did Eddie leave this morning?' she asked next.

'Oh, about quarter past seven, chick, somewhere round then. He had to get the kiddie's breakfast on.'

'Did you notice any strangers hanging around outside, or did you see a car you didn't know parked up anywhere?'

'No. No strangers, definitely,' Mabel said firmly. 'They'd stand out like a sore thumb in The Knott, wouldn't they? And no cars neither. I know all the neighbours' cars.' Mabel's eyes narrowed suspiciously. 'Here, why do you want to know that for? Did somebody do for Eddie?'

Hillary gently confirmed that somebody had. She reached into her jacket for her handkerchief as the old woman began to cry now in earnest. Then, when the sobbing had abated, she went to the forgotten kettle and made them both a hot drink. She added plenty of sugar to Mabel's tea.

When she was sure the old lady was recovered – and Hillary knew old ladies could be very resilient – she left Mabel to her memories, and stepped outside. It was now well past the lunch hour but her stomach wasn't rumbling.

She hadn't felt hungry in months. Not since Mel had been killed, in fact.

Pushing that thought away, she went back next door, surprised to see Steven Partridge's sporty little classic MG still parked on the other side of the road. As she went past the Philpott's cottage, however, she saw him coming out of the front door, and paused at the gate to let him catch up to her.

'You still here?'

Steven nodded. 'I don't like the look of that young woman. I insisted on calling her own medic in, but he couldn't get here until he'd seen the last of his patients. I waited with her until he arrived.'

'She's seriously ill, right?' Hillary asked.

'I'd say so. Though it's hard to tell without knowing some facts,' the medical man said with typical caution. 'Some people can just look rough but not be all that badly off, compared to some. Conversely, some people can look as healthy as a horse and be on the verge of dying. But yes, I'd say she's got something nasty wrong with her, all right.'

'Will he discuss her condition with you? You know, professional to professional?' Hillary asked hopefully.

'Not bloody likely,' Steven said glumly. 'When I talked to her, she seemed very cagey about talking about herself, and I reckon she's the sort who values her privacy. Which is something her GP would have picked up on. He's not likely to go blabbing to all and sundry.'

'Might he talk to me?'

'Maybe, but I doubt he'll have time right now. He was obviously in a rush, trying to fit in half a dozen things in his lunch hour. GPs nowadays work like maniacs. I tell you, Hill, I'm more and more relieved that I decided to work with the dead.'

Hillary nodded gloomily. 'I'll put in an appointment with him for later then.'

Reluctantly, she turned away from the cottage and trudged towards her own car. The sun still had a fair bit of power to it, and she felt a trickle of perspiration run down her back as she walked along the side of the road. She waved a hand as Doc Partridge tooted her on his way past in his low-slung car, and glanced around as she reached her own. She couldn't see a member of her team anywhere, and she reached into her bag for her mobile.

She speed-dialled a number, then heard a crisp voice answer. 'Gemma? It's me. I'm heading back into the office.'

'Right, Guv,' Gemma said smartly, obviously relieved to be left in charge of the crime scene once more.

Hillary hung up and climbed into the car. She had the beginnings of a major headache, and felt vaguely at a loss. She had the feeling that there was something she should be doing, but she had no idea what.

Frowning with disgust at herself, she started the car, and drove carefully back to Kidlington.

Inside the office, she took off her jacket and stared morosely at the towering pile that was her in-tray. Of course, the murder case that had landed on her lap today was only one of many cases that Gemma and the team would have been handling.

She sighed, and reached for the first folder, spending several hours just bringing herself up to date. A long-standing charge of assault with a deadly weapon, which she'd been overseeing before her leave, had been successfully concluded, with the perpetrator plea-bargaining for a lesser charge in return for dishing the dirt on a suspected rapist. Gemma's disgust at the CPS for doing the deal was easy to read between the lines. A succession of breaking and entering offences showed no sign of abating, nor of being solved, though she could see that Barrington had been working hard on them, and even Ross had successfully closed a sexual assault case at an Oxford nightclub.

She was just stretching her arms and shoulders to get some relief after hours spent leaning over the desk, when she noticed Danvers step out of his cubicle.

Instantly, she was on her feet. He spotted her at once, of course, his eyes seemingly attuned to the dark-russet colour of her hair. As she came closer, he saw that she'd lost some weight, and mourned the lessening of her magnificent curves. But he'd schooled his face into a blank mask by the time she reached him, knowing that she didn't like it when he ogled her.

'Hillary.'

'Sir. Got a minute?'

'For you, always,' he said, smiling to take the *double entendre* out of it – and not quite succeeding. He was glad that she was no longer seeing Mike Regis, the vice detective out of St Aldates, but he knew, for all that, that he was no closer to being able to ask her out on a date than he was before.

There was always something that seemed to be thwarting him. He wondered, with a vague sense of superstitious uneasiness, if something or someone was trying to tell him something. But he'd been pursuing Hillary patiently and persistently for far too long to give up now.

'How's the case looking?' he asked, when they were both inside his office, and he was sitting behind his desk.

Briefly, Hillary filled him in. 'But that wasn't really what I wanted to see you about,' she finished impatiently. 'It's about Frank Ross. I want him gone,' she demanded.

Danvers blinked at the vehemence of her tone. He leaned back in his chair, trying to deny his sudden feeling of fear.

'Why now?' he asked, careful to keep his voice mild. 'You've put up with him for all these years, after all,' he pointed out.

'That's just it,' Hillary said. 'I have, and I'm not prepared to do it any longer. He's eligible for retirement under the new rules, isn't he?' she asked, almost belligerently.

Danvers nodded. 'Yes, he is.'

'Then I want you to have a word in his ear. Tell him how it is. I know Donleavy will back me up on this. Hell, the whole station will celebrate.' Hillary smiled grimly.

Danvers laughed. Well, that was true. Cops and villains alike universally loathed Frank Ross. And yes, there were always ways and means of making it clear to an unpopular officer that it was time to retire.

It was the fact that Hillary was demanding that it happen that concerned him the most. It was not like her to be vindictive.

'Why now in particular?' he asked, watching her carefully, trying to track down the root cause of her anger.

'Why not now,' Hillary countered. 'There's change at the top, so we might as well make a clean sweep of it. And besides, with Vane being the new boss, I don't need Ross on my back as well.'

Danvers now felt a distinct chill creep up his back. 'What's the matter with Vane?' he asked sharply. He'd been reporting to the man for over a month now, and he seemed fairly OK. True, he was no Mellow Mallow, but who was?

Hillary frowned and shook her head. 'Nothing,' she lied quickly. 'Just forget I said anything. Look, I'm just not prepared to put up with Ross any longer, OK? Perhaps I'm running out of patience and forbearance in my old age.' She forced herself to smile. 'Maybe I'm just treating myself after going through a bad patch. I just need you to turf Ross out for me. You can do that, can't you?'

And with that appeal, Paul Danvers's heart began to swell. For the first time since meeting her, she was actually asking him for a favour; to do something for her. Treating him almost like an equal. And he was not going to look a gift horse in the mouth. Although he hadn't missed the fact that she obviously had some kind of a problem with the new super.

'Of course I can. I'll go now and get the paper work started, and I'll talk to Ross when they've been processed.'

'Fine,' Hillary said. She smiled briefly and left.

When she was gone, DCI Paul Danvers stared at the door and tried to convince himself that he was making progress with the woman at last. And that it was only to be expected that she'd want to get rid of Ross, now that at last she had the chance.

But he couldn't quite ignore the little voice inside his head that said that Hillary Greene was acting out of character. That she'd come back to work hard-hearted, instead of merely hard-headed. A voice that warned him that she was a woman still in mourning and, *ergo*, a woman who didn't need any kind of added pressure right now. Unfortunately, with a job such as hers, that was impossible to ensure.

He got up abruptly and walked across the large open-plan office to her desk. She was just putting the last of the folders into her out-tray.

'You look like you're all caught up,' he said casually.

'I am at last. I thought I'd head back out to Steeple Knott and see how Gemma's getting on.'

Danvers glanced at his watch. 'It's nearly five. And you're not even supposed to be here until tomorrow. Why don't you head back home and make an early night of it? DS Fordham is more than able to cope, you know.'

Hillary smiled wryly. Oh yes, she knew just how competent and able Gemma Fordham could be. She looked up at Danvers, about to tell him to forget it and that she was needed at the crime scene, but something in his face alerted her just in time.

She forced a brief, bright smile to her face instead, and said calmly, 'OK, sounds like a good idea. See you tomorrow.'

She felt his eyes on her all the way across the room as she walked to the door.

In the foyer, she nodded at the desk sergeant, then went through the door and walked across the sun-warmed car park to her car. It only took her five minutes to drive home. She felt tired, and her headache was worse. She thought that she might just have a glass of wine and stretch out on her bunk for an hour or so after all.

But as she walked along the towpath and saw a familiar figure waiting for her beside the *Mollern*, she knew that any respite would have to be postponed for a while yet.

Her face felt stiff and tight as she forced yet another smile upon it. When she was just a few yards from her narrowboat, the blonde-haired visitor heard her and turned to watch Hillary approach, her pretty face pale with tension.

'Hello, Janine,' Hillary said wearily.

CHAPTER FOUR

Philip Mallow's widow was now five months pregnant, and it was beginning to show, although the woman herself had none of the bloom or look of wellbeing normally associated with her condition. Janine managed a brief smile as Hillary stepped on to the rear of the boat.

'You've been in to HQ?' her one-time sergeant Janine Tyler, now DI Janine Mallow, asked flatly. 'I heard you weren't officially due in until tomorrow.'

'I wasn't,' Hillary agreed, reaching into her bag for the key to the padlock that kept the *Mollern*'s metal doors firmly locked. 'But I just wanted to touch base, then we had a murder case come up and,' Hillary shrugged helplessly, 'you know how it is.'

'This is a bad time then,' Janine said, knowing exactly how it was. 'I'll push off and let you get your breath.'

'Don't be daft,' Hillary countered. 'Come inside. I've got some fruit juice in the fridge.' In point of fact, she was dying for a glass – or two, or three – of wine, but wasn't going to open a bottle in front of Janine. She might just want to share it, and Hillary didn't think that would be a good idea. If the two of them got roaring drunk, Hillary had no idea where it could lead. But it would be to nowhere good, of that she was sure.

'OK,' Janine agreed, and stepped carefully on to the back of the narrowboat. She was wearing tailored cream slacks with a matching jacket, and a large sky-blue blouse that accommodated her growing bump. She followed her ex-boss down the few narrow steps, careful to duck her head, and into the cramped corridor below.

Hillary led her straight to the small lounge area at the front of the boat, slinging her bag and jacket into her bedroom as she passed it. Once inside the lounge, she indicated the one good armchair to Janine, then went into the galley for the cranberry juice.

When she came back, Janine was sitting down, and glancing out of the window. Because narrowboats are low in the water, her face was almost level with the towpath, where somebody was just going by, walking two golden retrievers.

'We haven't chatted since Mel's funeral,' Janine said when Hillary handed over her drink. The older woman nodded in reply, and reaching for a folded deck chair stashed against one wall, opened it up and sat down.

'No. I thought you'd probably want some time and space, and you know my number.' The words could have sounded brisk, even curt, but Hillary said them simply and from the heart.

Janine nodded. The two women had never been friends, as such, but Janine had – somewhat reluctantly – learned an immense respect for Hillary Greene. And she appreciated her straightforward strength and reliability. It was, in fact, why she was here now. From Hillary, at least, she would get no bullshit.

'Mel's case squad has been liaising with me, if you can call it that,' she began, without preamble. 'And it seems to me that for all it's been two months now, they're no further forward.'

'They've still got Myers under constant surveillance, and they've had him in to give him a grilling a number of times,' Hillary pointed out, but even to her own ears it sounded flat and pointless.

'And had to let him go again,' Janine shot back. 'They just can't seem to find any evidence linking him to Mel's shooting. But the more time that goes by with no other cops getting shot at, it's looking less and less likely that it could be a copycat sniper killer. Unless the bastard got cold feet after shooting Mel.'

Hillary sipped her fruit juice miserably.

'Do you think it was Myers?' Janine asked her sharply. Like everyone who knew and worked with her, Janine had a deep respect for Hillary's instincts.

Hillary glanced at Janine carefully. She did, in fact, think that it was Clive Myers who'd killed her best friend, and had thought so right from the beginning. But the fact was that even now, after two months, she still had no idea what she could do about it, and her feelings of helpless frustration were often unbearable. How much worse must it be for his pregnant widow she couldn't imagine.

She glanced away from Janine to the window, not knowing how to reply. It seemed to her that no matter what she said, it would only inflame the other woman, and the last thing anybody needed was impetuous behaviour by the hero's widow.

And Hillary knew of old just how impetuous Janine could be.

'You do, don't you?' Janine demanded, an edge to her voice now.

Hillary sighed. 'What I think is largely irrelevant. We just have to let the squad get on with it,' she said, and gave a mental wince. Even as she spoke the words, she could hear how defeatist and inadequate they sounded.

'That bloody Evans,' Janine muttered grimly. 'I don't trust him. He's supposed to have brains, but I haven't seen any evidence of it so far. He never even knew Mel, so how motivated is he going to be to catch the bastard who killed him?' Janine twisted her hands together in her lap and laughed bitterly. 'I wish you were heading the case.'

Hillary did too. Desperately. But that was, of course, impossible, and they were both just going to have to deal with it. 'You have to be patient,' Hillary heard herself say, and wondered why it was that she seemed to have nothing but clichés to utter.

'You know how much all this is costing, right?' Janine asked. 'And you know as well as I do how tightly the budget is stretched. How much longer do you think it'll be before they're forced to scale down the squad, cut the hours, and finally put the case on the back burner?'

Hillary's stomach clenched. She too had been aware of time remorselessly ticking away. But if the evidence wasn't there to convict, it simply wasn't there. Clive Myers was ex-army, intelligent and highly motivated. He'd been careful, clever and patient. Such people could be impossible to catch.

It was a galling fact to contemplate, but Hillary was beginning to suspect that they'd never get Mel's killer. Her only hope was that Myers was not yet finished, and would go after his daughter's rapists. At least then the team watching him would have a chance of getting him on something.

'I tell you, Hillary,' Janine said grimly, 'if they don't get a breakthrough soon …' She left the sentence unfinished, and it hung, as ominous as the sword of Damocles between them.

Hillary took another swallow of her fruit juice and wished it were wine. Or better yet – Scotch.

The next day dawned cloudy but still mild, and before setting off for work, Hillary swallowed two aspirins with her morning cup of coffee, in a last-ditch attempt to get rid of the vague headache that had plagued her all night.

She had the feeling the drug wouldn't work. She was sure that tension was the real culprit, and after her chat with Janine Mallow last night, the stress was only getting worse.

In her ex-sergeant Hillary could sense a ticking time bomb.

At her desk, she noticed Gemma had already arrived, and, right on her own heels came Barrington. Of Ross, naturally, there was as yet no sign. She hoped that Danvers had hurried Ross's resignation papers along, as he'd promised. With Vane at her back, just waiting for the opportunity to stick the knife in, she didn't want to have to keep her usual close eye on Ross as well. One enemy at a time was more than enough to deal with.

Barrington waited until his boss had settled a bit and dealt with the most urgent of her e-mails, before reporting in with his findings from yesterday.

'Guv. Rachel Warner delivered her youngest to the primary school at 8.35 a.m., and her eldest to her secondary at 8.45 a.m. A teacher at the secondary confirms she left immediately after the girl got out of the car.'

Hillary nodded. So the daughter's story checked out. There was no reason why it shouldn't, of course, and it meant that it was just one more thing ticked off her list.

'And I've spoken to the victim's solicitor. He's agreed to courier over a copy of the old man's last will and testament, but basically it all goes to the daughter, as you thought,' the young redhead added.

Hillary nodded. She doubted Eddie Philpott had had a lot to leave by way of hard cash, but the house alone was worth a bit. Although she didn't have the feeling that this one was going to come down to money, it wasn't something she could entirely ignore.

'Any sizeable bequests?' she asked sharply.

'No Guv. The old man had his pension and some savings but nothing out of the ordinary.'

Hillary grunted but said nothing.

'House to house, Guv,' Gemma put in, seeing that Barrington had finished. 'I've been getting repeated reports that the victim and a Mr Thomas Cleaves are at loggerheads, mostly over the village flower show.'

'Yeah, me too,' Barrington agreed. 'Apparently Cleaves put a rumour about that one of the judges had been biased in the victim's favour.' He flushed as Gemma gave him the evil eye, and smiled back an apology. Gemma Fordham didn't like to be interrupted when she was speaking, especially by still-green DCs. It was something Barrington had quickly learned since Gemma had been temporarily heading the team.

Hillary sighed. 'I suppose we'd better speak to Mr Cleaves then.' She didn't, somehow, think that Eddie Philpott had been killed over the length of his runner bean exhibit or what have you, but stranger things had happened in the past.

When she'd been new in uniform, there'd been a case at her first station house in which a man had killed his neighbour because she had, from time to time, been inclined to pinch the odd pint of milk from his doorstep.

'Does this Cleaves character live in the same hamlet?' she asked of Barrington, reaching down for her bag.

'Next village down the lane, Guv, Duns Tew,' Barrington said, consulting his notebook.

'Fine. You can drive. Janine … sorry, I mean Gemma, did you manage to catch every resident of The Knott at work?'

'All but two, Guv,' Gemma said, noting the slip but not commenting on it. 'One's a travelling salesman, due back in to the office today. The other was out showing a house to someone. I left a message at his office that he was to stay at his work once he got back there until I'd spoken to him.'

'OK. Once you've taken their statements you can start with the background research of the victim.'

'Guv,' Gemma said briefly.

Duns Tew and its more famous sisters of Great Tew and Little Tew, were firmly on the tourist map, situated as they were at easternmost approaches to the Cotswolds. But on a cloudy day in October there was little evidence of visitors as Barrington parked Puff the Tragic Wagon just off the village green, under the slightly yellowing leaves of a large horse chestnut tree.

'He lives in Deer Park Lane, Guv,' Barrington said, glancing around, looking in vain for any street signs.

'You head down there,' Hillary said, pointing. 'I'll try up here.'

Eventually a man walking a pair of excitable Jack Russells told Hillary the way. She collected her constable and quickly found number 8.

Thomas Cleaves, who answered the door promptly at the first ring, was a sprightly looking man, probably in his early seventies. He was carefully dressed in dark trousers with a pale mint-green, white and sky-blue knitted jumper, the kind with interlocking diamonds.

'Police? My word yes,' he said, as the two officers showed him their ID cards. 'This must be about Mr Philpott. Please, come on in.'

He lived in one of those small but tidy bungalows that sat in a small but carefully landscaped and sculptured garden. He showed them into a cream-coloured living room, and indicated two newish-looking cream leather armchairs that sat either side of a well-polished wooden table.

Hillary and Barrington obligingly sat down where he indicated.

'Were you in Steeple Knott yesterday morning, Mr Cleaves?' Hillary asked, immediately getting to the point, as Barrington obligingly scribbled down notes in his very fast and accurate shorthand.

'No, Inspector, I wasn't. I had no call to be.'

Hillary looked at the old man thoughtfully. She remembered Mabel Mobbs describing this man as being rather prim and proper, and Hillary could see what she meant. Even his mannerisms of speech seemed somehow prissy.

'You knew Mr Philpott well, sir?'

'Well, I wouldn't say that, exactly,' Tom Cleaves demurred judiciously. 'We knew each other, of course. From round and about, so to speak. But we were not friends, as such. We did not go out of the way to meet up, socially.'

Hillary nodded. 'You and he had a hobby in common, I think. Gardening, and the local villages' flower show?'

Tom Cleaves stiffened. He had a round, rather flat face, with deep-set, dark eyes and a whisper of a moustache. Now his whole countenance seemed to shut down.

'Yes,' he admitted, the monosyllable sounding diffident and yet impatient at the same time.

'Did you like Mr Philpott, sir?' Hillary asked bluntly, curious to hear what the man would say.

The man, in fact, said nothing for a considerable moment, obviously gathering his thoughts and arranging them to his satisfaction. 'No. I can't say that I did,' Tom Cleaves eventually said. 'But I did not kill him, Inspector.'

Well, that was plain enough, Hillary thought, hiding a wry smile. 'We've no reason to suppose that you did, sir,' she said blandly. 'Do you know of anyone who might have had reason to kill him?'

'No.'

'Have you ever heard him being threatened by anyone?'

'No.'

Hillary deliberately paused, determined not to let an exchange begin whereby the witness could indulge in his love of the monosyllabic. 'What did you think of Mr Philpott, sir?'

'I beg your pardon?' Tom Cleaves sounded mildly scandalized, as if she'd just told him a risqué joke.

'I merely wanted to have your opinion of the man, Mr Cleaves,' Hillary said mildly. 'It helps us if we can build up a mental picture of the murder victim, you see.'

'Oh.' Something flickered in those deep-set eyes, but his thin shoulders shrugged with elaborate nonchalance. 'He was, on the surface, a friendly, mild-mannered sort of man.'

'But?' Hillary pressed.

'But nothing, Inspector. He was well-liked by a lot of people.'

'But not by you?' Hillary persisted.

The old man shuffled on his chair, not liking the way she was backing him into a corner.

'No, Inspector, not by me.'

'Can you tell me why not? Surely rivalry over carrots and marrows wasn't the sole reason for your antipathy?'

Tom Cleaves sighed, and his eyes went once more to the windows. 'Let's just say I found him rather sly. And now, Inspector, if there's nothing else I can do for you …' He rose to his feet, effectively bringing the interview to an end.

Hillary decided to let him get away with it. After all, she

could always come back to him if she needed to. And something told her that she probably would need to, before the case was over.

'Well, thank you, Mr Cleaves,' she said pleasantly, as they parted on his doorstep.

The two police officers walked slowly and quietly back towards the car, before Barrington said carefully, 'What do you think, Guv?'

Hillary shrugged. 'I think Mr Cleaves seemed very ill at ease and unhappy about something,' she said thoughtfully.

Barrington sighed, wishing he didn't find that statement quite as enigmatic as he did. He'd been working with Hillary Greene for nearly a year now, and he knew he'd learned a lot in that time. But he still knew that she'd seen and heard something in that short, apparently profitless interview, that he'd missed. And it annoyed and worried him. Sometimes he wondered if he was really cut out for this job.

His lover would certainly be delighted if he quit. In fact, Gavin would be over the moon. His father was currently standing trial back in London, and their nightly phone calls had been becoming progressively chillier and chillier.

Keith could almost picture the look on his face if he should walk through Gavin's Belgravia door and tell him he'd left Oxford, and the police force for good.

Hastily, Keith pushed the fantasy to one side.

Barrington once again took the wheel and as she slipped into the car, Hillary said 'When you've got time, and working around your other priorities, I want you to do a full background check on Mr Cleaves.'

'Yes, Guv,' Keith said firmly.

Gemma Fordham had been able to return to Kidlington relatively quickly. Neither of her two errant interviewees had been hard to track down and, predictably, neither of them had had anything of use to say, and had said it quickly.

Nowadays, country villages were hardly viable communities, but a mere collection of wildly busy working types who used their houses as little more than sleeping places. The commute to work every weekday barely left them time to recognize, let alone get to know their neighbours. And at weekends most of the younger element were too busy enjoying their leisure time to stop and chat to the man who lived next door or the woman across the street.

One of her interviewees, the travelling salesman, hadn't even known who Eddie Philpott was – and he'd lived in the hamlet for nearly two years.

As she stepped through the station's big main doors, she noticed that two uniformed constables, loitering at the sergeant's reception desk, abruptly broke off their conversation when they saw her. Feigning indifference, she nodded briefly at the desk sergeant and headed for the stairs. Instead of climbing them, however, she walked only far enough to conceal her from view, then waited.

Sure enough, the men started talking again. True to form, although they started off whispering, they soon returned to their normal speaking voices, and she was able to overhear the odd sentence or two. When she was eventually able to understand what the gist of their talk was about, she felt a jolt of surprise go through her. Apparently, it was doing the rounds throughout the whole station house, that her boss, Hillary Greene, did not rate the new superintendent, Brian Vane.

This was news to Gemma. Apart from anything else, Hillary had barely been back at work a day. And as far as Gemma knew, she had only had the one brief meeting with the super anyway. Then one of the uniforms told the desk sergeant that a mate of his had a retired father who knew that Hillary and Vane had worked together before, back when Hillary was a new sergeant.

So obviously Inspector Greene had previous knowledge of the man. Gemma found that interesting.

It was hard to make out everything they were saying, for

Gemma would often miss words or even short sentences. But it soon became clear that the desk sergeant was insisting that Hillary Greene was never wrong about people, and that there was bound to be trouble, just watch and see.

When the doors opened to let a small band of plainclothes officers in, the trio at the desk broke up, and Gemma continued up the stairs, her face thoughtful.

If there was going to be trouble between the new super and her boss, could she make that work to her own advantage? Since Hillary had taken leave, it had been impossible for her to get back on DI Greene's boat, after her first abortive search a few weeks ago, and to search for a certain paperback novel that she was just itching to get her hands on. But now that her boss was back at work, she should be able to get a new impression made of her padlock key, since Hillary had changed the locks.

And then, who knew?

She found the cluster of desks by the window deserted. If Frank Ross had been in, he'd quickly gone out again, typically leaving nothing of interest or worth behind him.

She sighed, and headed out to the loos, momentarily disconcerted to find the place empty except for her boss. Hillary Greene looked up from the sink where she was washing her hands and caught her sergeant's eye.

'Gemma,' she said off-handedly.

Gemma Fordham walked slowly to the sink beside her, and turned on the tap. She wasn't sure why she was about to do what she was about to do, but some instinct told her that it was time to test the waters.

'Guv, I've been meaning to speak to you for some time now,' she began, her voice brisk and professional. 'It's about something personal,' she said, her words in total contradiction to her manner.

Hillary grunted. 'If it's about you and my ex, don't bother,' Hillary said mildly. 'I know you had a brief fling with him way back, and as far as I'm concerned, it's ancient history.'

Gemma felt her body sway slightly against the cold porcelain of the sink, and took a long, slow, steady breath. So, all those cold, nasty moments she'd had in the past when she'd guessed that her boss knew more than she was letting on, had been right on the button.

'How long have you known?' she asked quietly.

Hillary turned off the hot water tap, then the cold. 'That you had history with my old man? Almost since the first moment you joined the team.'

This shook Gemma, no two ways about it. She'd expected Hillary to say that she'd only found out about it a short time ago. She licked lips that had suddenly gone dry and raised a slightly unsteady hand to her head. Watching her reflection studiously in the mirror, Gemma faffed about unnecessarily with her hair.

If Hillary Greene had been that quick off the mark, was it possible … Gemma felt a cold shiver go through her. Was it really possible that she knew about the rest as well?

'I'm surprised you didn't object to working with me, Guv,' she tried out cautiously. Her voice, always husky after a child-hood accident, sounded gruffer than ever. She cleared her throat carefully.

'Why? It's not a problem as far as I'm concerned,' Hillary said casually. Then she added devastatingly, 'Although the fact that you seemed to be obsessed with finding Ronnie's dirty money can be a bit of a pain in the arse at times.'

Gemma Fordham's eyes widened and her gaze crashed into Hillary's in the mirror, and she swallowed hard. Ronnie Greene had stashed a fortune somewhere from his illegal animal-parts smuggling ring, and it had never been recovered. And she wanted it.

For a moment, it seemed as if time hung suspended between them as each dealt with their own thoughts.

Gemma's were mainly disjointed and slightly panic-stricken. It had never seriously occurred to her that Hillary Greene was on to her, and now that she knew that she was, Gemma had no idea what she should do next.

Hillary, for her part, was far more sanguine. This moment of reckoning had been coming for some time, and although the start of a new murder case was not a time she would have chosen to confront it, circumstances had seemed to make it inevitable.

'Just so you know,' Hillary said tonelessly, 'the money's all gone. A crooked officer found it and legged with it last year. So all your efforts have been wasted.'

Gemma opened her mouth, then closed it again.

'You can believe me or not,' Hillary continued in the same unemotional manner. 'But I will say this. I intend to force Frank Ross to retire, which will give you more scope to stretch yourself and practise your talents. If you stay with me, I'll see that you get the promotion you deserve, when you deserve it and can cope with it.

'If, on the other hand, you feel you want to leave, I won't stand in your way either.'

Gemma opened her mouth once more, then slowly closed it again. She felt humiliated, mortified, and frankly bewildered. And when she saw her reflection in the glass she was appalled to see the tell-tale high red colour of embarrassment staining her cheeks.

Hillary, also noticing it, sighed heavily. 'Gemma, as far as I'm concerned, you're smart, competent, very able and have a bright future in the force. I personally think you'd be mad to either quit, or apply for a transfer at this particular time. The brass would be bound to look down on either action.'

She reached for the hot-air hand-dryer and banged the big silver button, deliberately turning her back on the younger woman in order to give her some much needed privacy. 'Just think carefully about your options and don't do anything rash. You'd be a fool to let wounded pride drive any decisions you might make.'

Hillary rubbed her hands together under the hot air, and wondered if, at this rate, she'd have any of her team left.

Mel was gone, and the hole he left was gaping like a bottomless well ready for her to tumble into the moment she put a foot wrong.

Frank Ross was going, which, although a cause for celebration, was also, in it's own way, ringing in the end of an era.

Now, if Gemma Fordham decided to go too, she'd be left only with Barrington who, although keen and eager to learn, also had problems – and a secret of his own to deal with.

At this rate, she might be the only one left. The lone bloody ranger. Perfect.

She turned and walked from the ladies' loo, leaving behind her a stricken and silent Gemma Fordham.

CHAPTER FIVE

Hillary walked slowly to her desk and slipped off her jacket. She sat down at her chair and checked her e-mails, then pulled out of her in-tray the first of the forensic reports to reach her desk.

It was a SOCO report on the murder weapon. As expected, the spade bore the prints of both the murder victim and his daughter Rachel, and also a set of prints belonging to an as yet unidentified individual – possibly Eddie Philpott's grandson, Mark. With a pang she could picture the old man teaching the lad how to use the spade to dig up unwanted Brussels sprout plants or create trenches for the planting of new potatoes.

She made a note to get Gemma to oversee the taking of the children's fingerprints for elimination, and frowned thoughtfully as her telephone rang.

The lack of any other prints on the spade was faintly puzzling for it probably meant that the killer had worn gloves. But from her memory of the murder scene that morning, the victim had almost certainly been working with the spade himself on the onion and leek patch, which indicated that the killer had probably grabbed the spade to use as the first convenient weapon to hand. But if that was the case, why had he or she been wearing gloves? The day hadn't been a particularly cold one. Of course, either Rachel or her son could be the killer, but that seemed, on the face of it, vastly unlikely. A ten-year-old boy would almost certainly not have the upper body strength or height to be the culprit, and what possible motive could the victim's obviously ill daughter have?

She picked up the receiver, still puzzling over the problem. Of course, the killer might have been wearing gloves simply because he or she had to. Some sensitive skin condition perhaps, or some unsightly blemish on the hands? She'd have to remember to tell the team to watch out for any such person they might come across in the course of the investigation.

'DI Greene,' she said automatically into the receiver.

Of course, she hadn't actually seen Mark Warner yet – the lad might be exceptionally big and hefty for his age. But even if that turned out to be case, why would he want to kill his granddad?

'Hillary, it's me Janine. One of the rapists is missing.'

Hillary blinked, having to take a moment to switch her thoughts in mid-gallop. 'The Myers case, you mean?' she asked blankly, and heard Janine Mallow snort.

'Of course the Myers case,' she confirmed impatiently. 'I just got word from somebody who's keeping an eye on things for me. It's the break everybody's been waiting for,' she confirmed, her voice hot and tight with excitement. 'It's got to be.'

'Slow down a minute,' Hillary warned instinctively.

Janine swore under her breath, but Hillary caught it. 'It has to be Myers, now, right?' Janine Mallow pressed on. 'I mean, with Gregg in hiding, the only targets he can get to now are the bastards who raped his girl. This blows the sniper killer copycat theory right out of the water.'

Hillary rubbed a hand across her aching forehead. DI Gregg had been in investigative charge of the rape of young Evelyn Myers, and ever since the case had collapsed, and Detective Superintendent Philip Mallow had been shot, he'd been transferred out of the region, on the top brass's instructions, and was keeping his head down.

'I'm going over there,' she heard Janine say, and at once she tensed.

'No! Janine, don't be so stupid.' Hillary realized she was

almost shouting in her anxiety, and quickly lowered her voice. Even so, she knew those closest to her desk must have heard her. 'Mel's team are bound to be already on it. You need to keep out of it and let them do their job.'

'They've been and gone,' Janine shot back angrily, then muttered, 'or so I'd heard.'

Hillary didn't comment. She and Janine both knew that, officially, Janine wasn't supposed to be involving herself in her husband's murder investigation in any shape or form. But, of course, everyone also knew that the grieving widow had friends on the task force who were keeping her in the loop. Every copper had friends who knew the score, and Hillary herself could probably call on a half a dozen or more of the Oxford-based officers who were working Mel's case, and confidently expect to get the low-down.

'Then what's the problem?' Hillary hissed, casting a quick look around, but everyone was studiously ignoring her. Janine was still a working copper, and although she was on shortened hours, she was still pulling in a full salary from the Witney nick where she worked. If word got out that she was planning serious interference with the Myers case, she could find herself suspended.

'The problem is, I don't trust any of those cack-handed know-nothings to get anything useful out of the little shit-heel's parents, that's the problem,' Janine hissed back in her ear. She was sounding more and more uptight as the conversation wore on, which couldn't be good for her blood pressure. And a five-months pregnant woman needed to be careful.

It would be a tragedy upon a tragedy if Janine lost Mel's baby now.

Hillary sighed. 'Look, just sit tight. I'll call around and try and have a quiet word. See if I can see how the land lies. All right?'

From the end of the line came a few seconds of silence, and then a soft sigh. 'OK. Call me back as soon as you can.' It had, of course, been what Janine had been hoping for, and they both knew it.

Hillary muttered a few words of promise and then hung up. The last thing she wanted to do was go over to Blackbird Leys, where all three lads accused of raping Evelyn Myers still lived. But if she didn't, she knew her one-time sergeant was perfectly capable of barging round there herself and causing a huge cock-up, which was bound to come to the attention of the media and cause embarrassment all round.

She left her desk and went to the main stairwell, but instead of going down she climbed one flight to the canteen. There was something she needed to do first.

All coppers worked irregular hours, and she was fairly confident that she'd find someone on Mel's squad up there at any time in the day, snatching late or early breakfast, lunch or tea. As she pushed into the large, airy room, the usual food and coffee smells assaulted her nose, making her feel vaguely nauseated. As she'd thought, a quick scan of the half-full tables showed her one DS Charlie Gimmeck, a man who'd entered the force at the same time as herself. They weren't particularly close, but then, they didn't need to be.

She got a plate of salad from the counter, then walked over casually to join the DS and the two DCs sitting with him. The moment Charlie spotted her he said something to the two younger men, who got up and just as casually strolled away.

'Hey Charlie,' Hillary said, putting down her plate. Charlie was a portly, genial-looking man who could sometimes have a nasty temper, and had a reputation for coming up with surprising insights that his more so-called able, higher-ranking colleagues missed. As a choice for Mel's case he'd been inspired. Although he'd known Mel, he'd never worked under him nor could he be said to be a pal, so wouldn't be likely to have any emotional or psychological problems working on his murder. He also knew the area thoroughly, was known to be able to graft for long periods of time, and had no axe to grind with the Met man who was in charge.

'Hillary,' he responded amiably.

'I heard that one of the Myers rapists had gone missing,' she said very quietly, making no attempt to slide into the matter gracefully. They both knew why she was here, and they both knew Charlie was going to spill his guts.

So far, Hillary Greene had given Mel's case a wide berth – something that had both pleased and just ever so slightly puzzled the top brass. It was also something of a cause of speculation amongst the Oxford-based element, who knew Hillary and her reputation well. Now that she was at last calling in some markers, it made Charlie Gimmeck feel almost relieved.

'Right. Gary Firth. The chief instigator,' he confirmed at once.

Hillary's face tightened. It was well known that the sixteen-year-old Gary had been the only one to have actually forced sexual intercourse with the fifteen-year-old Evelyn Myers on that night, although two other, younger boys had been present to egg him on.

'Went missing late yesterday afternoon,' Charlie carried on, glancing around. Probably everyone in the canteen knew what was happening, but everybody was very carefully paying attention to eating their food or talking to each other, or looking out of the window. 'According to the parents, he gave them no warning he was going off, although scuttlebutt has it that the little scrote very often goes off for days at a time before coming back with dosh, booze or electrical equipment that he can't account for.'

Hillary nodded. 'And Myers?'

'Was under surveillance the whole time,' Charlie said positively. Hillary, who'd been listlessly pushing a tomato around her plate, looked up sharply at that.

'Reliable?'

'Hell yes! The teams watching him even have photos of him fiddling around with his lawn mower at the time Gary Firth was last seen leaving his parent's house. Whatever happened to him, Myers had nothing to do with it.'

Unless he has an accomplice, Hillary thought, but didn't say.

'So the team think Firth's just doing one of his usual thieving walkabouts?'

Charlie nodded. 'That's the Guv's thinking at the moment,' he confirmed.

Hillary smiled, pushed her plate away, and murmured her thanks. Charlie watched her go thoughtfully. He knew that a young DC way down the pecking order was Janine Mallow's pet, and had almost certainly reported to the widow by now. Unless he was totally losing his touch, he reckoned she'd then got straight on to her old boss, and demanded some action. He'd had to interview Janine Mallow on a few occasions before now, and guessed she could be volatile if not handled carefully.

He could only hope that she didn't land Hillary Greene in too much trouble.

Hillary parked in a park and ride service area a long way from the notorious Oxford estate and took the bus into town. She not only didn't want her car stolen by the roving gangs who saw any parked car as a source of scrap, but she didn't want her number plate noted and marked down by any plainclothes men who might still be hanging around.

She took the back roads on foot, and approached the house of Gary Firth's parents from the rear. As she walked up the back garden path, strewn with the usual decorations of dog shit, perennial weeds and scattered car engine parts she felt her chest tightening.

She knocked on the door and heard a huge dog, somewhere inside, set up a ferocious barking. It was probably an illegal pit bull, for the Firths and several other families around here were well known to be a part of the illegal dog-fighting fraternity.

She braced herself as, after some moments, the door opened. A man stood there, dressed in baggy brown trousers and a dirty vest. Unshaved and bleary-eyed, his pale-blue eyes narrowed on her aggressively.

'What the hell do you want?' he barked. 'I work nights, and

I'm trying to get some sleep. Been bloody impossible today, I can tell you. You better not be trying to sell me something. And if you're one of them bloody Jehovah's Witnesses I'm setting the dog on you.'

Hillary smiled grimly. 'None of the above sir,' she said pleasantly, reaching for her card, using a well-placed thumb to hide her actual name from sight. She felt her heartbeat rocket as he reached out and snatched it from her, scrutinizing it carefully.

'Another one of you bloody lot. I've had you here all morning. Why don't you just sod off?'

Hillary held out her hand for her card, and refused to wince as he slammed it down into her palm.

'You don't seem overly concerned about your missing son, sir,' she said, again mildly.

'Little sod's just gone off, ain't he?' the boy's father – or maybe stepfather or even 'uncle' – said flatly. 'He'll be back when he's ready.'

Behind him, she could see a young lad's face peering around an interior door.

'Do you have any idea where he may have gone, sir? A friend's place, perhaps, or a dossing-down site he likes to use?'

The man grunted and closed the door in her face. Through the wood, she could hear him swearing profusely, and heard a female voice reply. She sighed and turned, walking back up the path; but as she reached the gate, she heard the door behind her open again.

A young lad of about fourteen or so came through the door. Reaching behind a brown and a green wheelie bin, he emerged with a top-of-the-range mountain bike that was far too big for him. Cynically, she wondered where Gary Firth or his father had stolen it.

'Hey,' she said in greeting as he headed up the path towards her, wheeling the bike carefully. The boy shot her a quick, knowing glance.

'You're wasting your time back there,' the boy said, both his words and his world-weary attitude those of a much older individual. But then, Hillary supposed, growing up as a Firth on this estate probably made for a very short childhood indeed. If any.

'Dad won't say nothing, even if he was really worried, which he ain't. Speaking to the coppers will get him a thrashing see?'

Hillary nodded, not bothering to ask who'd be doing the thrashing. It would have been pointless.

'Besides, Gary's all right,' the boy said, nodding at the gate. Obligingly, Hillary opened it, stepping to one side to let him pass.

'Glad to hear it,' she said, not altogether truthfully, it had to be said. 'And you're sure of that, are you?'

'Oh yeah,' the boy said, sounding amused. 'I heard him on the phone to Johnno Dix last night. Johnno's got this motorbike, and he called round for Gary this morning. I was still in bed, but I heard 'em talking underneath me window, like. Johnno's gonna take Gary down to Wales to some poxy caravan his old man's got down there. Gonna buy some porn and pull a few jobs.'

The boy shrugged, climbed on to his expensive mountain bike, and, with some difficulty, got one foot on a pedal.

Hillary wondered what Gary Firth had done to piss off his little brother so much. It must have been something pretty dire for him to shop him to the cops. But then, sibling rivalry was a bitch. His brother had probably refused to steal a cool crash helmet for him, to go with the flash mountain bike.

'Hey, you tell the other coppers this?' she asked, before he could make off.

'Nah. Wasn't here then,' the boy tossed casually over his shoulder and, standing up on the pedals – since his arse couldn't reach the saddle – he shot off.

She got the bus back to the park and ride, wondering whether Mel's squad had managed to get the information of Gary Firth's probable whereabouts from anyone else. But it seemed unlikely, since they'd hardly be the kind to talk to the cops. So, the chances were, she was in possession of knowledge that Mel's team didn't have. Of course, the little sod on the mountain bike might just have been feeding her a line. Winding up the cops and setting them on a wild-goose chase probably passed for entertainment in the Firth family circle.

She sighed as she pulled into HQ and climbed the stairs wearily back to her office. She'd been gone for less than an hour, and didn't need to phone Janine yet. She was just heading towards her desk when Danvers caught her eye from his cubicle, and beckoned her over.

She knocked on his door and walked in.

'Hillary. Glad I caught you. I've got Frank's papers.' He reached into his tray and withdrew a slim beige folder. 'All he needs to do is sign. I've had a word with the admin and pensions people, and they'll make sure it's plain sailing.' He grinned widely. 'None of them wanted to put any obstacles in the way of finally getting rid of him.'

Hillary smiled her thanks and took the papers. She was just turning to the door, when her DCI's desk phone rang. She stepped through and was turning to shut the door behind her when Danvers said sharply, 'Hang on,' and she paused, raising an eyebrow in query.

'Yes sir, she's just here now,' Danvers said, lifting a finger to detain her. 'I'll send her right up,' he added. He hung up and met her eye thoughtfully.

'Donleavy wants to see you in his office.'

Hillary smiled a brief greeting at Donleavy's secretary as she walked past her desk, then knocked briefly on his door and received a curt invitation to come in. She shot the secretary a quick look, and because of the way the normally friendly woman avoided her eyes, felt her heart sink.

Not a friendly call then.

When she opened the door and walked in, her eyes went straight to the man rising to his feet in front of the detective chief superintendent's desk and, with a distinct sense of *déjà vu* she felt her face smooth out into blank insolence.

Brian Vane watched her approach with a tight look of his own. Marcus Donleavy didn't rise, and didn't indicate the chair next to Vane's own for her to sit down, either. The unusual lack of courtesy amused Hillary more than anything. She really *was* in the dog house about something.

What a pity she just didn't seem to care.

'Sir?' She met Donleavy's gaze placidly.

'We've received a complaint about you, Hillary,' Marcus Donleavy said, coming straight to the point.

'Oh?' she asked mildly, and without curiosity.

'From the parents of Gary Firth,' Brian Vane took over smoothly, in what was obviously a prearranged move. 'Have you just been over there to interview them?' he demanded.

Hillary met his gaze blankly. 'I've never set eyes on Mrs Firth in my life, sir,' she said, utterly truthfully.

Vane blinked.

'But you were over at their house just now?' he pressed. 'Don't deny it – you were seen by two officers who were watching the Firth residence.'

Hillary smiled. 'I wasn't about to deny it sir. I spoke, very briefly, with Mr Firth, and then with a young lad, presumably a younger son.'

Vane let out his breath in a slow, careful exhale. His brown eyes gleamed briefly. He might just as well have said *Gotcha* out loud. 'You've no right to be anywhere near that residence, Detective Inspector Greene,' Vane said severely, as Donleavy watched the interplay between them with growing concern.

It was clear now that Vane had some kind of serious issue with Hillary Greene, and obviously didn't like her, but, potentially catastrophic as that was, it was Hillary Greene's reaction – or lack of it – that was worrying him far more.

She seemed almost totally indifferent. And this was not a feigned indifference either, employed as a defensive measure to either enrage or disconcert her superior officer.

'No sir,' she agreed placidly.

Vane looked momentarily nonplussed by the admission. He shot a quick glance at Donleavy, who looked on, blank faced.

'I don't want you interfering in any way with DCI Evans's investigation. Is that clear?' Vane said sharply, feeling as if, somehow, this situation was getting away from him. Greene was clearly in the wrong, but for some reason, it was he who was feeling discomfited.

'Yes sir,' Hillary said clearly.

'Very well. In that case, so long as it's clearly understood, I'd best be getting back to my office.' Vane glanced at Donleavy, who nodded. He turned and held a hand out to Hillary for her to precede him. She'd just started to do so when Donleavy's voice halted her.

'Just a few quick words, DI Greene.'

Hillary turned back. Vane carried on walking. Hillary let him get to the door before saying softly, 'Sir, do you want me to pass on the information I gained from my visit to the Firth house this morning to DCI Evans and his team, or would you like to?'

Donleavy quickly hid a smile by placing his hand over his mouth. Now this, he thought, with some relief, was more like it.

Vane hesitated at the doorway. 'What do you mean? What information?' he asked suspiciously.

Hillary smiled briefly. 'According to the lad I talked to, Gary Firth has gone to Wales, riding pillion on the motorbike of a pal of his named Johnno Dix. Dix has a caravan somewhere down there. They intend to get up to some mischief or other, no doubt.'

Vane hesitated, glanced at Donleavy, then nodded. 'I'll relay that to DCI Evans,' he agreed. 'Although I'm sure he and his team are already conversant with those facts.'

Hillary doubted it, and the look on her face said so. When the door slammed behind him, she turned back to Donleavy, who looked at her warily.

'What's the problem between you and Vane?' he asked abruptly.

Hillary looked at him levelly, and said quietly, 'Are you sure you want to know, sir?'

Marcus Donleavy thought about that for a moment, and then sighed. Obviously Hillary could handle the man, and whatever the problem was, it was bound to be something that could cause trouble. 'Probably not,' he said, without apology. Then his gaze sharpened.

'You've been keeping well clear of Mel's case so far,' he said cautiously. 'And it's not like you to go off half-cocked like this. What on earth possessed you to go and talk to the Firths?'

It was not an idle question, and they both knew it. Hillary was no fool, and knew that she was, to a certain extent, on unofficial probation here. Not only had she been standing next to her best friend and superior officer when he'd been shot and killed, she'd also been on leave for nearly two months. She was bound to come under close scrutiny until she'd proved to everyone's satisfaction that she was back to her old self and fighting fit – both mentally and emotionally, as well as physically.

The last thing she could afford to do was show signs of bad judgement.

Hillary sighed heavily. Ever since she'd stepped into Donleavy's office she knew he'd ask her that question, and she'd been deliberating the pros and cons of telling him the truth all the time she'd been dealing with Vane.

On the one hand, instinct and loyalty said she should keep Janine's name out of this. But Hillary hadn't got where she was without learning a thing or two. And sometimes, you just simply had to cover your own arse. Besides, she trusted Donleavy – to a certain degree – and knew that, with Janine gradually getting more and more dangerous, she might just need some heavy hitter on her side in the near future.

'I got a call from Janine Mallow sir,' Hillary said at last, making sure she let her reluctance show. After all, nobody liked a snitch. 'She was going to go over to the Firth house to interview the family herself. Naturally, I talked her out of it, but I could only get her to agree to calm down if I promised to go and talk to them myself.'

Donleavy sighed heavily. 'And with good results by the sound of it. Damn. I've spoken to DI Mallow myself. I have to say, I got the impression that she could be rather unpredictable.'

Hillary shrugged. 'She's pregnant, a widow, a serving police officer, and her husband's killer is still wandering about as free as a bird. I think unpredictable is the best we can hope for. Sir.'

It was a loud and clear warning, and Donleavy felt himself tense. DI Greene knew the woman well, of course, having been her commanding officer for several years. And if she saw fireworks ahead, then it was time to start ordering the asbestos suit.

'I'll have a discreet word with DCI Evans,' Donleavy said quietly. 'Tell him the situation, and be sure to explain that you'll be acting as a brake and restraint on DI Mallow. It'll keep him off your back if you have to wander on to his turf again.'

Hillary nodded. 'Thank you, sir.'

Marcus nodded. In spite of all the unforeseen problems with Vane and Janine Mallow, Marcus Donleavy felt it was good to have Hillary Greene back in the saddle again, and obviously bearing up well. He'd been worried, for a minute there, that she was finding it a struggle to get back in harness.

At least that worry had finally been put to rest.

'Try to keep the woman from doing anything dire, DI Greene,' he said flatly.

Hillary sighed. As if she didn't have enough on her plate already.

'Yes sir,' she said grimly.

CHAPTER SIX

The moment Hillary walked back into the large open-plan office she noticed that Gemma Fordham was back at her desk. She wondered, briefly, how the younger woman was going to handle it, now that they'd at last dragged everything out into the open. To say that things could be a bit awkward from now on was putting it mildly.

Hillary gave a mental shrug, walked straight to her desk and sat down. 'Keith, before I forget,' she turned to Barrington, careful to keep her voice casual, 'I want you to ask around in the Philpott circle of friends and family, and see if there's been any known trouble between Rachel and her father.'

Barrington blinked. 'Right Guv. But you don't really rate her as a contender, do you?'

Briefly, she explained the SOCO results of the fingerprints found on the spade handle. 'Which means that it was either Rachel, the as yet unknown juvenile, or a killer who wore gloves. The last seems most likely at this point, I admit, which means that Eddie Philpott's murder was almost certainly premeditated,' Hillary concluded. 'I think it's more than likely that the killer came prepared, and simply used the spade, because it was already there and handy at the scene. Gemma,' she turned and looked deliberately at her sergeant, 'at some point, we need to take the Warner kids' fingerprints.' SOCO had probably taken Rachel Warner's prints on the morning of the original call out, but her children had been at school at that time.

'I'll get on it, Guv,' Gemma said, wooden faced.

'Guv, before I forget,' Barrington said. 'Rachel's GP. I tracked him down, and he can either see us today, this afternoon at 3.30, when the afternoon surgery ends, or the day after tomorrow.'

Hillary grunted and checked her watch. 'We'd better get our skates on then,' she said briskly.

Gemma watched them leave, and slumped in her chair in relief. She was still reeling from the revelations piled on her by her boss, and was relieved to have some time to herself at the deserted island of desks.

Frank Ross, as usual, was AWOL, but nobody cared about that.

Now that she'd had some time to get over the initial shock, Gemma stared blankly down at her desk. Just what did she do now?

Funnily enough, she believed Hillary Greene when she said that her late husband Ronnie's dirty money was gone, and that another bent cop had found and taken it. On the face of it, it seemed such an unlikely story, but the alternative was that Hillary Greene knew its whereabouts and was intending to retire on it at some point to a nice sunny clime where extradition was a bit of a grey area.

And that just didn't fit with the woman she knew.

So Gemma's dream of her future was over. Gone. There'd be no independent wealthy lifestyle, free of a rich lover or husband. Of course, she still had her man Guy. The blind music don drew in a healthy stipend from his college and, besides which, came from a well-heeled family and had investments galore. He would, Gemma knew, marry her on the spot if she indicated that she'd say yes, if asked.

But was that really what she wanted?

She sighed, and turned to stare out of the window, at the uninspiring view of the vast car park. It was cloudy and dull, a bit like how she felt.

Slowly her mind turned to what else Hillary Greene had

told her in the ladies' loo. With Frank Ross gone, she'd be the sole DS on Hillary's team. And she'd also believed her boss when she promised to give Gemma more and more responsibility and kudos. Which meant that within another year, maybe two, she could sit her Boards for DI. And be confident of passing, and of Hillary Greene's written recommendations for promotion into the next available position. Which could mean a nick many miles from here. And a brand-new start felt attractive right now.

But could she hack it for another year or two? Knowing that Hillary Greene had been on to her from the moment she started work at Kidlington HQ and had always been one step ahead, was seriously messing with her head. Shit, the older woman must have been laughing up her sleeve all the time that Gemma had been sneaking around, trying to get a handle on that bastard Ronnie Greene's money.

Just the thought of it made her burn with shame and humiliation.

And yet Hillary had also hit the nail on the head when she'd warned Gemma that to ask for a transfer right now could do serious damage to her career. With Mel dead, and Ross retiring, it would smack very much of a rat deserting a sinking ship. And with Hillary's status at HQ never having been higher – given an award for bravery only last year, a murder clearance rate second to none, and now back after two months' leave – Gemma would be universally hated if she asked for a transfer now.

So, the only other option she had was to quit. Marry Guy and live a life of ease and comfort. Gemma gave a mental snort of bitter laugher. She could just imagine what her fireman father and all her fireman brothers would say about that! The teasing would never stop. No, she simply couldn't quit. Apart from anything else, she'd be bored out of her skull within a month, living in Guy's big house off the Woodstock Road.

So the decision was really made for her. She'd stay, get her promotion, and move on.

She supposed she was lucky really. If Hillary Greene had been a different sort of a woman, she could have made Gemma's life miserable. But during their devastating chat in the ladies' loo, there'd been no hint of one-upmanship, no trace of triumph or hidden smirking glee in her superior officer. And somehow that fact only added to Gemma's discomfort. She felt shabby and small, and she didn't like it.

Slowly, her chin lifted. Well, there'd be no running away from it, that was for sure. And the only way she could win back her self-respect and get back on target was to be the best damn sergeant Hillary Greene had ever had.

With that in mind, she grabbed her coat and left the office.

Rachel's GP was situated in Deddington's health centre, and driving back through the pretty ironstone village recalled to Hillary's mind an earlier case. It had been just outside this village that a young artist had been found dead in a beautiful flower-strewn water meadow. A case she'd been able to bring to a quick and successful conclusion.

She only hoped she'd be able to do the same with her current case. It would send a clear and resounding message that she still had the old magic.

But did she? Somewhere, lurking at the back of her mind, was the niggling feeling that she wasn't operating at anything like her best. And to make matters worse, she had the not unfamiliar feeling that something somebody had said to her was mightily significant, and she was damned if she could think what it was. If she could only handle Mel's death better than she was doing would she already know who had killed Eddie Philpott? But last night she'd tossed and turned for hours, and now felt tired and muzzy-headed.

Maybe she shouldn't be in charge of this investigation.

Pushing aside such painful thoughts – after all, a crisis of confidence now would really put the kibosh on her work – she looked around as Barrington carefully parked her ancient

Volkswagen Golf. The car park was virtually empty, and a faint flurry of rain suddenly splashed across the windscreen.

'It's going to get dark early tonight, Guv,' Barrington said, turning off the ignition.

Hillary agreed, and after that, the two police officers walked in silence to the open surgery door. After Barrington had pressed a large pad on the inside corridor wall the inner door opened and Barrington approached the reception desk.

'Hello. DC Barrington. We're here to see Dr Scudamore-Blaire.'

'Oh yes. Straight down the corridor, fourth on the left.' The receptionist watched them pass her glass-fronted window with interested eyes, then turned to her fellow receptionist for a gossip. On a wet and miserable quiet Tuesday afternoon, a little piquancy was always welcome.

Dr Martin Scudamore-Blaire was a tired-looking man in his early sixties, lean and rather desiccated in appearance. He checked both Hillary's and Barrington's IDs carefully, and smiled a brief welcome over his gold-rimmed spectacles.

Hillary pulled up a chair, but Barrington preferred to sit on the edge of the high examination couch, where he pulled out his notebook and waited.

'Doctor, thank you for seeing us. Constable Barrington explained the circumstances?' Hillary began easily.

'Yes. I have to say, Inspector, I'm not totally comfortable discussing a patient with you.'

Hillary nodded. 'I understand, doctor. But as you know, Rachel Warner's father has been brutally murdered.'

'Yes, I treated her for shock at the time.'

'I noticed that she looked very ill,' Hillary said, deliberately vaguely.

'That's self-evident,' the GP agreed cautiously.

'Would I be right in thinking that it's a very serious illness?'
'Yes.'

'Terminal?'

'Yes.'

'And she's aware of this?'

'Yes.'

Hillary nodded. 'Does she have much time left?'

Dr Scudamore-Blaire frowned. 'I really don't like talking about a patient, as I said.'

'Six months?' Hillary pressed calmly. The doctor's grey eyebrows rose impatiently.

'Less than six months? Four?'

'Let's just say you're not far wrong,' the GP agreed reluctantly.

Hillary quickly decided that pressing for medical details would be futile, and deliberately changed her tone to one of sympathetic concern instead.

'She's a widow, I believe. So she must, I imagine, have been relying on her father to look after her children until they came of age?'

Dr Scudamore-Blaire sighed heavily. 'Yes. We talked about it not so long ago. And I was able to reassure her that her father was still a very fit and active man. After all, in this day and age, sixty-five can't really be considered old. She seemed anxious to know if the authorities would be likely to leave her children in their grandfather's care. I did my best to reassure her that they would.'

Hillary nodded. 'Her eldest, Julie, is already twelve, so she only has four years to go until she's sixteen. And even if you consider that the boy had another six years to go until he was independent, Edward Philpott would still only have been seventy-one.'

Yes, she thought, the social services probably *would* have consented to such an arrangement all right. What with fostering and care services stretched to breaking point, they'd probably have been only too happy to go along with such a neat and mutually agreeable solution.

'Had Mr Philpott agreed to look after the children, do you know?' Hillary asked, always liking to get her facts confirmed.

'Oh yes. He doted on those two. They were his only grand-children, you see. And having lived in his house for a good deal of their childhood anyway, he was used to having them around.' The GP sighed grimly. 'But now this had to happen.'

Hillary shook her head. 'The poor woman must be distraught,' she said, with genuine pity now. 'So what's the alternative? Fostering?'

The GP shrugged his shoulders helplessly. 'I believe Rachel has two cousins, one in Bath, the other up north somewhere. But I have no idea how they're placed financially or familywise. From what I can gather, they're neither of them particularly close to Mrs Warner, and the likelihood of them wanting to take on the responsibility of two grieving youngsters, well!' He spread his hands and shrugged helplessly again.

'She's not had an easy life, has she,' Hillary mused. 'Firstly she loses her husband, then she's diagnosed with, well, I'm assuming it's cancer?' Hillary fished delicately, but the doctor merely raised his eyebrows at her again. 'And now her father is murdered. Have you ever noticed how tragedy seems to plague some people? I notice it a lot in my profession.'

'Mine too,' the GP agreed gloomily. 'And of course, in Rachel's case, there was also that other trouble she went through, when only a youngster herself.'

Hillary blinked. 'Trouble?'

'Yes, surely you remember the case. Linda Quirke.'

The name rang a very faint bell. 'I'm not sure I follow you, Doctor,' Hillary prompted.

'Linda Quirke went missing – oh, it must be twenty-five years ago now. They never found her.'

Hillary nodded. 'Yes. I remember now.' She hadn't been in the force at the time, as she recalled, but it had made a splash in the papers, and along with everyone else at the time, the picture of Linda Quirke's long dark plaits and plaintive dark eyes had tugged at her heartstrings. 'But how did this affect Rachel Warner?' she asked, puzzled.

'Oh they were best friends, Inspector,' the GP explained. 'They went to the same primary school, and had just gone up to secondary school at the time of the incident. They were, by all accounts, virtually inseparable.'

Hillary nodded. So the officer in charge of the missing child's case would have questioned the young Rachel Philpott quite closely.

And something like that was bound to leave a mark.

Of course, there had been so many other similar cases since then. They broke into the public consciousness with a scream of outraged media attention and gut-wrenching misery on the part of the parents, only, over the years, to fade back into obscurity until the next tragedy happened to bring it back to mind.

But for people affected by it, people like Rachel, and Linda Quirke's parents, there would be no forgetting.

'They never found her, as you said,' Hillary mused thoughtfully. 'I think the general opinion at the time was that she'd almost certainly been abducted and killed.'

'Yes. Alas, that nearly always seems to be the case,' the doctor said heavily.

'Not always, Doctor. I've known several cases where missing children have been found, unmolested and unharmed, quite some time after they'd gone missing,' Hillary contradicted. 'In one case, a young lad of six had crawled into a washing machine in a dump near his home and had been locked in. Sniffer dogs found him, as I recall. Then there was another case where a young girl of ten, I think it was, was found by a farmer who was uprooting a tree blown down in a gale. The young girl had taken shelter underneath it, and become trapped in the roots when it toppled over.'

'Happy endings, Inspector,' the doctor agreed. 'But alas, Linda Quirke was never found. Her parents moved from the area some years ago now.'

'It must have affected Rachel tremendously,' Hillary agreed. 'Losing a best friend in those circumstances, and at that age, must have had a long-lasting psychological effect on her.'

'Yes,' the doctor agreed, somewhat cautiously. 'But don't forget, she put that all behind her, got married and had a family. Most people are resilient, you know.'

Hillary smiled grimly. 'It's a good thing they are, Doctor, isn't it?' she agreed.

Outside, they hurried through the rain to her car, and Hillary sat shivering slightly as Barrington turned on the ignition. She reached across to the dashboard and pulled the lever on the heater down to maximum. Obediently, a vague waft of warm air eddied around her feet.

'It makes you wonder why some people seem to have so much misery dumped on them, doesn't it, Guv,' Barrington said bleakly. 'What on earth's that poor woman going to do now?'

Hillary shook her head. 'Get in touch with the cousins, I suppose. See how the land lies. And if that doesn't work, I imagine she'll try and get social services to let her have a say in where her children go, after she's gone.'

Barrington shook his head. 'We've got to get the bastard who did this, Guv,' he said grimly. 'Whoever killed Eddie Philpott didn't just do in an old man. They wrecked an entire family.'

Hillary felt her stomach clench. Yes, they had to get this killer all right. Far more than on any of her other murder cases, Hillary could feel a growing pressure on her to get the man or woman responsible.

So wasn't it just sod's law, with bells on, that she was feeling on her worst form ever?

Back at HQ, she found Frank Ross at his desk, and told him to pull out the old Linda Quirke file when he had five minutes, more to satisfy her curiosity than anything else. The GP's revelations about the old case had piqued her interest.

Making herself comfortable at her desk, she read through the latest bunch of reports and paperwork, including the uniform's witness statement forms that had now been taken from every inhabitant of The Knott.

As expected, nothing of interest stood out. No strangers observed or unknown cars reported, no unusual behaviour noted on the part of either the victim or any neighbour. Nobody had stood out as someone who obviously disliked the victim, and no one knew of anything detrimental about him.

No motive, no witnesses, no nothing.

She sighed and tossed the reports aside. Her headache, which had never really gone away, was beginning to throb anew, and she felt hideously tired.

She grabbed her bag. 'I'm going to make an early night of it and start afresh in the morning.'

Barrington shot her a startled look. He'd never known her to leave much before eight o'clock in the evening when working on a murder case, and the fact that it was barely five now made him uneasy. Even Frank Ross frowned, but, as could be expected of Frank Ross, he took advantage of the boss's early departure to bugger off himself.

Back on board the *Mollern*, Hillary Greene poured herself a large glass of wine, and reached for her mobile.

Reluctantly, she telephoned Janine Mallow's number and filled her in on what she'd found out at the Firth residence. She managed to extract a promise from her ex-sergeant that she'd keep her distance from DCI Evans and his team, but Hillary would not have been surprised if Janine had got in the car and headed for Wales the moment Hillary hung up.

She sipped her glass of wine, finished it, and poured another one. With precise movements, she recorked the bottle and put it away in the fridge, firmly out of sight, and stood staring out on to the darkening towpath.

A light spilled out from the neighbouring boat, *Willowsands*, belonging to her old friend Nancy Walker. But she wasn't in the mood for company right now. With a sigh, she drew the small scrap of turquoise fabric that passed for a curtain across the porthole, and took her glass of wine to bed. She also took a novel with her to help her while away the hours before she could strip, and crawl under the bedclothes.

Unknown to her, several miles away in the attractive town of Thame, somebody else was also making a good show of turning in for an early night.

But Clive Myers had no intention of sleeping that night. He was simply waiting for the wet and dark night to become even darker, before giving his watchers the slip.

The next morning, Wednesday, 8 October, dawned blustery but bright, and Hillary was in the office by a quarter to eight. She used the quiet time to catch up on the other caseloads, complete some paperwork, and marshal her thoughts into some sort of order.

Gemma Fordham arrived, and gave Hillary her usual brief nod. So, we're going to play it as if nothing had ever happened, Hillary mused. Well, that was fine by her.

'Any joy on the fingerprints?' she asked curiously.

'I went over to the Philpott residence early yesterday evening and got the boy's prints – the daughter's too. I dropped them straight off at SOCO, and they said they'd let you know if the prints match as soon as they can. They've got quite a backlog of stuff to get through.'

Hillary grunted. It went without saying that the police laboratories were always backlogged, but murder cases were given a high priority, and Hillary knew they'd get around to her as soon as they humanly could.

'Any ideas so far?' Hillary asked, not to put Gemma on the spot, but because she genuinely wanted to hear her thoughts on the case. Gemma was bright and never missed a trick, and Hillary was relying heavily on her dynamic young blonde sergeant to catch anything she might overlook.

'Nothing obvious, Guv,' Gemma answered, after a moment's

thought. 'Although I went down to Eddie Philpott's old post office depot yesterday afternoon to ask around and see what I could nose out.'

Hillary nodded. 'Good idea.' She hadn't asked her to do it, but probably would have, sooner or later. The fact that she'd anticipated her gave Hillary a distinct feeling of security. Ridiculous as it might seem, Hillary was actually relieved to have this woman at her back.

'I couldn't find anybody who had anything bad to say about the man,' Gemma said slowly. 'No hint of dishonesty, that's for sure. His bosses saw him as reliable, very rarely off sick and, for the most part, a trustworthy plodder. Somebody who didn't moan too much and just got on with it. Most of his cronies seemed to think the same, and most said that he'd been counting down the days to retirement – the same as the rest of them.'

Hillary nodded, getting the picture at once. 'Eddie was a man who lived for his garden, his hobbies and his family,' she agreed. 'Definitely not a career-minded individual. He'd have been upset about his daughter's condition, and worried, I daresay about having to rear his grandkids alone. Not having to hold down a full-time job as well must have been a load off his mind.'

Gemma nodded. 'So, who'd want to kill a man like that? That's the question, isn't it?'

Hillary sighed. 'No obvious history of financial trouble?'

'No,' Gemma replied. 'He banked his salary straight away, and didn't spend much of it, after paying the bills. He retired on a full pension too. No signs of gambling, drinking, or any other of the favourite vices.'

Hillary shook her head. It wasn't what she wanted to hear. This was the third day into her enquiries, and they were still short of any solid leads.

It was, surprisingly enough, Frank Ross who provided them with something new. He rolled in around half past nine, almost shaved, and in a nearly clean suit. He helped himself to a mug of coffee from Barrington's personal carafe, and sat down at his desk, slurping.

'Found out something interesting, Guv,' he said, when both Gemma and the red-headed DC had finished filling her in on their findings.

'Oh?' Hillary said. 'Care to share it, Frank?' she pressed, when he continued to slurp coffee noisily.

Fully aware of her impatience, he grinned wolfishly. 'Our victim had a bit on the side,' he said gleefully.

Hillary sighed. Of course he did. As Scudamore-Blaire had pointed out yesterday, Eddie Philpott had been a still relatively young and fit, active man. It was hardly likely he'd been living the life of a celibate monk ever since his wife left him. Damn, why hadn't she thought of that earlier?

'Going to tell us her name any time soon, Frank?' Hillary asked drily.

'Martha Hepton, Guv.'

'I know that name,' Gemma said at once, her voice turning grim. 'I'm pretty sure I talked to her on Monday evening.' She reached for her notebook, a fierce scowl on her narrow, striking face, and began to riffle through the pages frantically.

Ross grinned, enjoying her discomfort. 'You probably did. She lives in Steeple Knott itself. In fact, she lives in our victim's old family home. The cottage his parents left him.'

Gemma found her notes and read them with a scowl. 'The crafty old cat never mentioned a word about knowing the victim as anything more than a neighbour.'

Frank Ross laughed and touched the side of his nose with a finger. Gemma flushed faintly, furious at being outdone by Ross, of all people.

'Let's go, Frank,' Hillary said calmly. Left alone at the office, he'd only wind everybody up. Besides, she wanted to talk to him alone.

*

Outside, they took her car and she drove, since she didn't really trust Frank to pass a breathalyzer test if they were ever pulled over.

Martha Hepton's cottage was one of the smallest in the hamlet, and on the furthest side from the Philpott family home. Even so, in so small a community, surely somebody must have known what had been going on? Unless Frank had got it wrong, of course. An event not entirely unheard of.

'You're sure about this, Frank?' she asked, as she climbed out of the car and glanced around. The hamlet was totally deserted. Not even a cat moved to disturb the scene. Of course, most of the inhabitants had left for work, leaving just a few old folk behind. So perhaps it had been relatively easy, after all, for two canny and seasoned lovers to conduct an affair in secret in a place as remote and quiet as this.

'I have my sources, Guv,' Frank answered firmly. In this case, a nosy old man in a pub in the next village down the road, whose missus was gossip monger in chief for the county.

The front garden of Honeysuckle Cottage was tiny, and totally gravelled. Two plant pots, each bearing a rather dry-looking yucca, stood at either side of the path, which consisted of just four flagstones. If her lover had been a gardener *par excellence*, it was not a passion shared by his mistress it appeared, Hillary thought wryly. Although, to be fair, a large honeysuckle did cascade picturesquely over the upside down V of the front porch.

Hillary knocked loudly. The door was opened after a few moments by an attractive, fifty-something woman, with dyed auburn hair and bright green eyes. She was wearing a large white smock, covered with daubs of paint and held a paintbrush in her hand.

She eyed Hillary and Frank warily, then sighed. 'Oh hell,' she said bluntly. 'I knew I should just have come clean when that first rozzer came asking about Eddie.'

Hillary smiled brightly. 'It's usually a good idea, madam,' she advised.

The woman nodded glumly. 'The truth was, I was just so damned surprised to hear that Eddie was dead. It sort of addled what little brains I already have, and I just stood there like a lemon, spouting all sorts of guff.'

She blinked, then took a deep breath. 'Oh well. You'd better come in, then. Welcome to the house of sin.'

So saying, she held the door open wider to admit them.

CHAPTER SEVEN

F ar from a house of sin, Honeysuckle Cottage looked very much like a small, charming country dwelling. Original flagstones in the cramped hall led to similar flooring in a small but functional kitchen. Martha Hepton led them into that room but then surprised them by continuing on and into a small glass conservatory attached to the sunny side of the cottage.

Apart from a few tubs of unremarkable greenery though, the space was bare of plants. Instead, a large easel was set up in the centre of the room, and ranks of finished canvasses lined the walls. A white-painted wrought-iron table and matching garden chairs were placed to one side.

'Sorry for the squeeze. Margery is due to collect a batch later today,' Martha said, indicating the paintings and then the cramped quarters with an apology. 'She owns a gallery in Woodstock, which isn't quite as grand as it sounds. She caters strictly to the tourists, nothing well paid or pretentious,' she added with a grin. 'Which is why I can't afford a decent studio, but please, pull up a chair, if you can make room.'

She tossed the paintbrush she was holding into a jam jar full of murky-looking liquid, as Hillary approached the canvas on the easel. It was a rather good watercolour of an English water meadow, with a church spire in the background, and placidly grazing cattle everywhere else. It was very nearly complete, save for a patch of buttercups and daisies the artist was high-lighting in the bottom right-hand corner.

'Nice,' Hillary said. And that's all it was. She personally wouldn't give it house room, and the artist seemed to sense it, for Martha shrugged helplessly.

'What can I do? I have just enough talent to know that I don't have enough talent. If I was honest, I'd go out and get a job in a supermarket, but instead I churn these out, and my pal Margery flogs them on to the Yanks and vast ranks of Japanese. You'd be surprised how many of them want something just a bit more original than a pottery thimble or a brass plaque of the dreaming spires of Oxford to take home as a keepsake. It doesn't earn me a fortune – hell, it barely earns me a living, but it still beats stacking shelves.' Martha sighed. 'Lemonade?'

In spite of the fact that autumn was well under way, it was understandably warm in the glasshouse. Hillary assumed that in the summer, Martha must be forced into another room in the house.

'Thanks,' she accepted gratefully. She watched Martha as she poured three glasses, and handed one to Frank Ross, who took it reluctantly. Unless it was secretly dosed with vodka or gin, she doubted he'd take more than a token swallow.

They all sat around the table, elbows touching, and Hillary drank the tart, refreshing liquid with pleasure. 'So, you and Eddie Philpott.'

Martha sighed heavily. 'Yes. Well, we've been lovers for nearly twenty years now, but I suppose you've already found that out. Hell, I can't believe it's been that long. Well, maybe I can.' She looked around somewhat bemusedly. 'Time seems to just go,' she added forlornly.

Hillary nodded. 'I understand you rent this property from him?'

Martha snorted a rather inelegant laugh, and then shook her head. 'Sorry. But yes, or well, sort of. It's strictly of the peppercorn variety, I'm afraid, since I couldn't afford to pay anything like what the cottage is worth in today's market.' She gave a very real shudder. 'But Eddie, bless him, was always big-hearted. And, well, I did provide him with his comforts.'

Hillary nodded. 'It sounds like a mutually beneficial arrange-ment.'

Martha nodded. 'It is. Sorry, *was*.' Her mop of dyed auburn curls bounced around her head as she shook her head. 'I just can't believe Eddie's dead. I just can't seem to make it real, somehow, do you know what I mean?'

Hillary did. She'd been hearing statements like that from the victims of violent crime throughout her long career. The wording might change, but the meaning was always the same. Sheer disbelief.

'When was the last time you saw him?' she asked quietly.

'Saturday night, as usual. Saturdays and Wednesdays were "our" nights. Not that he ever stayed overnight, you under-stand. I think he was rather keen not to upset his daughter. Although why Rachel would be upset by her father staying out all night beats me. As I told him, she was a married woman with kids of her own. It's not as if she doesn't know what he gets up to when he calls in here. And why would she care?' Martha laughed abruptly. 'Silly sod he could be, sometimes.' She stared miserably at her canvas and then let her eyes drift back to Hillary.

'Do you have any idea who did it?' she asked.

Hillary smiled briefly. 'Our enquiries are still ongoing,' she said, her standard phrase whenever asked that question by a member of the public. 'Did your last meeting with Edward Philpott go as usual?' she asked casually. 'Did he seem agitated or upset for example. Preoccupied, maybe?'

'Oh no. Nothing like that,' Martha shook her head vigorously. 'He was just the same as ever.'

'He didn't confide in you that he had anything on his mind, something worrying him, maybe? An argument with a friend, family troubles, threatening letters or phone calls. Anything of that kind?'

Martha looked genuinely astonished. *'Eddie?'* she squeaked. 'No. No, if you knew Eddie, you wouldn't ask that. The man was always the same. Used to drive me nuts, sometimes. You know, I've known that man all that time and I don't think I've ever seen him really lose his temper, or laugh with sheer joy. He just always plodded along, same old Eddie, day in, day out.'

Hillary could see how the more volatile nature of the artist would chafe against something like that.

'Of course, he was worried about his daughter,' Martha mused thoughtfully. 'And I have to say, the last time I saw her she wasn't looking well.'

Hillary nodded. So the very serious nature of Rachel Warner's illness wasn't in the public arena yet. She wondered why not. For all that Martha and Eddie had been an item for more than two decades, her lover seemed to have been unusually reticent.

'Did you go to Eddie's place last Monday morning, Mrs Hepton?' she asked curiously.

'Miss. And no, I didn't. I never went to Eddie's place, he always came here. Like I said, he could be a bit old-fashioned. And what with his grandkids living with him, I expect he'd have been a bit embarrassed at having to try and explain me to them.'

There was just a touch of bitterness there, Hillary mused, catching the pain behind the smile. But not too much. Martha was a woman who obviously knew when she was well off, and had no intention of letting any injured feelings that she might have lead her into rocking the boat.

'Did you kill Eddie?' Hillary asked casually.

Martha Hepton blinked rapidly. *'Me?* Why would I kill Eddie?'

Hillary smiled blandly. Why indeed?

A few minutes later, Hillary and Frank walked away from Honeysuckle Cottage and went back to her car.

'So what do you think?' Hillary asked routinely, and Frank Ross shrugged.

'Seems unlikely, Guv. She gets to live rent-free, and he got to have his bit of no-hassle rumpy-pumpy twice a week. Like she said, why would she kill the old sod off?'

Hillary nodded. It was very much what she'd been thinking too. 'Of course, something might have changed. Perhaps with his daughter about to die, he might have told her the arrangement was off. Social services would have been keeping an eye on the kids after Rachel was gone, and he might have been frightened that they'd see him as an unfit guardian if they found out about Martha.'

'The social wouldn't give a toss,' Frank Ross snorted, opening the door and slipping inside.

'I agree,' Hillary said, getting behind the steering wheel herself. 'But Eddie might not have known that. You heard his mistress – he had old-fashioned ideas.'

'Huh. So he gives her the elbow, and in a fit of passionate rage, she offs him?' Ross laughed. 'Don't think so, Guv. She's a comfortable middle-aged body, who was probably bored stiff with the old goat anyway. Hardly the sort to get into a tizzy over spurned love.'

Hillary felt her spirits drop. Ross's summary was identical to her own feelings on the matter. Which meant, in all likelihood, that another promising lead had just gone west.

To cheer herself up, Hillary reached into the back seat and handed Ross a slim, A4 beige envelope. 'Here, these are for you. Sign them and get them back to me.'

Ross opened the envelope and pulled out the papers. Hillary started the car, checked her mirrors, and pulled out.

'Are you having a laugh?' Ross asked a few minutes later, as they cruised down the narrow country lane. The ash trees lining the road were just beginning to turn, giving a faint tinge of orange and a hint of russet to the unrelenting green.

Hillary concentrated on her driving. 'Nope. You're eligible to retire on a full pension, and that's what you're going to do.'

She felt the man tense beside her, and ignored the colourful curse he came out with. She reached the main road, indicated, and turned right, heading back towards Kidlington.

'And what if I don't want to retire?' Ross asked, slapping the offending papers down on his knee with a resounding thwack.

Hillary took her eyes off the road long enough to shoot him a quick glance. He looked flushed with anger and his jaw was clenched so tight she could actually hear his teeth grind.

She sighed heavily. 'Come on Frank, what do you care? You don't give a shit about the job, and we both know it. Even if you ever did care, you've just been going through the motions for years now. You're barely in the office, and when you are, your paperwork is sloppy and always late, and more often than not you smell of a brewery. So why not just make it official?'

'I've still got bills to pay, the same as everyone else,' Ross snarled. 'And a full pension doesn't go far in this day and age.'

'Then get a part-time job, like everyone else,' Hillary snarled back. 'Hell, a night watchman's job is a doddle. Or you can sit in a car park all day on your fat arse and check vehicles coming and going, right? You and I both know there's plenty of firms about who hire ex-coppers for a show of security. Even you can manage that.'

Ross swore again. By the time they reached HQ Ross was still raging. After she'd parked in the lot and got out of the car Ross still effing and blinding beside her, ranting about how she wasn't going to push him out.

In no mood for his histrionics, she shouted him down. 'You're going,' she yelled across the roof of the car at him. 'You can either go with a bit of dignity and save some face by going quietly, or you'll get pushed out by the brass anyway. Both Danvers and Donleavy are behind me on this.'

Frank paled, finally understanding that she meant business. They both knew that no sergeant could stay in the force if enough people wanted him out. And of course both the men she mentioned would back her up. Danvers wanted to get into her knickers, and Donleavy, for some reason, had always rated her.

'You bitch!' he said at last.

'I expect those papers on my desk by the end of day tomorrow,' Hillary said flatly. When she turned and headed across the car park, she was aware of two uniformed officers smartly stepping out of her way. No doubt they'd heard everything she'd said, and the news would spread through the station like wildfire.

Hillary nodded at them grimly, without breaking stride.

She was still feeling tight-faced as she crossed the lobby, and for once the desk sergeant, sensing the atmosphere, didn't call her over for a chat.

Upstairs, she went to her desk and sat down. She'd barely put her bag away under the desk, however, when the phone rang.

'DI Greene.'

'Hill.' The desk sergeant's voice filled her ear. 'Thought I'd better warn you. DI Mallow's in the building. I just saw her go past.'

Hillary bit back a groan. 'Thanks, Sarge,' she said, and hung up.

Since her husband's murder, Janine had only been to HQ to give her interviews with DCI Evans, and everyone had felt both relieved and ashamed of their relief, at not having to face the bereaved widow. Now, when the door to the office opened and Janine walked in to her old stamping ground, Hillary felt every eye go to her. The noise level, always of a certain level, dropped audibly.

Hillary got up quickly and moved to the centre of the room to intercept her. She smiled as Janine approached and held out her hand. 'Janine. Good to see you,' she lied. 'Come and sit down.'

She saw Paul Danvers standing up behind his desk, a look of enquiry on his face, and with a discreet hand signal that the entire room of officers noted, she indicated for him to sit back down.

'Coffee?'

'You got decaff?' Janine asked, sitting down, somewhat ponderously, in Barrington's empty chair. 'The doctors are nagging me about my hypertension levels.'

Hillary gulped and reached for a jar of decaff that was Gemma Fordham's personal stash. Janine glanced around the empty desks and smiled grimly. 'Got all the troops out in the field, then?'

Hillary nodded. 'Milk and sugar still?'

'Yeah, thanks.'

Hillary made the coffee and handed it over. She sat down in her chair warily. Janine smiled wryly. 'Don't worry. I won't bite,' she said grimly. 'It's just that I'm going insane at home. My boss in Witney has given me a week's leave, whether I want it or not, and I can't just sit at home, staring at the walls.'

Hillary nodded. Mel Mallow had lived in a very desirable residence in the Moors area of Kidlington, an acquisition from his divorce from his second, extremely wealthy wife. And Hillary well remembered how much Janine Tyler, her young blonde sergeant at the time, had coveted it.

Now it had become somewhere she wanted escape from.

Hillary felt the familiar mix of bile and helpless rage begin to assail her whenever she was forced to think about her old friend, and quickly pushed it back down.

'I need something to do,' Janine said, the appeal in her voice cutting Hillary to the quick. 'And by that I mean something useful. Something that could help. Don't tell me to take up bloody Scrabble or something. I've got enough well-meaning do-gooders in my life as it is.'

Hillary smiled briefly. She knew just what Janine was asking for, but it was almost impossible to give her. She eyed the pregnant, wan-faced woman with some apprehension.

Never having experienced much illness herself, Hillary didn't know about hypertension, but it didn't sound good. What Janine needed was something to take her out of the house, and make her feel good about herself. Which meant helping out on her husband's case. But anything of that kind would instantly rile DCI Evans and the top brass for miles around.

'You could always go and do a bit of house-to-house,' Hillary said slowly. It was a fine day now and some gentle exercise would probably help. 'You know, do the rounds of the houses out there.' She turned and pointed out of the window. The sniper who'd shot Mel must have been holed up in one of the ordinary, run-of-the-mill residences that surrounded Thames Valley police headquarters.

Janine snorted. 'Oh come on, Hill. Evans had his team scouring those houses for weeks after Mel died, and came up with absolutely squat. No witnesses to put Myers or anyone else at the scene, and they never found any indication of where the bastard had set up his nest. You know that as well as I do.'

Hillary did. It was one of the reasons why she'd suggested it. Even if word did get back to Evans about what Janine had been doing, nobody would much care. She wouldn't be standing on anyone's toes or doing any damage.

But she had to convince Janine that the idea had some merit. Even if it didn't. But Janine was wily. She'd have to play it carefully. 'Sure, he had uniforms up and down the streets, making a right pest of themselves,' Hillary agreed airily. 'People probably got fed up with seeing them and being asked the same damn thing, over and over.'

Janine opened her mouth to say something sarcastic, then remembered just who it was she was dealing with, and closed her mouth again. In all the years she'd worked under Hillary Greene she'd never known the woman to do something without a good reason.

'So what's the point in going over old ground?' she asked cautiously.

'You know as well as I do that memories can be jogged after a certain amount of time has passed,' Hillary said, then held up her hand as Janine prepared to blast that down. 'Yes, I know it's a long shot, but it's still a shot. But that's not the main reason I'm suggesting it.'

Janine subsided back in her chair, but she was still looking suspicious.

'Just stop for a minute and think,' Hillary said softly, slipping back into the old teaching mode she'd used with Janine when she'd been a raw green recruit. 'It was early clocking-off time, just gone five,' Hillary said, having to force the words out now.

Briefly her mind went back to that afternoon. How they'd all spilled out into the car park, and the pervading feeling of celebration, and good-natured camaraderie. Mel still alive and smiling. And then the shot and Mel's body hitting the ground. The stunned silence that followed. And then … Hillary forced her mind to stop right there and concentrate on the living instead.

'Who would be at home around that time?' she asked Janine, who frowned in puzzlement for a moment, then shrugged.

'Anyone who'd clocked off work early, I suppose. Young mothers with kids home from school. Nannies looking after kids. The retired. People making last-minute deliveries.'

'OK. Now who, out of that lot, would be the most likely to lie about anything they saw that day?' Hillary pressed.

Janine shrugged. 'Anyone with a record, or a reason to be wary of the cops.'

Hillary nodded patiently. No doubt Evans had put any such individuals under a microscope long since. 'And who else?' she pressed gently.

Janine blinked and then sighed, suddenly catching on. 'The elderly. Especially if they live alone.'

Hillary nodded. Most old people tended to act like ostriches whenever trouble came knocking at the door. 'OK. So say you're an old man or woman, living alone. A knock comes at the door, which immediately makes you wonder what's up. You go to the door and, horror of horrors, there's a man or woman in uniform standing at your door. Asking you questions. What's your first reaction?'

Janine began to look more interested now. 'Three wise monkeys, boss,' she said, using her old title for Hillary without thinking. 'Saw nothing, heard nothing, say nothing.'

'OK. So you do your helpless old man or woman act, and the copper goes away. Next day you read about Mel in the papers. How do you feel?'

'Shocked and scared,' Janine said promptly, slowly nodding. 'A man's been killed right on your back doorstep. You might even have seen this man out and about. It's too close to home. You hunker down and batten down the hatches.'

Hillary nodded. 'OK. So, the next day, or the day after that, another uniform lands on your doorstep, asking you the same things again.'

Janine nodded. That was standard. You always covered the same ground twice, just in case.

'What do you do?' Hillary pressed.

'Batten down the hatches even more. If you've lied already, you just keep on telling the same lie, until it's set in cement.' Janine, who'd seen that particular phenomenon often during her days in uniform, grimaced.

'OK. Now months go by. It all seems to be dying down. You start to feel safe again. And then someone comes knocking on your door. But it's not some faceless copper in uniform this time. This time it's the widow herself. The brave, pregnant heroine of the day. Asking you if you saw anything on the day her hero husband is shot. What might you be tempted to do then?'

Janine slowly began to smile. 'Confess.'

Hillary got slowly to her feet. 'Do a few houses at a time. Concentrate on the old or those living alone. Wear something that shows off that bump. Hell, Janine, you know what signs to look for as well as I do.'

Janine's smile widened. 'I'll do it. Thanks boss.'

And Hillary, feeling about as low as a worm's belly, watched her go off on her wild-goose chase, and sighed heavily.

Whilst Hillary Greene watched her one-time sergeant set off on her mission, Clive Myers crossed the border into Wales.

The ex-soldier had set off at 3.30 that morning, a time which his stint in the army had told him was the optimum time for catching people unawares. He'd found it easy to give his watchers the slip, and then he'd walked for two miles out of Thame to a deserted country barn where he'd stashed a dented old van, days before shooting and killing Superintendent Philip Mallow.

It had only taken him a few hours to service the van and give the batteries a bit of a charge before taking it on the road. He doubted the coppers back at his house were even aware that he'd gone yet, and wouldn't be for some time, especially with his usual car still parked harmlessly in front of the house.

Nevertheless, he'd kept off the motorways and taken the winding, scenic, country route into Wales.

It was such forward planning that had earned him the praise of his instructors and superior officers in the army. And it was that mentality that had enabled him to get so many things in place beforehand, ready for the time when they'd be needed.

Before even getting into his disguised van to set out for police HQ on the day Mel Mallow died, for instance, he'd planted tiny bugs on the vehicles of all those closest to the trio of animals who'd raped his daughter. Knowing a man who could kit him out with all the latest gear was another huge help, and along with practising his marksmanship, he'd also been updating himself with everything that modern technology had to offer.

What else did he have to spend his money on? With his wife dead, and his daughter confined to a psychiatric institution, he hardly needed the money for anything else.

And so, when the motorbike of one of Gary Firth's closest pals suddenly took off for the wilds of Wales, not only did Clive

Myers know about it, he was able to track it accurately, due to the wonders of the Global Positioning System.

Now, keeping to the back roads, his eyes glued to the electronic map and the steadily bleeping green dot that told him where his quarry was holed up, Clive Myers drove calmly and placidly into Wales.

Beside him, under the passenger seat of his van, was a carefully concealed sniper rifle.

It was time to put phase 2 of his plan into operation.

Whilst Clive Myers contemplated killing the rapist of his fifteen year old daughter, Keith Barrington fairly skipped up the stairs of police HQ back in Kidlington.

'Guv. I've found someone who says they overheard Eddie Philpott and Tom Cleaves quarrelling in Eddie's garden the day before he was killed.'

Hillary, still feeling guilty over what she'd done to Janine Mallow, looked at him bleakly.

'OK.'

Barrington blinked, somewhat taken aback by her lack of enthusiasm. 'So do we go and see Tom Cleaves?' he asked uncertainly.

Hillary sighed. 'What time did this argument take place, according to your witness?'

'Early Sunday morning, Guv.'

'OK. Let's go back to The Knott. I want to see first if Rachel Warner or either of her kids heard the rumpus. If not, Tom Cleaves can flatly deny it, and we won't be able to prove otherwise.'

Barrington saw the logic of that, and, his faith in his boss restored, he followed her out into the car park.

Rachel Warner opened the door to their knock, rubbing her face with one hand.

'I'm sorry. Were you sleeping?' Hillary asked, her level of guilt, which was already high, abruptly sky-rocketing.

'No, that's all right. I needed to get up anyway.' The woman turned her wrist to look at her watch, then made an annoyed *tch* sound. 'Damn watch, it needs a new battery. I've been meaning to replace it for days. I never know what time it is.'

Hillary glanced obligingly at her own watch. 'It's just gone three.'

'I'll have to pick Mark up from school soon,' said Rachel, standing reluctantly to one side to show them in.

'That's OK, we won't keep you,' Hillary said quickly, taking the decision not to go inside. 'I just need to ask a few quick questions. Can you remember if you heard your father arguing with someone in his garden on Sunday morning? That would be the day before he died.'

Rachel yawned hugely, apologized, then nodded. 'Sorry. It's the pills I'm on. Er, yes, I did hear Dad talking to someone. It sounded a bit heated, too. I was still in bed, though, but I had the top window open a notch. I find fresh air helps.'

'Did you recognize the man he was speaking to?'

Rachel shook her head. 'No. Sorry.'

'Could you tell what the argument was about?'

Rachel smiled wanly. 'Yes. That's why I stayed in bed and didn't bother to get up and have a look. They were arguing about tomatoes. That's why I wasn't worried. I expect it was that man Dad was always ruffling up the wrong way.'

Hillary smiled. 'You took no notice of them?'

'Oh no. They've been feuding for years. I think they both enjoy it.' Then her face seemed to collapse in on itself. 'Or rather, *did* enjoy it. *Once.*' Her mouth began to do that wobbling thing that mouths do when tears are imminent, and Hillary hastily thanked her and backed away, leaving her alone with her grief.

Beside her, Barrington looked as miserable as she felt.

'Now we go and interview Cleaves?' he asked eagerly.

But as they climbed into the car, Hillary sighed and shook her head. 'Not right now. He'll keep.' She had the depressing feeling that talking to Tom Cleaves wouldn't get them an inch further in their case.

And she'd had just about enough gloom for one day.

Back at HQ, Ross's desk was still empty, which was not a huge surprise.

In Wales, Clive Myers pulled off a narrow and deserted country lane, and took to open grassland, parking his well-sprung van in a small spinney.

He got out his camping equipment, and set about making himself comfortable. Later, he'd check out the lie of the land and use his binoculars to pinpoint the nearest farms.

But with luck, when it came time to scout out Gary Firth's hidy-hole, he would find it in a nice, quiet little spot, well away from prying eyes and human ears.

CHAPTER EIGHT

The next morning, Hillary got in early and finally put paid to the backlog of papers in her in-tray. Another largely sleepless night had left her feeling lethargic and yet another vague headache loomed on the horizon.

With the arrival of Barrington and Gemma, she reached for her third cup of coffee of the morning, and told them both to update the murder book and refamiliarize themselves with it. The murder book was a file they kept up to the date with reports, witness statements and personal thoughts, so that any one member of the team could look at it and get a comprehensive view of the case.

The post mortem report had only just reached her, the delay due to a multi-car pile-up on the M40 two days ago. The sudden blitz of bodies arriving at the morgue had postponed Edward Philpott's autopsy for more than thirty-two hours, but as she read the report through, carefully translating the pathologist's medicalese as she went, she realized that it told them precisely nothing they didn't already know.

Cause of death, predictably, had been severe blunt force trauma to the back of the head. Apart from that, Edward Philpott had been a fit and healthy man for his age, with only the onset of a slight touch of rheumatism that might have caused him problems, had he lived.

She sighed and tossed the report to one side. Catching Gemma Fordham's eye, she shook her head. 'Nothing useful.'

Just then she became aware of a slight stirring in the office, and her heart fell, her first thought being that Janine Mallow was back. But when she looked up it was to see DS Frank Ross weaving his way through the room – and the weaving was not due entirely to his having to negotiate his way through the archipelago of desks.

Paul Danvers had also spotted him, and came out of his cubicle fast, on an intercept path. Hillary felt her shoulder muscles tense, for her soon to be ex-sergeant had his nasty eyes fixed on her face, and he didn't look in any fit state to be prudent.

'Well, bitch, here they are,' he all but shouted, bringing the entire office to a standstill. Telephone conversations were cut off in mid-sentence and keypads were ignored as everyone looked their way to watch the up-coming entertainment. The building was already buzzing, of course, with news of Ross's long-anticipated ejection, and nobody wanted to miss the fun.

'I take it that is your application for retirement, Sergeant.' Paul Danvers's icy voice cut across the room. Frank reeled around and glared at the sartorially elegant, blond-haired man reaching out with an imperious hand. 'I'll take those.'

'Screw you,' Frank Ross sneered.

'You're drunk,' Danvers said blandly.

'What a loss you are to the detective ranks, sir,' Frank slurred, with a drunken smile. He threw the papers towards Danvers who, surprisingly, managed to catch them before they had a chance to disperse and scatter.

'Go home and sober up,' Danvers said. 'You're a bloody disgrace and no damned good to anyone in this state.'

Somebody, somewhere in the room muttered soto voce *he never was, in any state*, and a few people sniggered. Frank Ross flushed, then gave an elaborate shrug followed by an over-dramatic V sign to Hillary, which made him stagger, then turned and weaved his way back to the door.

'Class all the way,' Hillary said quietly. Keith Barrington

grinned, then turned it into a cough and hid it behind his hand. Gemma watched Ross's departure with narrowed eyes. So he was definitely going, she mused with satisfaction. There was no possible way back from that. Which meant that Hillary had been sincere in what she'd said about the shake-up to her team.

It made Gemma feel better about herself and her decision to stay on. For the time being, anyway.

'Thank you sir,' Hillary said quietly to Danvers, who looked at her with a searching gaze, then smiled briefly, nodded, and returned to his desk. Once there, he gave Ross's papers the quick once over, just to make sure the stupid sod hadn't deliberately sabotaged them with a false signature or incorrect data – something of which he was thoroughly capable.

But the papers were all in order, and DCI Paul Danvers tossed them into his out-tray with a sense of relief. Well, that was one problem solved. Then he glanced through the plexiglass cubicle towards Hillary and her team, and sighed heavily.

She was looking desperately tired, and was still steadily losing weight. But she'd hold it together. The thought of her doing anything else was unthinkable.

Martha Hepton crossed her ankles nervously under her solicitor's admiring glance, and licked her lips unhappily.

'So there's nothing you can do?' she appealed.

'Not really, Miss Hepton. The death of your landlord doesn't really change anything from a legal point of view. His estate will be probated, and his executors will deal with all the issues arising from his last will and testament. Unfortunately, Mr Philpott had already made the matter concerning your lease formal by writing to his own solicitor. Who will, of course, be sure to pass Mr Philpott's expressed wishes on to the executors of the estate.'

Martha Hepton swallowed hard. 'But he was going to change his mind. I know he was. He told me so only a few days before he died,' she lied.

'Did he say this in front of a witness?' the solicitor asked hopefully. He was a lean, grey-haired man, who was trying hard to be sympathetic to his newest client, but finding it difficult.

'No. We were alone,' Martha said vaguely.

'Did he ever write a letter to you, a dated letter, stating his intention of changing his mind in the matter of Honeysuckle Cottage?'

Martha shook her head miserably. Of course he hadn't. Eddie had been determined not to renew her lease of the cottage. He'd told her weeks ago that, come the end of November, he needed the cottage empty, so that he could sell it.

When he'd first told her about it, she'd thought he'd been joking. After so many years, she'd come to think of the small stone cottage as her own, and it had come as a complete shock to her to realize that comfortable old Eddie would even *consider* making her homeless. Let alone *do* so.

At first, she'd pleaded and cajoled and tried every womanly wile she could think of to get him to change his mind.

After that came vague, veiled threats.

Then open tears and recriminations.

Then the withholding of sex.

Nothing had changed his mind, and by the time he'd died, they were barely on speaking terms. And Eddie hadn't been to her cottage for their usual twice-weekly get-togethers for more than a month. Something she had not been going to tell that nosy female copper, or her smirking git of a sidekick. It didn't take a genius to figure out what *they'd* have made of it all.

They'd have had her in cuffs and down the station before she could draw breath.

'But surely I'll have a bit more time now, won't I? I mean, doesn't probate take time?' Martha asked plaintively.

The solicitor shrugged helplessly. 'It depends on how straightforward things are. The clarity of the last will and testament, and the attitude of the heirs, for instance, can make a great deal of difference.'

'But he was murdered,' Martha pointed out. 'Doesn't all that slow things down?'

The solicitor cleared his throat. The potential for complications in this case was slowly becoming clear to him. 'Well, much of that would depend on how quickly the police conclude their investigations, and, of course, the identity of Mr Philpott's killer. For instance, for it to affect probate at all, it would have to be proved that one or more of the people mentioned in Mr Philpott's will had been culpable in his homicide. As you may know, it is against the law for somebody to profit financially from an unlawful killing.'

Martha sighed heavily. That was hardly helpful.

'Do you know who the main heirs are in Mr Philpott's will?' he asked curiously. Martha shrugged.

'Well, he only has the one child, a daughter. She's been living with him for a long while now, so I expect she'll get the bulk of it. Or he might have left it in trust for his grandchildren. I'm not sure.'

'In that case, I suggest it might prove prudent to try and have a confidential talk with Mr Philpott's daughter. She might well be amenable to you staying on at Honeysuckle Cottage. If the property does revert to her, she might prefer to have the steady income of a rent coming in, rather than the one-off large payment that would result from a sale.'

Martha's heart plummeted. She hadn't told this dry old stick that she'd never paid a penny in rent all the years she'd lived in Honeysuckle Cottage – or why. And again, it didn't take a genius to realize that Rachel Warner would hardly be likely to let such an arrangement stand. After all, Martha could hardly provide the same sort of service for her that she had for Rachel's father, could she?

'Well, thank you, Mr Mainwaring, for your advice.'

The solicitor stood and shook hands, and watched her go with a slight sigh.

Outside on the pavement, Martha Hepton saw the busy street

in front of her shimmer and waver, and realized she was on the verge of very public tears. Taking a big gulp of air, she set off across a pedestrian crossing towards a large church, and the quiet graveyard that surrounded it. If she was going to make a spectacle of herself, better that only the dead would see it.

But as she stumbled through the gravestones and all but fell down on to a wooden bench overlooking a gloomy, marble rectangle dedicated to the memory of one Elijah Cranwarry, Martha felt the first glimmerings of real despair.

What was she going to do?

She was hardly likely to get a council home, was she? Not at her age, not with her being single and not with the waiting lists like they were. And she didn't even know anybody who'd be willing to rent her a room. Most of her friends were married, had moved away, or had families or problems of their own.

She might end up in a caravan park somewhere. The spectre of homelessness loomed. She'd be forced to get a real job, find a poky hole somewhere, and skimp and save.

Damn Edward Philpott. She was glad the old bastard was dead.

Clive Myers paused in his digging and glanced around. Despite its being a damp and just slightly chilly day up in the Welsh hills, he was stripped to the waist and sweating.

It was the tree roots that were the problem.

The deep hole he was digging in the small spinney was choc-a-bloc with stubborn, ironlike roots that resisted the spade. But he was determined to get down to at least five feet. He knew that bodies were found mostly because the lazy sods who were disposing of them were too panic-stricken, too physically unfit, or too stupid to dig down far enough. Foxes and dogs had good noses, and liked to dig for buried treasure. Their scavenging instincts were always on the alert.

He took a swig of water from a supermarket-brand bottle, and flexed his tired arms and shoulders. A few more hours should do it. In his mid-fifties, he was no longer in his prime, but he'd always kept himself in trim. His wife had always teased him about that, although he knew she'd been secretly pleased by his lack of a beer belly. It had allowed her to show him off to her friends.

Friends who'd come to her funeral and spoke meaningless words at him, all the while looking at him speculatively, and gossiping at the first opportunity.

Clive Myers thrust such thoughts aside, and began digging with renewed energy and grim determination. He'd never been a man to contemplate things too thoroughly. A plain and simple man, he preferred plain and simple deeds.

Janine Mallow felt the desk sergeant's eyes on her as she walked across the foyer and to the lift. A few weeks ago she'd have taken the stairs, but just recently her back had been playing her up, and her legs felt heavy. It was almost as if she could feel the growing baby inside her sucking her juices dry of all stamina and energy.

As she got in the lift she saw him reach for his telephone, and knew he'd be calling Hillary to give her the heads up. For some reason she'd never quite been able to fathom, Hillary Greene had always, and seemingly effortlessly, commanded the respect of the rank and file. Young people in uniforms, old geezers like the desk sergeants, the retired legends, the up-and-comers. It seemed to make no difference. Hillary seemed to know them all.

But for once, Janine had got it wrong. The desk sergeant wasn't calling Hillary Greene, but only because he'd seen her leave the building about an hour before. Instead, he was calling a retired mate from Traffic to tell him the news about Frank Ross.

By now, the tale of Ross's drunken stunt upstairs was taking on the aura of legend. So much so, that by the time Janine had got halfway across the large open-plan office towards her old hunting grounds, she'd been told the news by no fewer than five people.

It made her smile. She'd never understood why Hillary Greene had put up with Frank Ross for so long, and she could only imagine the joy and relief everyone must feel finally to get rid of the waste of space.

As she approached Hillary's desk, however, her spirits abruptly fell. There was only one person seated behind a computer terminal, and Janine didn't know her. As Janine approached, she checked the stranger out cautiously. The woman was in her late twenties, with a long, lean body that was currently wearing a smart charcoal trouser suit with a grey pinstripe, and a man's white shirt. She had very pale blonde hair, cut short and tufted into attractive spikes all around her well-shaped head. Her face was fine-boned and almost striking enough to be called beautiful. When she spotted Janine and looked up, her eyes were like lasers.

So this was her replacement. Janine couldn't make up her mind whether to be amused or irked.

'Hello. Hillary not here?' she asked, then could have kicked herself for saying something so inane.

'No, she's just gone out to follow up a witness statement with DC Barrington,' Gemma Fordham said. Her voice had been deep and gravelled ever since a childhood accident, but most people assumed it was the side effects of a bad smoking addiction.

Janine smiled grimly. 'So she's still insisting on working in the field, is she?' Janine asked. 'Used to drive me nuts, that. I mean, why couldn't she just ride her desk like every other DI? I don't suppose our office Adonis has got anywhere with her since I've been gone?' she asked, tossing her head towards Paul Danvers' office – which was currently empty.

Gemma Fordham shook her head. She knew who the pretty, pregnant blonde woman was, of course. She just didn't know why DI Janine Mallow felt so compelled to stake her own claim by coming on so strong with all the nostalgia.

'Do you know when the boss will be back?'

Gemma shrugged. 'She shouldn't be long. I don't think the witness statement was that significant.'

Janine shrugged and pulled out a chair. 'Do you mind if I sit? My feet are killing me.'

Gemma shrugged and smiled briefly.

'Sounds like the case is stalled,' Janine said, obviously fishing.

Gemma shrugged again.

'I remember how that could be,' Janine carried on, glancing around. 'There were many times I used to think we were going to fall flat on our faces this time, and then, hey presto, the boss pulled a rabbit out of the hat. It always annoyed the hell out of me, because I could never figure out how she did it.'

Gemma blinked. So she wasn't the only one who'd been taken by surprise by the magic Hillary Greene seemed to be able to work.

'You'll get used to it,' Janine said, recognizing the sudden shading in the other woman's eye. 'She casts a hell of a long shadow, does our Hill, but it's worth putting up with the chill. I learned more about the job during the few years I was with her than I ever did before or have since.'

Gemma's gaze flickered to a spot just over her left shoulder, and Janine tensed. When she turned, she found Hillary Greene and a ginger-haired lanky chap walking towards her.

'Janine, don't get up,' Hillary greeted her, her face bland and vaguely welcoming. 'Keith, get another chair,' she said to the young man, whose seat Janine suddenly realized she must have taken.

'I've found her,' Janine said without preamble, the moment Hillary sat down. Hillary blinked, took just a moment to understand what she meant, then tossed her bag under the desk and looked at her thoughtfully.

'You sure?' she asked warily.

Janine nodded. 'As sure as I can be. She acted squirrelly right from the moment she set eyes on me. I could tell she recognized me, and what's more, her house has one of the best views of the car park of any of the residences out there.'

For Gemma and Keith following the conversation was all but impossible, but at the mention of the HQ parking lot, both of them stiffened.

Hillary's mind was racing. She'd sent Janine off on what she'd been sure would be a wild-goose chase. Was it possible that Mel's widow had found a reluctant witness after all? Or was her ex-sergeant just reading more into things than were actually there. It had been known to happen before.

'She might just have been feeling uneasy because you are who you are,' Hillary pointed out, further baffling the two onlookers. 'You know as well as I do, witnesses can act in the most bizarre way for no apparent reason.'

'I know. That's why I want you to talk to her. Everybody knows you have a way with witnesses,' Janine pointed out. It was true. Hillary's interview technique was something everyone commented on. She just seemed to have a way of getting on her mark's level and using whichever method worked best to get them talking.

'OK. Give me her name and address and I'll check her out,' Hillary promised reluctantly.

Janine reached into her bag and handed her a slip of paper, already prepared. 'I know you're up to your eyes on a case,' she said apologetically, but Hillary waved her to a stop.

Janine, her eyes suddenly suspiciously bright, swallowed hard, then got abruptly to her feet. 'Thanks. So you'll call me?' she said, her voice a little husky now.

'Yes. As soon as I can,' Hillary agreed.

Janine nodded to Gemma and Keith, then turned and walked carefully away.

'Guv,' Gemma said uneasily. She had a bloody good idea now that Janine Mallow had somehow persuaded Hillary to allow her to work covertly on Superintendent Mallow's killing. That could blow up in Hillary's face like a defective firework. And for some strange reason that she didn't want to contemplate, Gemma didn't want to see her boss humiliated.

'You never heard that conversation,' Hillary said sharply, looking first at Gemma, then at Keith, who averted his eyes and looked unhappy.

'Guv,' Keith muttered.

Hillary fixed Gemma with a steady stare. Eventually the other woman sighed reluctantly.

'Guv.'

DC Trevor Fields rubbed a hand across his mouth and glanced across at his mate, Harry Hastings.

'It's been bloody hours. We should have seen some sign of him by now.'

Fields was a young man, not long out of uniform and anxious to make a good impression. He had the shaved head that a lot of youngsters seemed to go in for nowadays, and a tattoo of a spider on the back of his hand.

Harry Hastings, in contrast, was a sergeant with over twenty years' experience behind him. Solidly built and mostly placid by nature, he sighed now as Field repeated himself for about the tenth time in the last hour.

They were currently sitting in a nondescript Fiat Uno, parked a little way across from Clive Myers' respectable semi in Thame. Two other officers were watching the back, and were in constant radio contract. None of them had spotted Myers moving around inside the house all day.

'I've informed Evans, and we've been told to sit and watch,' Harry said patiently. 'You know that, you heard me make the call. Now just sit and watch, will you?'

Trevor Field shifted on his seat. It was driving Harry insane the way the man couldn't seem to sit still for ten minutes at a time. If he didn't learn to cope with observation better than this, Harry could see him being bumped back down into uniform pretty damned quick. Perhaps the short sharp shock would do him good.

'But he must have done a runner in the night, it's obvious,' Fields argued plaintively.

Harry shrugged. 'Maybe. Maybe not. With this canny bugger, you never can tell. Chances are, he's just holed up in there and is deliberately keeping out of sight just to wind us up. He's done that before, you know. Once when I was on obbo, and twice more with other teams. It's a game of attrition with him. He's an old soldier, for Pete's sake. He knows we're watching him, and it's his way of telling us that we don't scare him.'

Trevor Fields sighed heavily. Restlessly, he reached for a stick of chewing gum from his trouser pocket, opened it and began to chew noisily.

Harry gritted his teeth and tried to think of football.

Clive Myers grunted as he hoisted the black bin-bagged weight into the hole. Inside it was the body of Gary Firth, the rapist of his daughter Evie.

It had taken him only one bullet to get the job done, as it had with Superintendent Philip Mallow.

As he'd surmised, Gary Firth had gone to ground in an out-of-the-way spot – to be precise, in a battered, 1950s model caravan at the bottom of a scraggy field, fit for nothing except grazing sheep. He imagined that the farmer who owned the field had either given up trying to evict the previous occupants, or had come to some sort of arrangement with them. Since the caravan's nearest neighbour was a small stone cottage nearly three miles away, Clive supposed that nobody had cause to complain about the eyesore. And the sheep wouldn't care.

He'd observed Gary Firth for over an hour, watching him drink beer and smoke pot. Sometimes he talked for long periods of time on his mobile phone, probably to the same friend whose motorbike he'd ridden down on. And it was during one of his quiet periods, whilst he'd been sitting on the step of the caravan smoking a reefer, that Clive Myers had shot him.

Always a neat man, Clive had cleaned up the minimal

amount of mess in the caravan doorway and steps, and locked the caravan carefully after him.

Now, job done, he began patiently to fill in the hole. It was a lot easier to fill it in that it had been to dig it out.

As the shovels of earth hit the black plastic with a scattering sound that reminded him of heavy rain, he remembered the last time he'd visited his daughter in the psychiatric institution that was now her home. It had been raining heavily then. Perhaps that was what had brought the thought to mind.

Evie hadn't known who he was, and if he tried to touch her, she'd start up a high-pitched keening that would bring the nurses running.

So he'd learned not to try and touch her.

As he levelled off the ground where Gary Firth lay, he hunted around for small sapplings and pieces of bracken, which he planted carefully in the earth. Within a month, the spot would be taken over by nature, and nobody would ever find it.

Sweating, dirty, numb and tired, Clive Myers began erasing all traces of his brief occupation of the woods. Afterwards he would need to drive back to Oxfordshire, timing his arrival just right. To get back into his home unseen, it needed to be fully dark. He never even contemplated getting caught. The back roads beckoned, and his anonymous van would attract no attention.

In fact, he rarely gave the police a thought. It had been their job to protect his family and they had failed. It had been their remit to catch the criminals and punish them. And they had failed.

Now it was his turn. And he would not fail.

The man in overall charge of his daughter's case had paid. The lad who'd raped his daughter had just paid. Now there was one more who needed to pay, and after that – well Clive wasn't sure.

Things were bound to hot up now that Firth had gone missing, and once he'd killed DI Gregg, the cops would almost certainly charge him – regardless of how little evidence they had. So once he'd got rid of Gregg, he'd need to go into hiding. Whether or not he'd be able to rid the world of the other two animals who'd stood by and cheered whilst his Evie was violated, he wasn't sure. The cops would be bound to take them into hiding and protective custody. He might not be able to find them. Or get at them if he did.

But he'd have a damned good go at it. And if he died trying – well, so what?

He had nothing left to live for, after all.

DCI Gawain Evans sat at his desk, listening to the latest report from the teams watching the Myers house.

The man had still not been seen.

'I agree, he's probably playing silly buggers again,' Evans said. He was a thickset man, with dark, coarse hair and dark-brown eyes. He was missing his wife and kids, although he tried to get back to London every weekend. He was dogged and meticulous, but even he was beginning to wonder whether Superintendent Phillip Mallow's killer was ever going to make a mistake.

The man on the other end of the line, a Sergeant Harry Hastings, was a good solid man to have on the ground, and Evans listened to him closely. Since first heading up this investigation, he'd quickly come to learn the strengths and weaknesses of all those on his team. He worked best with the men and women he'd brought with him from the Met of course, because he knew them better than the Oxford contingent. But everyone on his team pulled their weight – and then some. This was, after all, personal. And working and all but living out of HQ at Thames Valley had impressed on them all just how much the dead super had been liked and was mourned.

In fact, although he'd never met the man, Gawain Evans had come to feel as if Mellow Mallow had been a personal friend too.

'But then again, he's clever enough to be doing this to set up a pattern. If he keeps playing hide-and-seek and then showing up, he might think he can lull us into a false sense of security,' Evans said, little realizing as he spoke, that Myers had already achieved his aim. 'I'll put in a requisition order for some night-sensitive cameras and goggles, but whether we'll get them at all, let alone any time soon, your guess is as good as mine.'

Evans didn't need to tell the ground troops just how tight the budget was. It was enough to make even the most stalwart of officers feel despondent.

He listened to the man on the scene for a moment, then sighed. 'No, better not go in. You know what happened last time.'

The last time Clive Myers had pulled this trick Evans had ordered the team to go to the house and physically reassure themselves of his presence on the premises. They had, but Myers had instantly called his solicitors, who'd filed a harassment charge. Although they could hardly serve the police officers with a restraining order, the message had come through loud and clear.

You didn't 'harass' Clive Myers unless you had a clear and good reason to do so.

'We'd better just watch and see,' Evans sighed wearily. 'Tell the teams relieving you tonight to keep extra alert. If he has gone AWOL he'll probably try to slip in again unobserved.' He listened to the rumbling voice on the other line, the voice of weary experience, and sighed in agreement. 'I know, without night-vision equipment it'll be hard. Yes, I know the man's ex-army. Just tell everyone to keep out of the cars and stay on foot, as close to all the exits and entrances as they can. Keep in constant contact. If he does try and creep back in, and we can catch him at it, at least it'll give us an excuse to have him back in for questioning. And his bloody solicitors can scream harassment as much as they like.'

He listened for a few more moments, grunted, then hung up. He rubbed his face wearily, and looked around the small office they'd assigned him. His team was still working flat out, and he dreaded telling them the news that he'd received just that morning.

Starting at the beginning of next week, the investigation into the murder of Detective Superintendent Phillip Mallow was being officially scaled down. He knew just how demoralizing an effect that would have on everyone at Thames Valley, and especially on his own team.

Damn it. Myers just had to slip up sometime soon. The man wasn't infallible. Was he?

CHAPTER NINE

Hillary Greene drove the now familiar route back to the hamlet of Steeple Knott. The weather was damp and grey without being too cold, and she wound down her window a bare inch as she made the turning off the dual carriageway on to the narrow country lane.

When she parked outside the Philpott's cottage she saw that Barrington was waiting for her just inside the open front door.

'Guv.' He closed the door after her and lead the way up the narrow flight of stairs. 'I found them in his wardrobe, in an old shoebox.'

Hillary sighed. 'It's a favourite hiding-place for old folks,' she acknowledged. 'Don't ask me why. But the next time you do a house search, remember it.'

'Yes Guv.' Barrington opened the door to a small bedroom with sloping eaves. Hillary supposed Eddie must have let his daughter have the biggest bedroom, whilst the two children must share one. Now if that didn't make a recipe ripe for sibling ructions, she didn't know what would.

'Let's have a look then,' Hillary said, sitting down on the side of the late Edward Philpott's bed, and Barrington proudly passed his find over to her.

'Hope you don't mind my calling you in, Guv, but I thought you'd like to see them straight away.'

Hillary nodded absently, her eyes scanning the legal documents quickly. They were not, as might be expected, a copy of

114

the victim's will, or even his copy of his pre-paid funeral arrangements – which was a trend that Hillary had noticed had been growing during the last few years. Instead, they were a series of letters between Edward Philpott and a Mr Clarence Greengage, of Phipps, Brown & Greengage, Solicitors. Their office, she noted from the headed paper, was in Banbury.

She read the letters silently, then sighed. 'So Philpott wasn't going to renew Martha Hepton's lease,' she mused. 'Funny, she never mentioned anything about it to me and Frank.'

'Maybe she didn't know, Guv,' Barrington said, half-heartedly playing devil's advocate. As he spoke he glanced at his watch.

He'd intended to give Gavin Moreland a call soon, knowing that his father was due to finish giving his testimony around about now. He could only hope that his lover's father had been able to put on a fair show and give a good account of himself, or Gavin would be beside himself with worry. But the thought of coping with his lover's possible histrionics with Hillary around didn't really appeal, and he uneasily decided to wait until he was at home this evening.

But no doubt that would be wrong too. He could almost hear Gavin's opening sarcastic remarks right now. It had been nearly a month since he'd been up to London, and although their reunions were everything Keith could hope for, he was coming, slowly but inexorably, to the conclusion that things couldn't go on like this for ever.

But, presumably, they wouldn't have to. Once Gavin's father, a prosperous but undeniably shady businessman had either been exonerated or convicted, things would change anyway. But Keith didn't like to think about how things would change should Gavin's father be sent down. Apart from anything else, Keith would almost certainly come in for some major flak, just because of his job; a job that Gavin loathed and for which he vilified him whenever the opportunity arose. But, even more worrying than that, Keith had come away from the capital after his last visit with the distinct impression that Gavin might just decide to give up his own dreams of a professional life on the tennis circuit, and buckle down to the family business.

And Keith had the unhappy feeling that, should that happen, Gavin was more than capable of expecting Keith to throw in his job here and join him in London. And maybe even accept some sort of sinecure job in the import-export, antiques business that he would be heading in the temporary absence of his father.

'I can't imagine that Mr Clarence Greengage would have kept her in ignorance,' Hillary Greene's ironic voice snapped him out of his reverie and brought his mind back to the task in hand. 'I think we'll pop down the road and bring our Miss Hepton in for a formal chat at the station. If nothing else, it will teach her not to tell porkies.'

Barrington smiled obligingly. Hillary gave him a searching look, and wondered what was eating him. She'd been aware for some time that her young DC's personal life was a never-ending source of *angst*, and wished that he'd get a grip on it soon. At least, now that Ross was on his way out, if it did become widely known that Barrington was gay there'd be no one on his immediate team to give him a hard time of it. Of course, he'd still have to weather the possible flak that would be bound to come his way.

As it stood, she could only hope that his personal commitment to the job would see him through. But sometimes she thought she sensed a wavering in her red-haired young officer that boded ill for his future.

'We'll just have another word with Rachel first,' Hillary said briskly, picking up the letters and heading for the door. 'See if she knew about this, and what she intends to do about it. And we might just pop in to see the victim's solicitor before we tackle the mistress.'

'Guv.'

Downstairs, she tapped gently on the door to the small lounge, and heard Rachel Warner's weary voice bidding them to come in. When they entered, she was sitting on the sofa, her legs up and drinking from a mug of tea.

'Please, don't get up,' Hillary said quickly, as the younger woman turned her head to look at them, and then started to bend her knees and swing her shoulders around.

Rachel smiled a thanks and relaxed back into her former position, and Hillary took a seat close to the sofa. 'Have you seen these before?' Hillary asked, handing over the letters.

Rachel read them quickly, the papers shaking in her hands just a little as she did so. Even the effort of holding the papers up seemed to be too much for her, and she slowly let them drop into her lap, still reading. When she'd finished she glanced up at Hillary and shrugged.

'No, I hadn't. But I'm not surprised. Dad talked about "realizing his assets" some time ago, but I have to say, I didn't really know what he meant until now.'

Hillary nodded. 'You know Miss Hepton?'

'I've seen her around, sure. We live in a hamlet – I couldn't not know her. But we're not friends – or enemies either.'

'You know she was renting Honeysuckle Cottage from your father?'

Rachel Warner smiled briefly. 'Yes.'

Hillary nodded. So she knew about the arrangement between the attractive artist and her father.

'Will you follow through with your father's plans?' Hillary asked curiously. 'I imagine he intended either to sell the cottage, or perhaps let it to another party for a, er, slightly higher rent.'

Rachel sighed and shrugged. 'I'll probably sell it. I've been looking into the possibility of boarding schools for Julie and Mark. There are schools where they'll be able to stay together. And who knows, it might be a better option than fostering, where the chances are, they'll be split up. I'm hoping to talk to my cousins soon – if they'd agree to take Mark and Julie on alternate holidays, and act as their guardians, I might have the problem solved. But boarding school for six and eight years respectively isn't going to be cheap. Then there's the question of higher education for them, if they want to go on to university. I'll need all the cash Dad's left me, as well as the money raised from the sale of this house and Honeysuckle Cottage. I'm just hoping that, properly invested, it'll see them both through.'

Barrington, standing by the door, shuffled his feet, deeply uncomfortable. To listen to a woman making plans for after her death, all the while not knowing what was to happen to her two young children, made his own problems fade into insignificance.

'Well, good luck with that,' Hillary said softly. 'I'll leave you in peace now. I'm just going to interview your father's solicitors. I take it you know the contents of his will?'

Rachel Warner sighed. 'He told me years ago that he'd left everything to me, but recently he was going to change his will to leave it all in trust for the kids. I'm not sure if he'd got around to it yet, or what it'll mean to my plans if he had. I suppose it'll depend on whom he nominated as trustees?'

Hillary didn't know the answer to that, but as they drove towards Banbury, Keith behind the wheel, she wondered why Rachel hadn't been on to her father's solicitors long before now. It had been three days since her father's death – time enough for her to recover somewhat from the shock and start planning things. Especially since she had so much to do, and presumably, so little time to do it in.

But then, perhaps the dying had their own way of doing things.

As Hillary and Keith made their way towards the attractive market town of Banbury, Janine Mallow parked carefully in a small side street in the equally attractive town of Thame and turned off the car engine. She muttered under her breath; she could almost feel her ankles swelling as the warmth from the car's heater slowly subsided.

A hundred yards up ahead, on the left, was the home of Clive

Myers. She'd easily spotted the 'undercover' car, parked just beyond it and on the right-hand side of the road, and had been careful to pull in behind a large Landrover, out of their line of sight. Now, as she watched, she could clearly see the outline of two male heads inside, as the officers on observation chatted to one another.

She didn't realize, however, that another car parked at the rear of the Myers house in a cul-de-sac that curved around also contained two officers who had noted her arrival. Or that they could clearly see her from their vantage point.

The man in the passenger seat, a DC Stephen Crane, frowned slightly, and put the binoculars to his eyes. For once, he wasn't looking at the house, but at the car behind the Landrover. For some reason, it was ringing a bell. And when he saw the familiar, pretty blonde woman behind the wheel, he cursed softly.

Damn it, what was *she* doing here? And close on that thought, came the next. *What the hell was he going to do about it?* His home patch was Oxford, out of St Aldates, and the thought of reporting one of their own to the Met man, Evans, even if he was in charge, stuck in his craw. Besides, his instinct was to avoid an almighty row if possible, and the appearance of Mel's widow on the scene was bound to cause that, at the very least.

On the other hand, he couldn't just sit there and do nothing. What if she got out of the car and approached Myers' place?

'Hey, Mike.' He nudged his partner, who'd been dozing off behind the wheel. 'Who do we know whom we can trust to deal with a madwoman?'

His partner, who worked out of HQ, grunted awake and said blearily, 'Huh?'

Clarence Greengage's offices were in a small, cobbled square, not far from the famous Banbury Cross, and down a narrow, medieval-looking street. Lead-paned windows and a black-and-white exterior gave the building the appearance of an old coaching inn, now long since converted into commercial premises. An undulating roof echoed undulating floorboards inside, and reinforced the atmosphere of antiquity.

No doubt it made the largely affluent clientele to which Phipps, Brown and Greengage catered feel cautiously reassured that their business and legal affairs were in safe hands.

Considering they didn't have an appointment, the pleasant-faced receptionist was very quick to show them in to a large office on the lower floor.

The man who rose from behind his desk, somewhat to Hillary's surprise, was very much the antithesis of his old-fashioned-sounding name, however. Barely twenty-five, Hillary guessed, and wearing a smart suit and Armani aftershave.

'DI Greene, DC Barrington,' he echoed the receptionist's introduction of them. 'Please, take a seat. This is concerning Mr Philpott, I imagine?'

'Yes,' Hillary agreed.

'I read all about it in the papers. Shocking. He was such a nice man.'

With Hillary and Barrington seated, the young Mr Greengage retook his own chair. He had a smartly barbered haircut that suited his lean face, and his intelligent hazel eyes flickered from one to the other of the two police officers.

'I've just come from his residence,' Hillary began. 'As you may know, he shares it with his daughter. She's given her permission for you to speak freely to us. I understand that she herself has not yet been in touch?'

'No. But I understood from her father that the lady is rather seriously ill?'

Hillary nodded, tight-faced. 'She tells me that Edward Philpott had left all his property to her in his will but that, in the light of the circumstances, was going to alter it in favour of her children.'

'Quite true,' the solicitor agreed at once. 'I'd drawn the papers up, but Mr Philpott hadn't yet been in to sign them. He was due in tomorrow to do so, in fact.'

'So, legally, the old will still stands?'

'It does, yes. Unless, of course, in the unlikely event that Mr Philpott made yet a third will, not with this company, that was properly signed, dated and witnessed. But that, I imagine, is very unlikely.'

Hillary agreed that it was. 'So Rachel, Mrs Warner, gets every-thing? Were there any other major bequests we should know about?'

'Not a one,' Clarence Greengage assured her. 'It was one of the most simple wills I've ever drawn up. The second will, the one that left his estate to his grandchildren was much more complicated, of course.'

Hillary nodded, and Barrington took down notes as the solic-itor obliged by outlining it.

'So an old friend of his, his local vicar, and one of his own cousins were due to act as legal guardians for Mark and Julie, should he die before they reached maturity?' she recapped succinctly.

'Yes. And, of course, there were the usual safeguards in place to ensure that any residue of the estate went to the children on their maturity.' In other words, the guardians wouldn't be able to snaffle it with some clever accountancy.

So there were no obvious provisions in Edward Philpott's will that might provoke a motive for his murder, Hillary mused grimly. True, Rachel Warner got everything, but the fact that she would probably be dead herself in a few months' time rather ruled her out as a suspect.

Unless, of course, there was some as yet unknown urgent reason for her to want to get her hands on her father's money and property? It seemed so unlikely as to be hardly worth investi-gating, but she'd tell Keith to work systematically on researching the theory, when he had time between more urgent priorities.

'Now, there's another matter I wanted to discuss with you, Mr Greengage,' Hillary said briskly, handing over the letters she'd taken from Eddie Philpott's shoebox.

The solicitor read them briefly. 'Oh yes. The tenancy of Honeysuckle Cottage.'

'I take it you informed Miss Hepton that her lease would not be renewed at the end of November?'

'Oh yes. Edward informed me that he'd already told her, and that she hadn't taken the news well. So I wrote a formal letter to her the same day. That would have been, let me see,' he briefly riffled the pages of a large desk diary and nodded, 'yes, nearly eight weeks ago.'

'Has Miss Hepton been in touch?'

'No, she hasn't.'

'Has she got any legal recourse, to challenge her eviction, as it were? I take it you know that Mr Philpott and Miss Hepton were in a long-standing relationship?'

Mr Greengage, for the first time, looked rather surprised. 'No, I didn't know that. I simply assumed she was a regular tenant. Mr Philpott certainly never mentioned it. Hmmm, that might be awkward, should the lady challenge the will in court. The rights of a common-law wife, or partner, are somewhat shall we say, elastic?'

Hillary sighed. 'But what do you think her chances are of being allowed to stay on in the cottage?' Briefly, she explained the circumstances, as she knew them to be, and the solicitor frowned thoughtfully.

'On the face of it, there seems to be little the lady can do. If neither of them publicly acknowledged the liaison and there was no actual co-habitation … Then again, long-term tenancy is a bit of a nightmare. But no, on the whole, I think even if the lady should fight it, the courts would almost certainly side with Mrs Warner, or her heirs, in this particular case.'

So Martha Hepton, at least, had motive for wanting the old man dead.

At last, she was getting somewhere.

'Well, thank you very much for your time, sir,' Hillary said, getting to her feet and shaking hands.

'I don't suppose you know when the funeral is, do you, Inspector?' the young man asked. 'I would like to attend.'

Hillary admitted that she didn't know, but would be sure to inform him when she did.

Once outside they walked thoughtfully to her car, and got inside.

'Pick up the mistress, Guv?' Barrington asked brightly. He too, was glad to have something solid to go on at last.

'Pick up the mistress,' Hillary confirmed. 'And once you've dropped us off at HQ, I want you to talk to every resident of The Knott again, and see if anyone can place Martha Hepton at Edward Philpott's cottage that morning. Don't forget, she could have gone through the gardens and not walked down the main road at all. And while you're at it, see if there are any footpaths or rights-of-way she could have used that would take her round the back of the houses. Very often in old, small villages, there are secret little paths that outsiders like us don't know about.'

'Guv.'

Back in Steeple Knott they found Martha Hepton about to tackle a field of poppies on her latest canvas. She looked more annoyed than afraid when Hillary insisted that she come with them to Kidlington for a formal interview; she washed her hands and pulled off her painter's smock with ill grace.

She was curiously quiet on the drive back into town. Most suspects, Hillary knew from experience, liked to talk in the car on the way to the station. Either to protest their ignorance or innocence, or to nervously make joking observations, or even to throw angry abuse and threats of suit for wrongful arrest.

Very few simply sat quietly in the back and watched the scenery pass. She wondered what the other woman was thinking, and it made her feel suspicious. It would be interesting to see which way Martha Hepton jumped when confronted with the fact that they knew her long-term lover had been in the process of making her homeless.

Gemma Fordham glanced up as her boss walked through the crowded office to her desk. 'I've just brought Martha Hepton in,' Hillary said coolly by way of greeting, and briefly brought Gemma up to date. 'I'm letting Barrington sit in with me, but I'd like you to observe. I've got a feeling she's going to be a wily one.' And another set of eyes and ears might come in very handy.

Gemma felt her heart-rate skip. 'Right, Guv,' she picked up her notebook and headed for the door. She liked to watch Hillary in action, and this was the first real lead they'd had since starting the investigation. Who knew, she mused: if Hillary could break her down they might get a confession and have the case wrapped up by teatime.

Hillary collected her favourite personal mini-cassette recorder and slipped it into her bag, then glanced across at Danvers' cubicle and saw that it was empty. She started to write out an update for him concerning their new suspect when her phone rang.

'DI Greene.'

'Hello, DI Greene? This is DC Stephen Crane, ma'am. You don't know me, ma'am, but I'm one of the officers in Thame.'

Hillary jerked upright. What the hell was going on now? 'Yes, Constable?' she said warily. She wouldn't put it past Brian Vane to be setting her up for something. After all, he'd warned her in front of Donleavy to stay out of Mel's case, and she didn't know this DC Crane from Adam.

'I think you should know, ma'am, that I've just seen an ex-sergeant of yours,' Stephen Crane said, carefully, and unhappily. 'In fact, I'm looking at her right now.'

Hillary caught her breath. Shit! Janine was in the vicinity of Myers' house? What the hell was she thinking of?

'Is she on foot?' Hillary asked sharply.

'No ma'am. In her car.'

'I'll be right there. If she tries to leave the car, please tell her I'll be there shortly.'

'Yes ma'am,' came the relieved reply.

Hillary swore colourfully as she hung up and grabbed her coat. She all but ran across the office, down the stairs and into the interview rooms in the basement.

She didn't go immediately to interview room 2 however, where she'd left Martha Hepton not five minutes ago, but rather to the adjoining observation room. There she stuck her head around the door.

'Gemma, it's all yours,' she told her startled sergeant. 'I have to go out. I want you to get Barrington out here and let him fill you in more fully, then start the interview without me. I expect to be back within the hour, so keep her talking if you can.'

'Guv, what if she wants to walk?' Gemma asked in alarm. They both knew that unless a suspect was actually under arrest, he or she could leave at any time they liked. 'Do I charge her?'

'Hell no,' Hillary said forcefully. 'We don't have anything like the evidence for that yet. Just get a feel for her. See if you can draw her out.'

Damn it, Hillary fumed. This was going to be a difficult inter view, even for a seasoned veteran like herself. She shouldn't be putting it all on Gemma and running off after Janine like this, but doing her job, damn it.

'Just think of it as a chance to perfect your technique,' Hillary said, somewhat desperately, and gave Gemma a brief smile.

She wasn't surprised to see her savvy sergeant give her a searching look in return. But she also knew that she could rely on Gemma's ambition to smooth things over. This was a big chance for Gemma to show what she was made of, and Hillary knew she'd grasp it with both hands.

'Guv.' Gemma gave a dutiful nod.

She leaned forward and pressed a button, which sounded a buzzer inside the interview room. Barrington looked up, briefly surprised by the summons, but came out obediently. He was just in time to see Hillary disappearing down the end of the corridor.

In the observation room, Gemma told him of the change of plans. She listened carefully as Keith gave her the full run down of what they'd learned at Phipps, Brown & Greengage, and Gemma felt her heart beat rising.

Even so, as she pushed open the door to the interview room, and felt a rush of power wash over her as Martha Hepton watched her nervously, she wondered what could be so important as to make Hillary Greene leave such an important interview up in the air like this.

And she only hoped that Danvers, or worse yet, Superintendent Vane, didn't get to hear about it. There was growing scuttlebutt going around that Vane and Hillary were not seeing eye to eye. And if that was the case, then the last thing Hillary could afford to do was give the new superintendent ammunition with which to blast her.

Janine jumped as the door to her car opened, then she swore softly as Hillary Greene slipped in beside her. 'Damn, I was sure I hadn't been spotted,' Janine said ruefully.

'What the hell are you doing here?' Hillary demanded, her tone making it clear that she was in no mood for the softly-softly approach.

'I heard that Gary Firth's whereabouts have been traced to a caravan in Wales,' Janine said, a hint of defiance in her voice.

Hillary almost groaned aloud. 'I know. I gave them the bloody tip.'

'But did you know that they can't find Firth at the site? Oh, there's plenty of evidence that he's been there. But of the boy himself – not a dicky-bird.'

Hillary frowned. 'So? He's probably somewhere in the nearest town getting drunk in a pub.'

'Nope.' Janine shook her head. 'Apparently, the caravan's in the middle of nowhere – literally. No bus routes, no taxis, nothing. And the little scrote who drove him down there had already come back on his bike. He was due to fetch Firth more supplies today. Word has it they were probably planning some rural post office job. And I doubt Gary Firth's the kind to hike for miles – lazy little scrotes won't walk for a hundred yards if they can ride. So where is he?'

Hillary ran a hand through her hair, trying to get a grip on what Janine was saying.

'So they think – what, exactly?'

Janine shrugged. 'They've asked for cadaver dogs,' she said. 'And guess what? Clive Myers wasn't seen in his house all day yesterday.'

Hillary chewed her bottom lip angrily. 'So, you think sitting here, watching his house, is going to help – how – exactly?'

Janine swore loudly. 'I can't just sit at home all day. I'm going bloody insane.'

Hillary closed her eyes and took a long, slow, breath. Yes, she knew all about how that felt. Hadn't the same sensation of agonizing helplessness been driving her similarly insane all these weeks?

'I know Myers killed Mel,' Janine said now, her voice hard and tight and about to break. 'He's taken out Firth, he'll take out the other two lads, and maybe even go for DI Gregg. It was no sniper killer copycat, Hill. It was that bastard in there. I know it. And you know it too.'

Hillary looked numbly out of the windscreen. It had begun to rain: slow, fat heavy raindrops that made her vision of the street outside shimmer.

'Come on, Janine, they'll get him,' she said, but without much conviction. The truth was, the investigation into Mel's murder was showing all the signs of stalling and winding down, and Hillary knew it. But she had to convince Janine otherwise. 'Look, I want you to promise me you'll follow me back to Kidlington. If you don't, you know Evans doesn't have any option but to have you removed, so save yourself the hassle, yeah?'

Janine turned and looked at Hillary out of dead-looking eyes. The lack of expression in them made Hillary's hands go cold.

'Sure Hill,' she said. 'I understand perfectly. You've given up. But just because you won't do anything to avenge Mel, don't think that I won't.'

She started the car engine, and revved the accelerator, forcing Hillary to get out of the car quickly.

She's coming unravelled, Hillary thought helplessly, as she watched Janine Mallow's car pull out on to the road with a noisy squeal of rubber. She felt a huge wave of guilt and panic wash over her. First she'd had to watch as her best friend was killed in front of her, and had then been forced to take a back seat whilst someone else investigated his case. Without any tangible results.

And now his widow was headed for disaster.

Well, nothing she could do would bring Mel back or put that situation right, but Janine was not yet beyond help. And Hillary owed it to Mel to see that she looked after Janine, and that unborn baby of his.

Somehow.

Grimly she walked back to Puff the Tragic Wagon and headed back to HQ. On top of everything else, she still had a murder case on her hands. She could only hope that Gemma had managed to get somewhere with Martha Hepton.

As she drove, she had no idea that the officers in the car in front of the house had noted Janine's tyre-squealing exit from the scene. Or that they'd run the number plate of her car, and had already informed DCI Gawain Evans of Janine Mallow's unauthorized presence at their suspect's house.

And that of one DI Hillary Greene.

CHAPTER TEN

Once back at HQ, Hillary went straight to the observation room to try and get a feeling for how things had gone in the interview.

Martha Hepton was sitting in her chair, her arms crossed over her chest in a classic protective/defiant gesture. So whatever stance Gemma had taken had certainly rattled her. But from the stubborn look on her face, Hillary doubted it had netted results.

'Miss Hepton, Mr Greengage told DI Greene not two hours ago that he wrote and sent you a letter telling you that Mr Philpott was not going to renew your lease. He'll be sure to have kept a copy of it. Do I really have to send for it for you to see?' Gemma asked. Her voice, although calm enough, had a sharp edge to it, and her words, all too grimly, confirmed Hillary's pessimism.

Things had not gone well.

Martha Hepton shrugged petulantly. 'He may have *sent* it, Sergeant, I'm sure, but that doesn't mean to say I received it, does it?' she asked, sweetly and reasonably. 'I mean, the post office is hardly infallible, you know. Things *do* go missing.'

Hillary had heard enough. She quickly stepped through and pushed open the door.

'The firm of solicitors that Edward Philpott used always send their important mail by registered post, Miss Hepton,' she said tightly, even before she'd sat down.

Gemma glanced across at her, and muttered into the tape, 'DI

129

Greene has just entered the room.' She cited the time and then took a mental step back. Although her face wore a blank look, Hillary was sure that she could see relief glimmer in those cool grey eyes of hers.

'That means you must have signed for it,' Hillary continued, fixing her gimlet eyes on Martha, who flushed. 'Which also means that there will be a record of it at the post office. All there in black and white, with your signature on it.'

Hillary took a seat, and got out a pen and a notebook from her bag. 'Now, I suggest you stop being so silly and start co-operating, or you'll find yourself charged with wasting police time and trying to pervert the cause of justice. And that's just for starters.'

Hillary pressed the top of her pen down with a decisive 'snick' and glowered at the woman opposite. Her message was loud and clear. She was in no mood to play silly buggers.

Martha Hepton bit her lip, no doubt trying desperately to remember whether or not she'd signed for the solicitor's letter on the day it came. Hillary was banking on her not being able to, and she thought her chances were fairly good. No doubt the arrival of an official letter had come as a shock, and a barrage of emotions would have followed – rage, disbelief, fear. All of which were pretty good for clouding the memory about other, specific details.

'Oh, for Pete's sake, what does it matter anyway?' Martha huffed, caving in. Beside her, she felt Gemma relax.

'So you knew your lover was intending to make you homeless?' Hillary stated baldly.

'Don't be so dramatic, will you?' Martha asked with an unconvincing laugh, looking at the tape recorder nervously. 'So he wasn't going to let me stay on at the cottage. It's hardly the end of the world, is it?'

Hillary allowed herself a bleak smile. 'So you had no problem with it then?'

Martha, realizing how absurd that sounded, shifted uncomfortably on her chair. 'Well, I can't say as I liked it, no. But so what? Things happen in life.'

'It must have made you very angry. I mean, you'd been inti-mate with this man for years. And after all that time, you must have come to look on the cottage as your own. And then Mr Philpott turns you out without a qualm,' Hillary pressed on.

'Hey, you don't know that!' Martha objected. 'And as it turns out, Eddie was really cut up about it. But he said that with his daughter like she was, and with the kids to think about and all, he needed to have capital. Just in case, like. He said family came first. And he's right – family always does,' she added with false piety.

'A pretty speech, Miss Hepton. But don't you count as family too? After twenty years?'

Martha flushed hotly and opened her mouth, no doubt to say something rather pithy in the affirmative, then caught herself just in time and closed her lips with a snap. She gave Hillary a tight smile.

'He wasn't going to just abandon me, was he?' she said with a bright smile. 'He was going to help me find a new place; he said so. Put some feelers out, find a little part time job for me. He even offered to loan me some money, if I needed it.'

She leaned back and crossed her arms across her chest a little tighter. It was all lies, of course, and Hillary knew it. And Martha Hepton knew that Hillary knew it. But with Eddie Philpott dead, who was left to gainsay her?

'So I had no reason for wanting Eddie dead, did I?' Martha swept on breezily. 'He was going to help me, so he was. And now he's gone, I've lost everything.'

She even managed to shed a few tears.

Hillary watched her silently for a few moments, then closed her notebook with a snap. 'That'll be all for the moment, Miss Hepton,' she said briskly. 'DC Barrington will drive you home.'

Gemma followed her glumly out of the interview room. Once on the stairs, she sighed slightly. 'She's a tough old bat.'

Hillary nodded.

'And she won't budge?' Gemma tried again.

'No.' She saw her sergeant shoot her a quick look, realized what the problem was, and smiled briefly. 'Some interviews are just a waste of time and effort. It's not anybody's fault. You did fine.'

Gemma nodded, but her lips felt tight and stiff. Hillary was right, she knew. And not even the boss herself had been able to do much more than get Martha grudgingly to admit to knowing about the eviction notice. But still, a sense of failure nagged at her innards.

'It's a good job that solicitors' outfit uses registered mail, Guv,' she said thoughtfully.

Hillary shot her a blank look. 'Do they?'

Gemma felt her mouth drop open, and then she gave a reluctant laugh. And made a mental note to herself: never play poker with Hillary Greene.

Back at her desk, Hillary sat down with a sigh. She reached for Edward Philpott's biography, now as up to date as modern technology and records could make it, and began to read. She'd barely read a few paragraphs, however, when something leapt out at her.

Edward Philpott's marriage date. To one Frances Gaye Miller. Shit! *The ex-wife*. She'd never given her a thought! But *why* hadn't she? It was standard practice always to check out the spouse.

'The ex-wife,' Hillary said guiltily to Gemma, who nodded. She picked up her notebook and began to riffle through it.

'Divorced when the daughter was thirteen Guv,' Gemma said calmly, totally missing Hillary's relieved gasp. 'She moved back to Leicester, her home town, and married again to a man called Bruce Lorrimer, but he died four years later. She then moved again, to Weston-super-Mare. I tracked her down to a hospice there. Cancer. Probably runs in the family, Guv, that's why her daughter is like she is. I didn't interview her over the phone, but spoke to the matron on duty there. She went in on the four-teenth of August this year. They don't think she'll see Christmas. According to her, there's no way Mrs Lorrimer was strong enough even to catch a train, let alone bash someone over the head. Besides, I had her check her records, and Mrs Lorrimer never left the hospice.'

Hillary let out a long slow breath. 'Fine.'

So Gemma had followed up on her as a matter of routine. Of course she had. She probably hadn't even given it a thought that Hillary hadn't bothered to ask her to, but had taken it for granted.

It came to something when your sergeant was more on the ball than you were. And the irony of relying on Gemma Fordham, of all people, to stop her fumbling her own murder case was not lost on her.

But a cold feeling of unease was tickling her spine. She needed to get her mind off Mel and Janine and Clive bloody Myers, and concentrate on Eddie Philpott.

Just then her telephone rang.

'DI Greene.'

'Superintendent Vane. My office now, please.'

Hillary heard the dial tone in her ear and hung up. Gemma was looking at her curiously, and Hillary realized that the distaste must show on her face. 'Wanted in the super's office,' she explained succinctly.

As she reached for her bag she saw that Frank Ross's desk was still empty. Had he even been in today? But then, she thought, what did it really matter? And as she made her way up the stairs to the super's office, she wondered if Ross wasn't the only one who'd end up out of a job.

If she carried on like this, she might be leaving before he did!

The thought made her smile, and her grim smile was noted by a young male PC as she knocked on Vane's door.

So the rumours were true, he thought, with a tinge of excite-ment. DI Greene and the super were at loggerheads already.

Nobody could understand why. It wasn't like DI Greene to make trouble, and so far, nobody could find any faults with Superintendent Vane. Rumour and speculation was running wild. He hurried on down the steps to get back to the lockers and report the latest to his mates in traffic.

Unaware of the interest in her, Hillary tapped on the superintendent's door and waited for the summons to come in. When it came, she closed the door carefully behind her and was careful not to sit.

Brian Vane finished scribbling on the memo he was reading and then looked up.

'I've had a report from Thame that Janine Mallow was seen near Clive Myers' house this morning. Do you know anything about that?'

Hillary nodded quickly. She was too canny to be caught out in a lie. 'Yes sir. I received an anonymous tip that she was there. I went there myself, and persuaded her to leave.'

Vane's already thin lips tightened at the words 'anonymous tip' but he wisely let it ride. Every DI worth their salt had eyes and ears everywhere – both on the force, and in the criminal world. Besides, this was technically DCI Evans's problem, and making a complaint about one of his men keeping Hillary Greene informed wouldn't make him, Vane, popular with anyone.

'I hope you aren't encouraging Mrs Mallow in her understandable desire to keep tabs on the inquiry into her husband's murder, DI Greene,' Vane said bleakly. 'Because if I find out that you have, I will take the matter seriously. Very seriously indeed. Do you understand?'

So Donleavy hadn't told Vane that he'd given her instructions on the q.t. to keep a close eye on Janine, Hillary thought. Now that was interesting.

'Yes sir,' she answered in a level tone.

Vane nodded a silent dismissal and Hillary left. He could just as easily have said what he wanted to say over the phone, she knew. But that wasn't the point.

As she walked out of his office and back down the stairs, Hillary knew that she was supposed to feel both chastised and uneasy for making it on to the super's shit list. But that would require too much energy. Besides, Donleavy was looking out for her. It was not the same as having Mel watching her back, of course. Donleavy was very much the politician, and if it became politic to let her go, then go she would. But, in the absence of her oldest and dearest friend, Donleavy's support was some small comfort.

When she got back, Barrington was pacing restlessly beside her desk.

'Guv. Tom Cleaves was found collapsed on his allotment this morning. A fellow allotment holder, Jim Goulder, found him and called 999 thinking he'd had a heart attack. But when the medics arrived, it seems they found the old man was just drunk.'

Hillary slowly pulled out her chair and sat down. 'Does he have a history of drinking? I think I asked you to do a background check on him, didn't I?'

'Yes, Guv, still working on it,' Barrington said. 'And no, there's no history of his having a drink problem. I talked briefly to Goulder, the allotment holder who found him, and he was surprised too. He said he'd never known Tom to have more than one pint in the pub, and hardly ever spirits.'

Hillary sighed. 'Where is he now?'

'Back home, sleeping it off. The paramedics got him round, and Goulder got some of Tom's friends to rally round. They got him home in a wheelbarrow apparently. They're probably still siphoning strong black coffee into him now.'

Hillary sighed. 'We'd better go and see what he has to say for himself, then.'

Tom Cleaves, it turned out, wasn't in the mood to say much about anything. A tall, grey-haired and lanky man, who looked slightly sheepish when Hillary identified herself, answered the knock on Tom's door.

'Tom's in the living room,' he said. 'He's got a bit of a hang-over, and is feeling rather sorry for himself at the moment,' he added nervously. He opened the door to the living room, but didn't come in, murmuring something instead about making tea.

Tom Cleaves opened his eyes briefly, saw police officers, and flushed. He made an effort to sit up straighter, then seemed to think better of it.

'Hello, Mr Cleaves. I understand you've been under the weather?' Hillary said, taking a seat unasked.

'Huh. Making a fool of myself, more like.'

'A bit too much to drink?'

'Yes.'

'You were found by a Mr Jim Goulder, I understand?' Hillary pressed.

'He's got the allotment next to mine. Decent feller.'

Hillary waited. Barrington waited. Tom Cleaves closed his eyes and looked as if he was going to go back to sleep.

'I understand you're not known for being a big drinker, Mr Cleaves,' Hillary said, a shade more loudly than normal. The man on the chair jerked slightly and opened his eyes.

'I'm not.'

'And yet this morning you'd been drinking,' said Hillary, assuming a tone of mild curiosity. 'Rather an odd time, isn't it? Most people drink at night.'

Tom Cleaves shrugged.

Hillary sighed. First Martha Hepton, now Tom Cleaves – recalcitrant witnesses were thick on the ground today. 'Would your drinking have anything to do with the death of Edward Philpott, Mr Cleaves?'

'No, it wouldn't.'

'Is there something on your conscience, perhaps?'

'My conscience is fine, thank you.'

'You know, Mr Cleaves, alcohol isn't the answer to any problem. It only makes a problem even worse. If something's preying on your mind, you should talk to someone.'

Tom Cleaves began to close his eyes again, and a grim smile played around his lips. 'Talk to you, you mean?'

'Or a psychiatrist or counsellor perhaps. Maybe some kind of priest or pastor?' Hillary said casually.

Tom began to snore loudly. He was probably faking it, but then again, if the man really wasn't much of a drinker, it could be genuine.

Either way, she knew when she was flogging a dead horse. She got up, and with a head roll, indicated to Barrington to follow her out.

Outside, she sighed heavily. It was trying to rain. Around her, hawthorn hedges were red with old berries, and their leaves were just beginning to yellow. Give it another few weeks, and the autumn colours would be spectacular. Somehow, she couldn't work up any enthusiasm for that approaching natural treat.

'What do you think, Guv?' Barrington asked curiously.

Hillary shrugged. 'It doesn't take a genius to realize something's eating him. We'll just have to wait until he's got a clear head, then try again. In the meantime, get cracking on his background check.'

'Guv.'

Barrington drove them back to HQ, his eye on the clock. He knew that round about now the barristers in the Moreland trial would be giving their final arguments. On the telephone last night, Gavin had been like quicksilver – elated one moment, and crowing about how his father had made the prosecutor look like a know-nothing idiot, then downcast the next, and convinced that the jury would bring in a 'guilty' verdict.

Keith had been following the trial as best he could, and even from such a distance, had been able to tell that it was a complicated case. Fraud and financial cases often were. It largely depended on how much the jury had been able to understand about the complicated import and export laws, and the tax issues. But privately, Barrington thought that the actual physical evidence of the smuggled items found in Moreland's possession would alone be enough to convict him.

Of course, the sentence was something again. Moreland might get away with a non-custodial sentence.

But Keith rather doubted it.

He'd rung off, promising Gavin he'd try and get down that weekend. It was Friday tomorrow, and nobody expected the jury to want to have to stretch things out over the weekend. So a verdict seemed likely. But he doubted he'd be able to get time off, not with the case as stalled as it was. Besides, Moreland was bound to be home, and the last thing he'd want would be to have to make small talk with his son's policeman lover over the cold cucumber soup and smoked salmon.

'Have you had any luck placing either Hepton or Cleaves at the Philpott residence?' Hillary's sharp question made him draw a quick breath.

'No Guv. No sightings and no forensics either. At least not yet.'

Hillary nodded. Some forensic tests could take weeks, or even months. But just how much forensics would there be in a case like this? The killer walked up to Philpott, whacked him on the back of the head with the shovel, and walked away. How many fibres would have been shed, or microscopic skin particles? True, the killer might have got a blood spatter on his or her clothes, but until you had a reasonable case against someone it was hard to obtain a warrant to get clothes.

Rachel Warner's clothes had borne traces of her father's blood, of course, but then she'd found him. She'd admitted to bending down to touch him – indeed, she had been close enough to notice that his watch and ring were missing, so that didn't put them any further forward.

And that reminded her.

'Any trace of the watch and ring?'

'No, Guv. We've put out warnings to all the usual lot to be on the lookout. But so far, nobody's reported anything.'

Hillary sighed. The 'usual lot' consisted mostly of local jewellers, market stallholders and pawn shops, plus a few copper-friendly fences. But Hillary didn't think the killer of Edward Philpott would be stupid enough to try and flog his jewellery just yet. If at all. It seemed to her far more likely that the killer had simply robbed the body in an attempt to muddy the waters. If Edward Philpott had really been killed for profit by a passing opportunist, then the house would almost certainly have been ransacked as well, and valuable items stolen. No junkie would have let such an opportunity slip by.

But she knew from Gemma's and Barrington's careful research, and from Rachel Warner's own input, that nothing had been taken from the house.

'OK. Apply for a warrant to search both Tom Cleaves' and Martha Hepton's homes. Concentrate on their clothing. We need to examine what they were wearing that day.'

'Guv,' Keith said, without enthusiasm. Doing the paperwork for warrants was one of his pet hates. And he had the feeling that no judge was likely to grant such a request, not on the flimsy evidence they had to go on. But he could understand why Hillary had to try.

No matter which way they turned, they seemed to come up against dead ends, he thought, dispiritedly.

That night Gemma Fordham crawled under the covers, and snuggled up against Guy Brindley. The blind music don sighed contentedly, and moved his arm to one side to make it easier for her to nestle.

'Bad day at the office?' he asked sympathetically.

Gemma sighed softly. 'I'm not sure.'

'That sounds interesting,' he said cautiously. He knew that his lover had some issues with her boss, although he'd never enquired too closely. He was coming to know Gemma well, and knew that any probing into certain areas of her life on his part would net him a few mental bruises.

'Greene's not at her best,' Gemma said unhappily. 'She's distracted by Janine Mallow for a start, and there's something going on with the new super. Nobody's sure what.'

'Sounds ominous. But then, she's still grieving for her friend, so I suppose you can't expect her to be on tip-top form,' Guy pointed out reasonably.

Gemma sighed. 'No. What happened to Superintendent Mallow was a nightmare for me, and I didn't even know him that well. So what Hillary must have felt that afternoon ...' She broke off and shivered.

Guy had listened with growing horror, that evening just over two months ago, when his lover had come home, blood-spattered, shaking slightly, and grim-voiced as she told him that her superior officer had just been shot dead in front of her.

Being Gemma, of course, she'd tackled the trauma head on, and when Hillary Greene had taken two months' leave, had typically grasped the opportunity her superior's absence had afforded, to consolidate her own position.

It seemed unlike her now to be worrying about her boss's mental health. 'I thought you weren't looking forward to having her back,' Guy said casually. 'But from the tone of your voice, you sound sorry for her.'

'I am. And I'm not sorry she's back.' Gemma heard herself say the words with something close to shock. 'You know, two days ago I wrote out my resignation?'

Guy went very still. 'Really?' Ever since she'd agreed to move in with him, Guy had had a ringside seat from which to observe just how much his lover valued the identity her job gave her. So the bombshell of her words made his head spin.

'Let's just say, the issue between me and Hillary Greene came to a head, but not in the way I'd expected. Or hoped.' Although her voice sounded to Guy to be deeply ironic, he sensed something else underneath it.

Amusement, perhaps? A hint of grudging respect?

'Was the joke on you, my love?' Guy asked softly.

Gemma sighed deeply. 'Sometimes, *my love*,' Gemma mimicked him savagely, 'you can be too damned perspicacious for your own good.'

She turned and rolled away, presenting him with her back.

In the suddenly cool bed, Guy gave a small sigh, and closed his eyes.

After about five minutes, Gemma Fordham suddenly reached for him savagely.

But Guy didn't mind. Making love to Gemma always involved both pleasure and pain.

Whilst Hillary's current sergeant made love to her blind, wealthy partner, her ex-sergeant was doing something totally different.

Janine Mallow parked her car behind a deserted warehouse, and turned off the engine. She left the headlights on, however, and waited patiently. Out in the dark, she knew, a pair of nervous eyes was watching her in the surrounding darkness of the night. Here, in a run-down area of Cowley, there were barely any streetlights, and the only living things scuttling about in the dark were drunks and urban foxes.

After nearly ten minutes, Janine saw movement, and smiled grimly. Matthew 'Skunk' Peterson approached the car cautiously. He was wearing a hoodie and white trainers, and couldn't have looked more conspicuous if he'd tried.

He opened the door and slipped inside.

'Hello, Sarge,' he said nervously. He was in his early twenties, but had the acne of a teenager. The youngest of a family of nine, Skunk was on the fringes of the biggest Oxford gang. Once or twice, whilst in uniform, Janine had arrested him, and treated him decently.

She'd wanted eyes and ears in the gang, but although Skunk wasn't the brightest lamp in the lightbulb factory, even he'd been too canny to play along.

Still, they'd kept a vague sort of contact over the years, and Janine put the fear of something nasty into him every now and then. Which was why she'd called him a few hours ago. He'd be frightened enough of her to do as she asked, and just wise enough to keep quiet about it. He'd also be able to get his hands on what she wanted.

'You have it?'

Skunk looked around nervously, then unzipped his hoodie and let a chunky item, wrapped in newspaper, drop into his lap. He was sweating now, and Janine could smell the waft of sour body odour rising from him that gave him his nickname.

'What do you want it for, eh, Sarge? You being a copper and all, you could get your hands on one any time.'

'Never you mind,' Janine said sharply. 'Just hand it over, and keep your mouth shut.'

Skunk quickly did as he was told. Janine reached into her bag and withdrew a tightly folded roll of notes.

'Hey, thanks Sarge,' Skunk said, evidently surprised. He'd expected to have to do the favour for nothing.

Janine sighed heavily. 'Just remember – we never met. You know nothing. You say nothing. Otherwise you'll be behind bars faster than you can cough,' she bluffed grimly.

'Won't say a word, will I? I ain't no grass,' Skunk said indignantly.

Janine ignored his hurt feelings. 'How hot is it?'

'Not very.'

Janine shrugged. What did it matter. 'OK, Skunk, bugger off then, there's a good lad.'

The 'good lad' didn't need telling twice.

Janine Mallow drove back to her big, empty house in the Moors, and parked the car in her garage. Mel's car was still housed inside it, and the sight of it made her burst into a bout of weeping.

One day she'd have to sell it.

She got out, carrying the chunky, newspaper-wrapped parcel

with her. Inside the house, she laid it down on the kitchen counter, and unwrapped it.

It was an ugly, Russian-made ten-year-old weapon, but it would do. She checked it thoroughly, oiled it, and loaded it with bullets from a small store Mel had kept under lock and key in a gun cabinet.

That done, she poured herself a glass of lemonade, and tipped the rest of the fizzy drink down the drain. The now empty plastic bottle would make a crude but effective silencer.

She sipped her drink and wandered around the empty house, alternately weeping and then caressing the gun. Eventually at nearly three o'clock in the morning, she went to bed.

But she wouldn't sleep.

The next day, Friday 10 October, Detective Inspector Peter Gregg returned to his Kidlington home where, before the Myers case, he'd lived with his wife and three sons. It was nothing special – just a smart semi near the big Sainsbury shop by the roundabout. But it felt good to be back.

There were no fanfares, and no big welcome home. His wife and kids were still safely in hiding in the Forest of Dean, where he'd been for the past two months. And none of the neighbours had known about his imminent arrival.

But as he unpacked, drew back curtains, watered whatever houseplants were still alive, and generally began to reclaim his old habits, he was watched constantly.

Last night, DCI Evans, faced with the inevitable closure of his operations, had decided on one last big gamble. And DI Pete Gregg had gone along with it.

Myers was simply too cagey, too quick, too clever, or just too damned lucky to make a mistake. Which meant that the only way they were going to get him was to stake out a Judas goat and wait.

Today, the news of Gregg's return would be 'leaked' to the local papers, and Myers would then know where to find him.

And even if he guessed it was a trap, Evans and Gregg were willing to bet that the opportunity to get the man who'd led his daughter's rape case would be too tempting to pass up.

Hence the intense watch on Gregg's every move. Of course, a sniper rifle had a long range. And it was possible Myers might slip through the cordon. Consequently, his shoulder blades itched every time he walked past a window, even though Peter Gregg knew that Myers couldn't possible know of his return yet.

But when he did, it was a distinct possibility that Gregg might go the same way as Philip Mallow.

It was a chance Gregg was willing to take. Guilt gnawed constantly at his gut. The bullet that had taken Philip Mallow should, by rights, have had his name on it. Gregg knew it, and so did every other cop at HQ.

This was his one and only chance of redemption. And it was why he'd argued for it so passionately over the objections of the top brass.

Now, all he could do was wait. And try not to go insane. Or get shot.

CHAPTER ELEVEN

It wasn't often that Hillary Greene had breakfast in the canteen at HQ, but that morning she'd been running late and had left the boat without even a cup of coffee. When she parked Puff the Tragic Wagon, she felt the first faint stirrings of hunger. On impulse, she detoured to the canteen for some fresh fruit and toast.

Most of the tables were full, so she chose a free chair at a table where a solitary DS was finishing his fry-up. He looked up as she pulled the chair out, and nodded in recognition.

'Ma'am.'

Hillary gave him a second glance and fought for a name for him from her memory. 'DS Knighton, isn't it?' she said after a moment or two.

'Yes, ma'am. We worked together briefly on that ram-raiding case a few years back, out Woodstock way.'

Hillary nodded, then her eyes sharpened. 'Aren't you working with DCI Evans?'

'Yes ma'am,' Knighton replied. He was nearly forty, and had long since given up on trying to pass his Boards. But he was happy at the rank he held, since he'd never been too keen on paperwork, and preferred to be out and about and doing things, instead of riding a desk. It was one of the reasons he'd always admired Hillary Greene, who seemed to share his attitude.

He cleared his throat, then glanced around, and leant forward, lowering his voice. 'I just thought you might like to know, ma'am, that DI Gregg is back.'

Hillary blinked. 'Back? At HQ you mean?'

'No, ma'am. Not on active duty, as yet. But he's back in his own home.'

Hillary slowly unwrapped a pat of butter and began to spread it on her toast. It didn't take her long to figure out what was going on.

'And he agreed to this?' she asked, then made a disgusted grimace. 'Damn, what am I saying – of course he did. The brass can't be happy.'

'No, ma'am.'

Hillary met Knighton's bland hazel eyes, and nodded grimly. 'He's a brave man, DI Gregg. And obviously trying to do right by Mel.' She didn't say it lightly. She knew her words would be passed along the grapevine via Knighton, and she knew how people would take it.

Hillary and Phillip Mallow had been well known to be great friends, and if Hillary had officially put her seal of approval – and forgiveness – on DI Gregg, then it would go a long way towards helping Gregg get back in the good graces of the rank and file at HQ. Not that anyone openly blamed Gregg for what happened to Mel, but Hillary knew a lot of people were secretly thinking – and wishing – that it had been Gregg who'd taken the bullet. It was Gregg, after all, who'd been in operational charge of the Myers rape case.

Hillary also had felt a knee-jerk reaction of resentment at the mention of the man, but she was too honest not to admit to herself that Gregg had merely been unlucky. Or to acknowledge that Mel himself hadn't blamed Gregg for the foul-up. Still, to know that she would probably be bumping into Gregg some time in the future filled her with unease.

'Yes ma'am,' Knighton said quietly. 'DI Gregg wants Myers badly.'

Hillary grunted vaguely, then forced herself to eat the fruit she no longer had any appetite for, nodded pleasantly to Knighton and left the canteen.

For some reason her throat seemed to ache, and she realized she was on the verge of tears. She made a quick detour to the ladies' loo to splash cold water on her face and swallow back the tightness in her throat, then went to her desk.

She was surprised to see Frank Ross at his desk. He shot her a blank look as she took her seat, and she braced herself for some nastiness that never came. Perhaps he'd been on a bender and was now sober enough to face reality.

'Did you find those old case files I wanted, Frank?' she asked, as Gemma Fordham looked at him curiously. Briefly, she told her sergeant about the Linda Quirke case, and how the missing girl had been Rachel Warner's best friend. Gemma shrugged and went back to her keyboard, obviously finding it of little interest.

Wordlessly, Frank Ross searched his messy desk top, and came up with a somewhat dirty beige file. She wondered if the admin people who beavered away putting old cases on to the computer database had reached as far as the Quirke years yet, and decided, from a brief scan of the ancient-looking forms and typewritten reports within the folder, that they hadn't.

Quickly, she scanned the evidence, acquainting herself with the basics.

Linda Quirke, a thirteen-year-old with long brown pigtails and big eyes, had gone missing from her home in Duns Tew one Saturday morning in August 1981. She'd set out on her bike to pedal the three-quarters of a mile or so to her friend's house in the nearby hamlet of Steeple Knott, and had simply vanished.

Her bicycle had never been found. There'd been very little traffic on the roads, and none of the motorists who *had* been in the area on the isolated country roads had reported seeing the little girl.

An extensive search had come up with nothing of any use – no trace of the girl, her bike, car or lorry-tyre marks that might have been parked on the side of the road, or Linda's clothing.

Linda Quirke had simply vanished.

Hillary frowned. No doubt the friend she'd been going to see that morning had been Rachel. Had the little girl she'd been then been puzzled by the no-show of her friend? Had she hung around the house, watching from the windows, wondering what had kept Linda? And how had she felt when the news started to circulate, that her friend had gone?

Something in the file niggled at her, and she couldn't think what it was. All this had happened over twenty-five years ago. None of the names of the useless witnesses were familiar to her. The Quirke family themselves certainly didn't feature in the Philpott case, nearly thirty years later. So what was bugging her?

'Guv, I've got something!' Barrington's excited voice as he barrelled over towards her had her head snapping up. She tossed the file into her pending-tray, determined to go through it with a fine-tooth comb later and figure out what was teasing at her brain stem.

'Can you be more specific, Constable,' Hillary asked wryly, and Barrington smiled back just as wryly.

'Sorry, Guv. Tom Cleaves. The man's life has been as boring as anything, and I thought I'd never find anything interesting about him. He was the manager of a carpet warehouse company for nearly forty years, and had an exemplary work record. He and his wife Margaret have been married for nearly as long, and his three sons are all as respectable and boring as himself. All have left home now, of course, and there's not a sniff of naughtiness anywhere in the whole damned lot of them. No extra-marital affairs on either side as far as I can tell, and no run-ins with us either – not even a traffic ticket, Guv. Then, when I got back into his childhood, I finally struck gold.'

He sat down in his chair and shuffled back the leaves in his notebook. 'He was an only child, and his mother, Cecily Cleaves, née Crane, committed suicide when he was seven. There was something of a scandal about it,' Barrington said, aware that he had everyone's full attention now. Even Frank Ross was listening.

'Apparently, Cecily worked as a parliamentary secretary to the local Conservative MP. Well, it's the usual story. They had a fling and the press found out. The MP's wife "stood by her man" and the press had a field day painting Cecily Cleaves as the "scarlet woman". Anyway, the coverage, and the hounding of the press got so bad that Cecily's husband, Tom's father, George Cleaves, filed for divorce. Before the case could get to court, however, Cecily was found drowned in the local river.

'It turns out that somebody had been blackmailing her for months before the press got hold of the story, and had bled her dry. The copper assigned to the case found letters demanding more money in her wardrobe. Another secretary in the same office came under suspicion, but nothing could ever be proved.

'A sympathetic local coroner's court brought in a verdict of misadventure. But everyone at the time believed she'd committed suicide. There was even a bit of fuss over the local vicar having her buried in consecrated ground.'

He took a large breath, then looked across at Hillary.

Hillary thought it over. It was dramatic, yes, but did it really add anything to their case? 'Well, something like that will certainly scar a child for life,' she agreed pensively. 'And I dare say Tom Cleaves came away from it with several hang-ups.'

'The poor sod probably never goes fishing in the river,' Frank Ross said, and laughed.

Everyone ignored him.

'Well, he certainly never blamed his mother,' Gemma pointed out, with rather more relevance. 'Boys who turn against their mothers don't tend to have long happy marriages with another woman, twenty years down the line.'

'Right. But I imagine he has a knee-jerk reaction to blackmail of any kind,' Hillary said. And she could well understand why. Like most people, she found blackmailers to be particularly offensive.

'Guv,' Gemma said sharply. 'You remember at the beginning of the case, we kept running across examples of how Tom Cleaves and our victim came to loggerheads over the local flower show?'

Hillary nodded.

'I'm pretty sure one of the green-fingered brigade I spoke to said something about Eddie saying that Tom Cleaves and a certain judge were too pally for his liking.'

Hillary cocked her head to one side. 'Go on.'

'Well, Guv, I think he said that Eddie mentioned something in passing about how he had proof that Tom had won his prize dishonestly. I was just wondering …'

She let her voice trail off, and Hillary took up the thought obligingly. '… whether he spoke to Tom about it. And if he *did*, and was particularly clumsy about it, it *might* have sounded as if he was trying to blackmail Tom?'

'Well, it's possible, isn't it?' Gemma asked.

'Yes, it's possible,' Hillary agreed. It was even possible that Eddie Philpott *had* in fact used a little bit of blackmail to get his rival to back off in next year's show. From what they'd learned of Eddie, he might well have simply seen it as a bit of teasing fun, never knowing how devastating such a ploy might have seemed to the sensitive Tom Cleaves.

'And if Tom Cleaves does have a particular sensitivity about blackmail, it could have unbalanced him enough to make him act out of character,' she mused. All along she'd thought that the act of hitting a man over the head with a spade was an act of either rage, desperation, or some other extreme mental or emotional pressure.

'OK, reinterview your green-fingered friend. Try and pin him or her down on what Eddie Philpott actually said,' Hillary ordered Gemma.

'Guv. Should we bring in Cleaves?'

'No. Not yet. So far all we've got is speculation.'

'Guv.'

Hillary nodded across to Barrington. 'Good work. Any luck at placing either Cleaves or Hepton at the cottage on Monday morning?'

'No, Guv. And I can't see it happening either. I think in such a small place, if anyone had seen anything, we'd know about it by now.'

Hillary agreed, but didn't say so. Instead she nodded at him to continue, whilst Gemma grabbed her coat and walked quickly across the office. It amused Hillary to see several of her male colleagues follow her progress with their eyes.

She reached for her telephone and dialled Janine's number. There was no answer.

'Frank, go out and get a copy of the local papers, would you?' Hillary said.

Frank grunted, got up and left without a word. Nervously, Barrington watched him go.

Like Hillary, he was expecting fireworks at any minute. Frank Ross compliant and quiet was far more worrying than Frank Ross as his usual belligerent self.

The two constables watching the front of Clive Myers' house perked up when an extremely dirty red truck with an open flatbed trailer pulled up just past the house and began to reverse up the short drive.

PC Patrick Mulligan, a six-foot-six, almost bald youth, began furiously to take pictures with his digital camera, whilst his colleague, PC Ian Davis reached for the radio to report in.

Both of the men watched as Clive Myers walked from the house and opened up his garage obligingly.

'I don't like this,' Mulligan said grimly, as the rear end of the small, dirty truck began to disappear into the back of the garage. When only the nose of the truck was visible, the engine was turned off, and the driver's door opened.

A man dressed in dirty white painter's overalls, splotched with many colours, climbed out. He was wearing distinctive hobnailed boots, and had a large, dark blue baseball-style cap on his head. He also wore dark glasses.

'I really don't like this,' Mulligan repeated under his breath.

'Shit, they're going inside,' Ian Davis said, his voice rising in a squeak. Unlike his friend, he'd barely met the police height requirements and, again unlike his friend, had a mop of unruly brown curly hair. The two men had become firm friends, however, since being assigned to the same Panda car. And when they'd both been seconded to DCI Evans's team, they still tended to work together.

Grimly, Davis relayed the news back to HQ, asking for further instructions.

Hillary Greene thanked Ross as he tossed copies of the *Oxford Times* and the *Oxford Mail* on to her desk.

As expected, the *Oxford Mail* had a story on page two about the return of DI Peter Gregg.

Hillary grunted. So they had their goat well and truly staked out now.

She only hoped, for Gregg's sake, that they didn't botch it. She might never be able to warm to the man, but she didn't want any more dead coppers on her patch.

She tried dialling Janine Mallow again. Again, the telephone wasn't answered.

She hoped that it meant that Janine was having a long lie-in. But she rather doubted it.

'Sir, he's coming out again now,' Davis hissed into the car radio.

'Can you see his face?' DCI Evans's voice, tight with tension, crackled back over the line.

'Hold on,' Davis said. 'Pat, use the telephoto zoom. Can you see his face?'

Mulligan got the man emerging from the Myers house in the frame and swore. 'No, the crafty bugger's looking down at the ground.'

'Sir, all we can see are his clothes. He's wearing the same painter's overalls, boots, cap and sunglasses.'

'Shit!' Evans swore sibilantly. 'What's he doing?'

'Going to the truck, sir. Climbing in. Yes, the engine's turned over. Sir, what do we do?' the youngster asked anxiously.

'Follow him. Tell the other two in the car at the back to split up. One is to remain in the vehicle, the other is to walk around to the front and get a good view of the house. I wouldn't put it past Myers for this to be a double bluff. Lure us into following an obvious decoy, and then slip out of the house later.'

'Guv,' Davis said, and quickly contacted his colleagues to relay the message.

Mulligan started the car – an unremarkable Renault – and pulled out behind the truck.

'Sir, how long do we follow him?' Davis asked into the radio.

'Until I tell you otherwise,' Evans said curtly.

Janine Mallow pulled her car into a gap in the line of cars which were parked somewhat illegally on the road, and switched off the engine.

Compulsively, she reached a hand under the driving seat of her car, and felt the touch of cold metal and the slightly warmer plastic bottle, and gave a little sigh of relief. Not that she'd expected the gun to have magically disappeared or anything.

She glanced around the quiet, residential road, and settled back in her seat more comfortably. Her bloated stomach felt tight and slightly alien. She'd always been a slender, pretty blonde, and her distending stomach made her feel vaguely uneasy.

She glanced down at the open copy of the *Oxford Mail* beside her and read the story again. It had taken her a little longer than it had taken Hillary Greene to realize what was afoot, but once she had, nothing on earth would keep her out of it.

She reached into her bag, withdrew a small bottle of tonic water and took her pills. Her doctors had been nagging her about her hypertension for weeks now.

Duty done, Janine Mallow leaned her head back against her seat's headrest, and waited.

She'd wait all day if she had to. And all night. And all the next day, if it came to that.

After all, she had nowhere else to go and nothing else to do.

'Where the hell's he going?' Ian Davis muttered to his pal fifteen minutes later, and then, into the radio, 'We're still going vaguely north, Guv. He's taking the country roads, and isn't in any particular hurry.'

'You ask me, he knows we're following him and is just playing silly sods,' Patrick muttered darkly.

'Have you heard from the boys back at the house, sir?' Davis asked curiously.

'Yes. No sign of Myers, and the garage door is still standing open,' Evans told them. 'So either he's really not there, or he just wants us to think that he's not.'

'Well, we're not falling for that,' Mulligan muttered. 'Hold on, he's turning off here. Hey, Ian, doesn't this road lead back to that same village we passed about five minutes ago?'

Ian Davis wasn't sure, and quickly consulted the map. 'Yeah, it can do. Or it loops back on to the main road again.'

'That confirms it,' Mulligan said grimly. 'Tell the Guv this bloke's just leading us around in circles.'

Ian passed the message on to his superior officer. For a long while the radio was silent, then Evans said grimly, 'OK, pull him over. Make it a routine check. Have you got anything minor you can use as an excuse?'

'Not sure, Guv. His tail lights are working OK.'

'He's got a muddy number plate,' Mulligan pointed out with glee.

'I heard that,' Evans said. 'Use that.'

'Guv. What do we do if it *is* Myers?'

'Bring him in,' Evans said decisively. 'He'd expect us to, so let's not disappoint him.'

'And what do we do if it's *not* him, Guv?'

'Let him go with a warning,' Evans replied. 'But make sure you get his name and details. If nothing else, this bastard must know he's helping Myers to give us a hard time. He might not be so obliging once he learns what it means to make our shit list.'

'Guv,' Davis said, with a grin.

Patrick accelerated to get right behind the truck, then flicked his lights and beeped his horn. They were not in a panda car, and both coppers were aware that, legally, the man in the truck had no reason to stop. If asked why he hadn't, he could all too reasonably respond by asking how he was to know that it had been police in the car behind him? For all he knew, they could have been bandits out to rob him or steal his car.

But the truck in front slowed down immediately at their frantic signalling, and Mulligan carefully pulled up in front of the truck, blocking any quick exit he might make.

'Here we go,' he muttered nervously under his breath to his partner. Both men were well aware that this was almost certainly the man who'd killed Superintendent Philip Mallow. And as they approached the truck, both were unarmed, but knew that Clive Myers almost certainly had access to a high-velocity sniper rifle.

As an ex-army man, Clive Myers had probably had more hand-to-hand combat experience than both of them put together.

So it was not surprising that Ian Davis felt his palms sweating as they approached the truck, and he rubbed them nervously on the outside thighs of his trousers. Beside him, he could hear Patrick Mulligan breathing heavily.

Without a word, they split up as they got to the nose of the truck – Patrick to go to the driver's side, Ian to the passenger side. It was how they always did it when approaching any stopped motor vehicle, and it simply never occurred to them to change their routine this time.

So Patrick Mulligan was the first to see the driver's face as he turned to wind down the window and look out, and Ian plainly saw his partner's shoulders droop with the release of tension.

'Excuse me sir,' Patrick said, in his well-rehearsed policeman's voice. 'Were you aware that your rear number plate is all but unreadable?'

The man driving, a sixty-something man with a beaked nose and straggling grey moustache, blinked watery blue eyes at him.

'Is it? Oh damn, sorry about that. You coppers then?'

Patrick smiled briefly and flashed his ID. 'Would you like to step out of the vehicle sir?'

The older man obliged at once, and followed Mulligan around to the rear of the truck, leaving Davis free to give the cab a quick once over.

Nothing.

Casually, Ian Davis strolled around to join the two men at the back, who were earnestly discussing the number plate. Standing on tiptoe to see over the flatbed truck, his eyes darted everywhere. Tarpaulin covered what were obviously large round paint cans. There were several wooden ladders laid across it – pressing the tarpaulin down just enough to show that there was no possibility of anyone hiding underneath it. Just to be sure however, Davis passed behind his partner and the old house-painter and went around to the other side of the truck. There he reached in and lifted one corner of the tarpaulin and took a quick peek underneath.

The smell of paint wafted out at him. But nothing stared back at him apart from paint cans, rollers, trays and brushes.

He went back to join Patrick, giving a quick shake of his head.

'Well sir, be sure and wash off the mud when you get back. It's an offence to drive a vehicle without a properly displayed number plate.'

'Sorry again. And yes, I'll be sure to do that, Constable.'

Patrick gave him a hard look. 'I'll just take down the details from your driving licence sir.'

The old man, far from looking worried, merely nodded, and went back to the cab and reached into the glove compartment. Both coppers momentarily stiffened, then relaxed when his hand emerged with nothing more frightening in it than a plastic envelope encasing his driving licence.

Ponderously, Mulligan wrote the details down.

Many miles away, in a field in Wales, a cadaver dog called Millie, a beautiful black, glossy cocker spaniel, set off with her owner into a small copse, not far from the caravan where Gary Firth had gone missing.

It didn't take Millie long to sit down and bark sharply once, her indication to her handler that she wanted a treat for locating the smell her master seemed to like.

Her handler, PC Geoff Walker, put a hand to the radio attached to his shoulder and bent his head to talk into it.

Back in the car, Mulligan and Davis trailed the dirty truck back to a B road, and watched it drive away.

'Guv, nothing.' Davis was reporting in on the radio. 'The driver was not Myers. I repeat, he was *not* Myers.'

DCI Evans's sigh could clearly be heard over the radio. 'The vehicle was empty?'

'Yes Guv. I got a good look in the back. As you know, I couldn't officially ask to search it, but I had a good view of it. There were paint pots and the usual paraphernalia that goes with them and a couple of ladders, all covered by a tarpaulin.'

'Tarpaulin?' Evans repeated sharply.

'Don't worry, Guv, I got a peek underneath it. Nobody was hiding there, I'll swear to that in court.'

Back in HQ Evans mumbled under his breath that the young PC might have to, then gave him the curt order to return to the Myers house.

Next he contacted the two remaining constables still at the residence. 'OK, I want you to go in. Make sure Myers is there,' he informed them curtly. 'Use any excuse you like – you smelt gas, a neighbour reported a prowler, whatever. Just make sure you see and speak to Myers. Then radio back at once.'

In Wales, a team of grim-faced PCs with shovels stood back as the first waft of decomposing flesh hit them.

Two, more hardy than the others, got down on their knees and began to scrape away the soil carefully. They found the first hints of material a few minutes later. Then they unearthed a trainer – with a foot still inside it.

'OK, that'll do.' The sergeant in charge pulled them back. 'We've seen enough to know it's not a dead dog or sheep. Now we'll have to get the experts in. Cordon off the area. I'll go and report in.'

Back in Kidlington, DCI Evans waited impatiently. He glanced at his watch.

What the hell was keeping those two? They should have reported back by now. How long did it take for them to check that one man was still in his house?

In a narrow country lane, a dirty red truck pulled on to the grass verge near a five-barred gate and an old man dressed in painter's overalls turned off the engine. Somewhat stiffly, he climbed out and walked round to the side of the truck and glanced about him. The lane was single-track and deserted.

He listened for a few moments, then nodded, and banged on the side panel of the truck. A moment later, he heard a 'snick', then stood aside as the dirty panel dropped down, and a man's head emerged.

He watched, without offering to help, as Clive Myers wriggled out and, somewhat awkwardly, got one foot down on the ground, then hopped and jiggled to get the other one out.

Wordlessly, the old man looked up and down the road on lookout, whilst Clive Myers jogged on the spot and rotated his shoulders, stretching and staving off imminent cramp. Then he reached into the cavity in the truck and drew out a long, narrow, canvas bag. This he put down beside him, then reached into his jacket pocket and brought out a large, fat, white envelope. This he handed over to the old man.

'Cheers Clive.' The old man slammed the panel back in place. 'Thanks Dave.'

The old man gave a brief, somewhat ironic salute, climbed back into the cabin and pulled away.

Clive Myers waited until the truck was completely out of sight, before climbing the gate and making his way around the edge of the farmer's field.

A mile or so further on, down a rutted, stone track, he came across an empty barn. In the barn, hidden behind rusty doors, he climbed into a plain white van and carefully drove down the stone track.

He had places to go and things to do.

CHAPTER TWELVE

PC Ray Porter knocked on the door to Clive Myers house and glanced across at the man beside him. Porter, a slightly built man with thinning fair hair, had been drafted into this inquiry from DCI Evans's patch, and didn't know the Thames Valley man who'd been assigned to this watch with him all that well.

His partner was a large, quiet man, in his early forties, Ray supposed, with a distinct Oxford country burr to his voice and a thick mane of prematurely grey hair. His name was Mervyn Jones.

'Merv, can you hear anything?' Porter asked nervously, aware that, back at HQ, his guv'nor would be waiting for their report.

'Nope,' DS Jones said laconically.

'Shall I try the door?'

'Might as well. The Guv said to make sure Myers is definitely here,' Jones pointed out.

Ray nodded and turned the silver handle on the outer porch door. It turned easily, and allowed Porter to step into a tiny porch and knock on the inner door. There wasn't room for both of them in there, especially when one of them was built like Jones, so the older man stayed on the step.

'Mr Myers, sir, it's the police,' Ray shouted politely. 'Can we come in?'

Both men listened closely. It had been apparent for some time that the visit by the so-called house painter just a short while ago had been the prelude to some kind of funny business and both men now felt distinctly edgy.

'Mr Myers. We need to check that you're all right. A neighbour of yours reported the smell of gas,' Ray lied, bending down to shout through the letterbox.

Both men waited again. Still, only an unbroken silence met all their efforts.

'Try the door,' Jones ordered brusquely.

Ray nodded and tried the small metal button that indicated a Yale lock. Somewhat to his surprise, the small knob twisted easily under his hand, and the door gave a slight sighing 'snick' as it opened. Ray glanced across at his partner with a raised, enquiring eyebrow, and was glad for once of Jones's comforting bulk.

Everyone on the case knew that Myers was ex-army, and handy not only with a rifle, but could probably kill with his bare hands as well.

Jones gave a brief nod. 'Let's go in, then,' he prompted gruffly.

Since he was in front, Ray went in first, somewhat reluctantly, pushing the door wider open, and looking around warily before stepping into a tiny, neat hallway. He didn't know that the door had been rigged with an almost invisible fishing wire that tautened at the inward movement of the door. But even as the two policemen stood there, looking around, the tug on the line travelled along the base of the skirting board where Myers had rigged it, and all the way through the open door to the lounge. There it had been attached to a small device, connected to a switch that now turned, and set off the second phase of the mechanism.

In Wales, a forensics officer with a degree in medicine from Oxford, biochemistry from Durham and forensic anthropology from a redbrick university on the east coast of the United States of America, knelt down in the dirt and peered almost comically into the soil.

With his qualifications he could, of course, have been teaching anywhere in the world. But this was what he liked doing – so much so that he was willing to take a substantial cut in salary in order to indulge himself.

He was a whippet-lean man with a rather pointed head, and a chin capped by a little pointed goatee beard, to match. Nobody much liked him, but everyone respected him, and when the top brass back in Cardiff had been apprised of the situation, it had been Dr Norman Fielding who had been promptly dispatched to the scene.

Apart from his undoubted expertise, the man was also a demon in court, and was universally hated by all barristers, as he'd been known to tie them in knots. Furthermore, he could out-sarcasm the best of them, and had a rapier wit. He was, in short, the kind of man any police force would want on their side, should a contentious or controversial trial be likely to arise.

'Is it Gary Firth sir?' a young wet-behind-the-ears constable asked. He'd been assigned to the search party and was now, like the rest of them, hanging around to watch the proceedings. His question earned him the amazed stares of several of his more experienced colleagues, and a long, level look from Dr Fielding.

'We haven't even uncovered the face yet, son. Who do you think I am? Gypsy Rose Lee, the fortune teller?'

The youngster blushed and tried to melt into the background.

With a sigh, Fielding reached into his bag for a large brush, and began, painstakingly, to clear the dead leaves and rich dark humus from the face of the young man buried in the woods.

In Thame, Ray Porter nearly jumped out of his skin as he suddenly heard a voice.

'Hello? I'm in here, in the lounge. Come on through.' The voice was definitely that of Clive Myers. After spending hours of listening to his tapped phone calls, both men recognized it as such at once.

Ray breathed a sigh of relief, and led the way to the open door, relieved to find that Jones was right behind him. After he'd pushed the ajar door fully open and walked in, he stopped in the middle of the room and looked around in puzzlement.

The room, tastefully furnished and perfectly clean though it was, was also undeniably lacking its owner.

Unseen behind the two puzzled officers, a coiled spring, attached to a gizmo at the bottom of the lounge door, reacted to the ten-second delay on a timer, and contracted with a loud 'snap.'

'Shit! What was that?' Ray yelped, then leapt around as the lounge door crashed to with a resounding 'bang'. He felt the skin of his scalp contract with fear.

Jones looked at the door thoughtfully. Beside him, Ray held a hand over his fast-beating heart and patted his chest, swallowing down hard on the taste of bile that had risen to his throat. Being in this house was beginning to give him the willies.

'What the hell's going on?' Ray whined plaintively. Then, more sharply, 'Is that a note on the door?'

'Looks like it,' Mervyn Jones said. Slowly he approached the square of white paper that had been pinned to the door. As he did so, he reached into the top pocket of his jacket and withdrew a pair of old-fashioned, black plastic-framed reading glasses.

Ray stayed where he was in the centre of the room and looked around. The first thing he spotted was a small mini-cassette recorder in the middle of the coffee table. When he went to it and lifted it, he felt an unusual resistance, and discovered the fishing wire.

So that explained the invitation to come in. Myers had pre-taped his invitation, and rigged it up somehow to play when someone came through the front door. Unless it was a double-bluff, and he was waiting in ambush somewhere in the room!

Giving in to his incipient paranoia, Ray glanced swiftly around the room and checked behind the only large piece of furniture in it – a three-seater settee. Only when he'd satisfied himself that Myers was not in the room did he allow himself to relax.

So, somehow, Myers had booby-trapped the door to slam shut behind them as well. It made Ray wonder, anxiously, what other surprises the ex-army man had in store for them.

'Huh,' Mervyn Jones said.

'What?' Ray quickly joined his colleague at the door now, and read the note pinned on to the door over Jones's massive shoulder.

It wasn't particularly short, but it was very much to the point. And it made Ray's blood run cold.

Hello, Mr Policeman
You are now in a house rigged with more than fifty pounds of explosives.
Use your mobile phones to call in to HQ and we all go BOOM!
Try to open any of the doors or windows in this room, and we all go BOOM!
Try to use the landline to phone your superior office and – guess what? Yes, you've guessed it right.
We all go BOOM!
Just in case you're wondering, I'm upstairs in my bedroom, lying on the bed that I used to share with my wife. You may remember her – the woman who killed herself rather than live with the knowledge of what had happened to our poor, broken, mad daughter.
Of course I killed Superintendent Philip Mallow.
Of course I killed Gary Firth.
Of course I'm going to kill myself. What have I to live for? The only question now is – do I take some coppers with me, or not?
And do you know, Mr Policemen. I'm not sure.
Yours sincerely

And the note, which had been printed by a computer in large bold letters, was signed with a flourish in pen by the man himself.

'Oh shit,' Ray Porter whispered.

'Huh,' Mervyn Jones agreed.

Back at HQ, Hillary Greene picked up the now hefty bulk of the murder book, and began at the beginning.

Already her eyes felt gritty and tired, and the day was a long way from over yet.

She had no idea then of just how long a day it was going to be.

Dr Fielding, a white mask covering the lower half of his face, breathed carefully through his mouth. The putrefaction of the body was not yet too pronounced, leading him to suppose the body hadn't been in the ground all that long.

But he was not going to say so. Until he had the body fully unearthed, prepared and ready for autopsy on his table, he wouldn't be speaking to any high-ranking police officer.

And they all knew his stringent methods.

'The body looks to be that of a young male,' he felt prepared to say. 'He has brown hair, is roughly five feet nine inches tall, lean of build and,' he raised a swollen angry eyelid on the cadaver, and several of the curious young police officers around him, looked away hastily or took a step backwards. 'Yes, he has light brown eyes.'

'That matches Oxford's description of Gary Firth sir,' one of the constables said to a DS.

'Unfortunately, it also matches the description of another missing lad, one of our own, who left his home in Abergavenny Tuesday night,' the DS responded. 'Until the doc can run some tests, we won't know who the poor sod is. Not for sure.'

'Should we tell Oxford, sir?'

'Tell them what, laddie?' the sergeant asked testily. 'That we've found a young man's body? They already know that. We won't know who this is until the doc's got the body cleaned up and has run some tests. And I daresay the parents of the boy in Abergavenny will want to see the body without delay,' he added.

He didn't need to add that they looked after their own first.

'Well, that won't be until tomorrow morning at least,' Doctor Fielding broke in grimly. 'I have to take samples of fly eggs and lava, soil samples and take clothing scrapings, before we even move the body from this site.'

The DS sighed heavily. It would be dark, he reckoned, before this pernickity bugger was satisfied. He only hoped that the brass in Oxford weren't waiting too anxiously for news about this body. Because if so, they were going to be disappointed.

Janine Mallow took a sip of tonic water, and glanced at her watch. She could see DI Peter Gregg out in his front garden, spraying his paving with weedkiller.

She'd passed the time by playing 'spot the guards' and had already pinpointed five officers, in various guises, but imagined there were probably more scattered around, some of them in a rotating pattern. She had no idea if any of them had spotted her yet, and at this point, didn't much care.

She put the cap back on her bottle of tonic, and glanced up into her rear-view mirror as a plain white van turned left at the intersection behind her, and turned towards her.

She saw one of Gregg's guards, a woman walking a dog, lift her arm and take a crafty picture of it with a tiny digital camera which she had in the palm of her hand. Janine smiled, remembering doing duty just like this not so long ago.

The woman carried on walking, but Janine knew she probably had a 'round' that took in the same streets, and that within a half an hour, she'd be back where she was now, to report in any suspicious behaviour to her DS.

Janine glanced across without much interest as the white van passed her. There was a single white male driving, which was probably what had triggered off the woman officer's need to take the snapshot. It seemed, after all, unlikely that Myers would have an accomplice with him.

Not that the man driving this particular vehicle looked

anything like Myers, Janine noted dispiritedly. He had a thick patch of nearly black hair for a start, and a neatly trimmed black moustache to match. His face was much more rounded than Myers', too, and he wore gold-framed spectacles. As he drove past Janine had a view of him for about one and a half seconds.

And in those one and a half seconds she saw his earlobes.

And was instantly transported back about two years, and was listening to her old boss, DI Hillary Greene talking about disguises.

Janine couldn't quite remember how the conversation had started. But she remembered saying how unlikely it was that, given today's modern policing methods and the quality of the criminal fraternity, the chances of any officer having to follow a 'master of disguise' was practically zero. Such characters, she'd maintained, belonged to the era of Sherlock Holmes.

Hillary had agreed with her, but had then given her a brief lecture on how to spot disguised people – just in case.

Forget the hair, she'd said – the rise in the popularity of modern amateur theatrical societies made access to good-quality wigs and facial hair a doddle. Forget even the shapes of noses or faces – prosthetics, and simple cotton wool padding in the cheeks could radically alter an appearance.

It was no good either, Hillary had maintained, thinking about eyes – with coloured contact lenses easily available you could have bright-purple eyes if you wanted them, and the use of simple cosmetics could alter eyebrows and skin tones.

No, Hillary had said, if you wanted to spot a disguise, look to the ears. Ears were something that very few people thought to disguise, and they were – largely – unalterable anyway.

Janine sat up straighter in her car seat. The white van, travelling at a very modest twenty-five miles an hour, wasn't yet at the end of the road.

On impulse, she started her car engine and let a Vauxhall pass her before pulling out.

Janine Mallow had spent many long hours studying the face

of Clive Myers, the man she believed had murdered her husband. She'd seen pictures of him from his army days, snapshots of him on holiday with his wife and daughter. She'd even seen his wedding photos as well as photos of him taken by reporters who'd covered his daughter's trial.

And in all of those pictures she'd noticed something about him that reminded her of what Hillary Greene had said about ears. It wasn't a widely known fact, but something like ninety per cent of the population had hanging earlobes – that is, lobes that you could pinch between thumb and finger, and that hung loosely at the base of the ear.

Only a very small percentage of people had ears that actually fixed into the side of their face.

But Clive Myers was one of those.

As had been the driver of that white van.

OK, the chances weren't great that the man driving had been Clive Myers.

On the other hand, Janine had become bored, and she could always go back if it turned out the white van man was harmless.

Hillary Greene slogged her way to the end of the murder book, by which time Gemma had returned, and Frank Ross had left early. Nobody tried to stop him from leaving.

Only after she'd finished with the murder book did Hillary take up the Linda Quirke file again.

Once more something nagged at her but, yet again, she couldn't think what.

With a sigh, she leaned back in her chair and stretched her cramped shoulders. Gemma watched her, wondering when her boss had last had a decent night's sleep. She looked shattered.

'Guv. Randy Cauldicott, the chap who heard Eddie Philpott talking about Tom Cleaves,' she prompted.

Hillary dragged her mind away from the nagging worry of the Linda Quirke file and forced herself to concentrate. 'Right. You've just re-interviewed him?'

'Yes, Guv. He definitely had the impression that Eddie thought he had something on Tom. He said,' she consulted the immaculate shorthand in her notebook, 'that Eddie had been sort of "pleased as punch" and Randy got the feeling that he either had approached or was going to approach Tom about it.'

Hillary sighed. 'Might have. Got the feeling that ... Had the impression that ... All phrases that a defence lawyer would have a field day with.'

Gemma agreed miserably. 'But it does make it more of a possibility that Eddie might have set Tom off,' she insisted, reluctant to dismiss their only really solid lead. She knew that Keith Barrington liked Martha Hepton for it, but she had no idea what Hillary Greene was thinking.

'*If* Tom got the impression that Eddie was trying to blackmail him,' Hillary allowed drily. '*If*. Another word you never want to use at a criminal trial if you can help it.'

Gemma sighed grimly. 'So what do we do?'

'Keep plugging away,' Hillary answered briskly. What else could they do? They were stuck, and everyone on her team knew it.

And talking about plugging away Hillary reached for the Linda Quirke file again and began at the beginning. Gemma, puzzled by her boss's fascination with the decades-old file, gave her a rather aggrieved look, and began to type up her notes.

Hillary forced herself to breathe deeply and let her mind go blank. Then she began to read, starting with Linda Quirke's details. Sometimes, if she let her conscious mind wander off, it gave her subconscious mind a chance to ring a bell, loud enough for her to hear it.

Linda Mary Quirke. Her date of birth. Physical characteristics. School record.

Nothing sprang out at her.

Her mother's details. Her father's details. Her younger sister's details.

Still nothing.

Went missing on … As she read the date that Linda Quirke went missing, she felt a tiny tug on the back of her mind.

The date? Puzzled, Hillary stared at the date, but there was nothing about it that could possibly be significant.

She moved on, and felt another restless tug. Obediently she went back to that August day in 1981. It couldn't be the date, Hillary thought, frustrated enough to sigh out loud.

Barrington looked across at her and saw her frowning savagely.

Not the date. But every time Hillary tried to move on, her subconscious tugged her back to it.

All right, Hillary thought angrily, if it's not the date, what is it? Something to do with the date, without being the actual date itself. Oh, this is ridiculous, she thought shifting angrily on her seat. A date was a date was a date.

What was there about a date that wasn't necessarily a date?

Timing?

Timing.

Hillary suddenly went very still. Timing. Of course it was the timing. Damn it! She all but launched herself off her chair and grabbed the murder book, riffling through it frantically.

'I can't have been that stupid,' she thought, and then realized she'd spoken aloud when Gemma Fordham looked up at her, startled.

'Where the hell is it,' Hillary muttered, turning the pages so hard she almost ripped them.

And then she found it. Nearly at the beginning of the book, nestled within Eddie Philpott's biography.

The timing.

'I was right,' she said, astounded. 'It *is* all about the timing.' *How the hell*, a sharp angry voice shouted in the back of her mind, *could I have missed this?*

'Guv?' Gemma said sharply.

Hillary slumped back in her chair as it all came rushing up to her, like an eager puppy offering a bone. It was all so clear, so very damned obvious. In fact, it was so damned self-evident, she could have known on that very first day who'd killed Eddie Philpott.

If only she'd been paying attention. If only she didn't have her head up her arse worrying about other stuff.

She would have known after her first round of interviews. The killer had practically told her in no uncertain words that they'd done it. Hell, even the forensic evidence had been blatant and there for anyone with half a brain to see.

'I just can't believe I didn't see it,' Hillary said, still speaking out loud.

Gemma shot a quick, excited look at Barrington, for she knew what this meant. She'd seen this *'eureka'* moment once before, when her boss had solved her previous murder case.

Then, on the heels of her elation, she felt a distinct shaft of unease. If Hillary Greene had figured it all out and, from the looks of things, she obviously *had*, then Gemma should have figured it out too. Hillary had been consulting the murder book, and had seen something in it. Well, Gemma too, had had access to the murder book. More than that, Hillary Greene insisted on full disclosure in her team, with nobody holding anything back, or hugging facts to themselves. At the end of the day, it had become a habit with them to discuss what they'd done and learned during the day. So what Hillary knew, they all knew.

So damn it, why hadn't she seen it as well? Whatever it was. It was at times like this that Gemma felt incredibly inadequate.

Hillary Greene shook her head helplessly. She'd gone very pale, and Keith Barrington moved nervously to the edge of his seat. He might not understand it, but he sensed that his boss was having a crisis of confidence.

And he didn't like it.

For long, silent minutes, Hillary Greene continued to stare unseeingly in front of her, a growing look of horror on her face.

*

Janine Mallow frowned thoughtfully as the white van she was following turned left yet again, confirming what she'd only begun to suspect.

The driver was going in one big square. Moreover, a square that had DI Peter Gregg's house firmly in the middle of it.

She felt her heart-rate rise. Could this really be it? Was it just possible that Lady Luck had handed her a million-to-one-shot? Her hands felt slippery on the wheel, and she let a second car get between her and the van.

If it was Myers in that van, the last thing she wanted was for him to spot her.

In Thame, Ray Porter stared at the note on the door and swallowed hard.

'What the hell do we do, Mervyn?' he asked, his voice little more than a squeak.

Mervyn Jones shrugged his massive shoulders. 'Nothing,' he said simply.

Ray blinked. 'What do you mean, you great big lump? We've got to do something!' he yelped.

Mervyn Jones looked at the excitable cockney with interest. 'Such as what? Want to use your mobile or radio to contact Evans, do you?'

'Hell no. You read the note.'

'Boom!' Mervyn said, straight-faced.

'Shut up!' Ray pleaded.

'So do you want to try and crawl out the window, or open the door?' Mervyn persisted patiently.

'Hell no!'

'Well then. The only thing we can do is nothing, isn't it?' Mervyn pointed out with aggravating logic. And then, seeing that the youngster looked anxious enough to wet himself, he relented and added more kindly, 'Look lad, DCI Evans is going to get very impatient very quickly when we don't report in, right?'

Ray Porter agreed that he would.

'So he'll send someone round, or even come himself, to see why we don't report in, right?'

'Right,' Ray said, then went as green as pond slime. 'If he tries to come in the house, we'll all be blown sky high!'

'So we will,' Mervyn agreed baldly. 'So I suggest we get cracking on getting our notebooks out and making free with a pen. Then we can attract the attention of whoever comes, and get them to read our message through the front window.'

'Message?'

'Don't come in or we all go BOOM!' Mervyn Jones said, with nice resonance.

Ray Porter gulped like a cartoon mouse.

Janine Mallow fell back another hundred yards. This meant that the white van was able to turn corners and set off down different roads for several long seconds before she could get to them. But the trouble was, the van was driving so slowly that unless she pulled back even further, the driver was bound to spot her.

Already the two cars she'd let come between them had already overtaken, and there was very little traffic about to take their place. She reached the turning in the road that the van had taken and indicated left.

She felt the tension cramping her stomach as she peered ahead, and sighed in relief when she saw the back right-hand side of the van disappear down another road.

He'd turned left again. Heading back towards Gregg's house.

With a spurt of speed that made an old woman walking two terriers along the pavement jump in fright, Janine accelerated down the residential street and came to the junction.

When she looked left, the van was nowhere in sight.

Janine swore savagely and quickly turned left, her head swivelling left and right every time she spotted a turning into another road. She was almost bouncing up and down on her seat with tension.

Damn it. Where had he gone?

*

'I can see him,' Ray Porter said with an excited squeal. The two policemen were standing in the front window of the house and peering out on to the road.

Climbing from a large black Astra, DCI Gawain Evans glanced around angrily. From their position at the window both men began to wave frantically.

Evans spotted them almost at once. The expression on his face as he spotted his two officers waving at him like children spotting their daddy would, under other circumstances anyway, have made Mervyn Jones laugh out loud.

Ray Porter, though, was far beyond thoughts of humour. He quite simply had never been so scared in his life. The thought of Clive Myers, lying upstairs in his bed, his calloused thumb playing teasingly with a detonator switch, was wreaking havoc on his nervous system.

He just wanted to get out of there, and it was taking all his self-control to stop himself from trying to jump out of the window – regardless of whether or not it was open.

Janine saw the brake lights of the white van just in time, and indicated right. This time the van was travelling faster, but still not doing the forty-mile-an-hour speed limit that was the restriction in the area.

Janine allowed her own speedomoter to creep up, determined not to lose sight of him again. She didn't think her nerves could stand it.

Of course, there was still a possibility that white van man was an innocent, maybe an out of towner, lost and looking for a delivery address.

But Janine just didn't think so.

She could feel it in her bones.

This was it.

*

Hillary Greene slowly became aware that Keith Barrington and Gemma Fordham were staring at her, wearing varying looks of concern on their faces.

As well they might, Hillary thought bleakly. As SIO on this case, she'd totally botched it.

She'd always felt, since her first day back, that she wasn't operating at her best. But now, just when it was becoming clear to her how very much off her game she'd been, she had to admit that she'd been little short of incompetent.

And she surely shouldn't have been in charge of this case.

'Guv,' Gemma said softly.

Hillary smiled. 'I have to go and see Danvers,' she said grimly.

And she wasn't looking forward to it.

Barrington watched her walk across the office, noticing how stiff-legged and rigidly she held herself. Something about the sight of his boss made him want to cry.

'Is she going to be all right?' he heard himself ask. And when he looked across at his sergeant, he wasn't reassured to see a tight look of apprehension cross her face.

Clive Myers parked his white van just across from a large plot of allotments. He looked up as a mid-range dark-green saloon car drove quickly past him, a blonde woman at the wheel and talking on a mobile phone.

He shook his head, wondering why drivers *would* do it.

The saloon turned right at the end of the road and disappeared from view.

In the car, Janine Mallow put the switched-off phone back into her bag. She'd only held it up to her face in order to obscure her features from the van driver's view. After all, she'd reasoned, if she knew Myers by sight, he would almost certainly recognize *her*. Now she pulled her car into the first available space and switched off the engine.

Then she reached for the gun under the driver's seat and

shoved it into her voluminous bag. She got out of the car and, not even bothering to lock it, speed-walked to the end of the road.

There she cautiously looked back in the direction she'd just come, and was just in time to see the van driver, carrying a large, long canvas bag, cross the road and disappear into the allotments.

Puffing slightly, and feeling cramped and sick to her stomach, Janine Mallow walked quickly up the pavement towards the allotment gates.

In Thame, DCI Evans approached the Myers house cautiously, and saw the two clowns inside hold up a piece of paper to the window.

Suddenly, all his irritability fled. When they'd failed to report back to him at HQ, he'd taken the snap decision to drive out here, very much on impulse. The fact that everything was quiet on the Gregg front had helped his decision along, of course.

On spotting his two officers inside the house, his first reaction had been one of angry relief.

Now, as he approached the window, he felt the first grim tingle of warning. His eyes squinted as he tried to make out the block capitals that had been written on the small rectangle page of a policeman's notebook.

Something here seemed very wrong.

And when eventually he was close enough to read Mervyn Jones's short message, he felt the skin on the nape of his neck contract as if someone had placed an ice cube there.

He stepped back, and held both hands out in front of him, patting the air, indicating that the two men should stay put, stay calm and wait.

The habitually unflappable Mervyn Jones nodded. And, after an agonized moment, Ray Porter reluctantly followed suit.

DCI Gawain Evans ran back to his car. A DS sat behind the driver's wheel, where Evans had told him to wait.

Evans opened the passenger door and leaned in. 'Get the bomb squad,' he snapped grimly.

CHAPTER THIRTEEN

Although Janine had been living in her husband's house in Kidlington for nearly a year now, she still didn't know all the town's nooks and crannies that well. And as she peered cautiously over the allotment gates, she found it hard to get her bearings.

An old man further down the grass pathway was busy hoeing up some withered-looking plants, and barely glanced up as she opened a gate and stepped through. As she did so, she looked left and right, and saw the white van man further up the path that ran parallel with the road, heading east.

Janine saw him begin to turn his head. Quickly she ducked back through the gate, her heart pounding. The old man paused in his hoeing and watched her curiously. Janine managed to give him a weak smile, then cautiously looked around the hedge again.

The white van man had disappeared from view.

Quickly, she set off up the same path, her eyes scouting the area ahead as she did so. There, the allotments turned at right angles with the others, the chains of land heading east–west. Rows of sheds lined their length, obscuring her view of what lay beyond. She could only hope that the white van man had gone behind them. Otherwise she'd lost him.

She began to trot, rather awkwardly, her breath coming in harsh, hard gasps. A stitch in her side made her swear under her breath. She felt suddenly foolish, imagining herself through the old man's eyes. With her burgeoning belly and flat shoes, she was probably waddling along like a pregnant duck.

Then she reached the first shed, and had to lean against it to catch her breath. Shit, she was out of shape. Her stomach cramped warningly, and she bent over, taking long, deep breaths, waiting for the pain to subside. When it did, she moved cautiously between two sheds and, pressing her back to one of them, very slowly poked her head out for a better view.

All that met her gaze were yet more allotments, this time running all the way to the back gardens of a row of council houses that lined the road opposite.

She searched in vain for the sight of a medium-built man, wearing dark-blue overalls.

But the white van man had vanished.

Back in Thame, DCI Gawain Evans watched grimly as a large black van pulled up a few yards in front of him, releasing from its rear a swarm of men wearing black overalls and helmets with tinted visors. Each of them bore a stitched-on tag identifying them as bomb disposal officers.

Already the respectable residential street was awash with panda cars, and the whole street was in the process of being evacuated. A bewildered old lady from the house a few yards down was even now being led out through her garden gate by a solicitous WPC. It was only when they passed by his car that Evans could see that the woman was clutching an interested and friendly Yorkshire terrier close to her scrawny chest.

'Sir, Sergeant Blunkett reckons we'll be clear within the next five minutes.' The speaker was an anxious-faced PC, leaning down to speak through the open car window. He kept flicking his eyes towards the Myers house, as if expecting it to go up in a spectacular bloom of explosive flames at any second.

'Fine,' Evans said curtly. The youngster nodded and backed away, putting some distance between himself and Evans, who'd parked his car right out front and hadn't yet moved. Evans didn't blame him. If it weren't for the fact that he was in nominal charge of this shindig, he'd have put some distance between himself and the house as well.

But from the car he could see the tense forms of the two coppers inside, and he was damned if he was going to let them see him scuttle away and hide.

He'd already contacted the team leaders back at DI Gregg's house to warn them of the situation. Although it seemed likely that Myers *had* snapped at last and *was* upstairs in the house, contemplating the 'final scenario' where he got to go out in a blaze of glory, there *was* another option.

It was more than possible that this situation at his Thame house was just a diversion Myers had set up in order to keep them distracted. They had, after all, no positive proof that Myers was still in the house. True, he hadn't got out of the house painter's truck, but there was still the chance he'd managed to give his watchers the slip some other way.

And whilst everybody was busy here, Myers might be making a move on Gregg. Which is exactly what he'd told Gregg's protection squads. Consequently, they were on high alert back in Kidlington as well.

Evans fought off the urge to check in, yet again, and see if they'd spotted anything at the Gregg house. Instead he got out of the car as the leader of the new arrivals approached. He was a tall man, and although Evans couldn't see the colour of his hair, given the helmet, the man's eyebrows were a fierce ginger. He also had the pale freckled skin of a natural redhead. He observed Evans with large, watery grey eyes.

'DCI Evans? Neville Colt. Have you any idea what explosives we're talking about here? Or their likely deployment?'

Evans grunted. 'Not a bloody clue. Your best bet for assessing the situation is to write messages for those two in there,' Evans gestured towards the house, 'and see what they can tell you.'

The bomb disposal expert turned to look where he was pointing, and frowned. 'We've got people inside? That's just great,' he muttered under his breath. Then he shrugged.

'You've approached the house?' he asked sharply.

Evans smiled grimly. 'Only as far as the lawn beneath the front window. When I arrived, my men beckoned me over and held up a piece of paper for me to read, telling me the place was rigged to blow. They can't use their mobiles or the landline, apparently. Myers, that's the home owner, claims to have both of them rigged in some way.'

'You never leaned on the window glass?'

'No.'

'Or touched the actual glass?'

'No.'

Neville Colt nodded. 'Know much about this Myers character?'

'Ex-army,' Evans said briefly. 'And from what I've been able to prise out of his old regiment, although his area of expertise was firearms – namely high velocity sniper rifle fire – he'd know enough about explosives and their make-up to do a reasonable job.'

Neville Colt swore softly under his breath, and turned to two men, who were hovering behind him. 'OK lads, you heard the man. Let's set up the gear and get a preliminary view.'

'What's the game plan?' Evans asked, as the other two men trotted off.

'First we'll set up the roving cameras and do a recce of the perimeter,' Colt said, standing arms akimbo and looking at the house thoughtfully. 'See if we can see any wiring or little plastic boxes that shouldn't be there. Then we'll see about finding a hole somewhere where we can fit in an endoscopic camera, see if we can get a look inside. Your men aren't confined in any way, I see.'

'Only to the living room,' Evans said.

'Oh?' the bomb man said sharply.

'They tell me the door slammed shut behind them when they entered – they've found fishing line attached to a cassette recorder and stuff like that.'

Neville Colt sighed heavily. 'So the likelihood of booby traps has got to be high?'

Evans nodded. 'Oh yeah. This bastard likes to keep us on our toes. Oh yeah, and I haven't told you the best bit yet.'

Neville Colt's ginger eyebrows lifted.

'He could be lying on his bed upstairs with his finger on a detonator,' Evans told him.

Colt blinked and glanced back at the house. 'Well isn't that just dandy,' he said.

Hillary Greene tapped on the door to Danvers' office and heard him call for her to come in.

'Hillary, how's it going?' He looked up as she pushed open the door and stepped inside.

He'd taken off his dark-grey jacket, and his ice-blue tie was loosened, as was the top button of his shirt. His well-cut blond hair gleamed in the overhead lighting.

'Sir,' she said heavily, 'I'd like your permission to apply for a warrant of arrest in the Philpott case.'

Paul Danvers smiled widely. 'That's what I like to hear,' he said, and meant it. Since becoming Hillary Greene's immediate boss, she'd been making him look very good, solving all the murder cases he'd given her so far. And now, here it was without even a week having gone by, and she was ready to put another case to bed.

But when he looked up at her she was still standing by the door, having made no move to sit down, and for someone about to bring in a killer, she didn't seem to be very happy.

'Something wrong?'

Hillary Greene smiled grimly. Where to start? 'I should have known who it was from day one sir,' she said bleakly. 'But I missed it.'

Paul Danvers glanced sharply behind her, only relaxing when he saw that the door was firmly closed. Which meant that they couldn't be overheard. Good.

'Come in and sit down,' he ordered. 'If you're going to beat yourself up for not being perfect, you might as well be comfortable whilst you're at it.'

Hillary smiled weakly. 'Sir,' she said wearily, and started towards the chair.

On the other side of Kidlington, Janine Mallow carefully edged round one of the allotment sheds and looked inside the grimy window.

It was empty.

She moved to the next one. Also empty.

Then she heard something – a footfall, or some kind of movement, and froze. A moment or so later, at the end of the pathway, a middle-aged woman carrying a seed tray went into one of the sheds, and Janine let out her breath in a whoosh.

Where the hell had Myers gone?

She moved further down the grass path, listening intently. Over in the distance she could hear a steady, *scrape scrape* noise and realized that it must be the old man still doing his hoeing. From the shed further down, she could also hear the woman moving about. A few birds twittered and tweeted, and there was a faint *shush* of traffic from the roads.

And then she distinctly heard a human voice. It came from far away and sounded odd, then it was abruptly cut off. It sounded vaguely familiar, and yet, for the life of her, Janine couldn't understand what it was, exactly, that she was hearing.

She hesitated, listening hard, but the odd, distant human voice, was now silent. She gave a mental shrug and began her careful check of the allotment sheds once more. Grimly, they reminded her of a previous murder case, when Hillary Greene had solved the murder of a young teenage boy found stabbed to death in his father's allotment shed.

Relentlessly she turned her head and looked through yet another grimy window.

No murdered teenage boy and no white van man either. Janine sighed heavily. Dammit, where the hell could he have gone?

'OK, the perimeter's clear,' Neville Colt said to Gawain Evans as the two men studied the monitor in the back of the bomb disposal squad's van. 'Bring Rover back.'

The technician operating the radio-controlled mounted camera nodded and set the trundling device on a course back to the van.

Inside Clive Myers' house, Ray Porter watched the trolley head back for the van, and wished he were doing the same. It had seemed like days since they'd first stepped into this nightmare, although it had only been a few hours.

'What do you suppose they're going to do now?' he plaintively asked Mervyn Jones, who was sitting comfortably in one of the armchairs and staring morosely at a painting of a ship in full sail.

'Dunno. One of them will try and come in, I suppose,' he said. 'Anybody coming our way yet?'

'No,' Porter said, sounding aggrieved. 'They're still talking. Wait! One of them's starting to pad up. Shit, he looks like a walking michellin man. Come and see.'

Mervyn Jones heaved his bulk out of the chair and stood behind Porter's tense, quivering shoulders. And as he watched, a man who was indeed very well padded headed towards them.

In his hand he had a piece of paper.

When he was level with the window he looked carefully around, then stepped on to the lawn and, without actually letting the paper touch the window, held the piece of paper flat, so that it could be read.

I'M COMING IN THE FRONT DOOR.
BARRICADE YOURSELVES BEHIND HEAVY FURNITURE.

DON'T MOVE UNTIL A BOMB DISPOSAL OFFICER COMES
FOR YOU.
DON'T TOUCH ANYTHING.
GOOD LUCK.

'Oh shit,' Porter said gruffly. 'This is really it, then?' For the
past hour he'd been impatiently waiting for something –
anything – to happen, and for someone to rescue him from his
predicament.

But now that it was happening he suddenly felt so scared that
he could actually feel his knees going weak.

It was Mervyn Jones who raised both thumbs, pointing them
up in the universal sign of understanding, and turned away
from the window.

'Right then, let's get in a corner,' Jones said briskly. 'The
outside corner over there, I think,' he added, pointing to the
house wall that abutted on to the garden. In his opinion, if the
house *was* rigged to blow, then it was the inside of the house that
was most likely to provide the real danger spots. 'Let's get the
settee right in front of us, and an armchair either side. We can
use the back of the settee as a sort of roof, which should keep at
least some of the rubble off us if anything does blow.'

Ray Porter stared at him aghast.

Mervyn Jones took one end of the settee and glanced up at
him. 'Come on. Shift!' he said sharply.

Ray Porter jumped, then reached for the other end of the
settee.

Janine Mallow realized that the white van man was no longer on
the allotments. He couldn't be. She would have seen or found
him by now.

So the only place he could have gone was into the back
gardens of the houses opposite. But which one? And then it
occurred to her that it hardly mattered, since he'd almost
certainly gone right on through the garden, past the house and

thus out on to the road the other side. In which case, she'd lost him well and truly, and the sense of frustration made her want to scream out loud.

Grimly, she jogged down the path between two allotments, and saw a row of tall, wooden-planked doors leading off in a seemingly endless row. Apparently, all the houses here gave access from their back gardens to the allotments.

She headed to the far right, and started to try the handles.

The first was locked.

As was the second.

As was the third.

Then she heard that strangely tinny, distant human voice again – and this time caught some words. Amongst them was 'aisle one', and 'trained cashiers', and 'checkout'. And it suddenly hit her.

The voice was the voice she heard when shopping in her local Sainsbury's.

And suddenly she knew where she was. She was close enough to the big shop near the roundabout to be able to hear the voice within whenever the front doors opened to admit a customer.

And DI Peter Gregg's house was within spitting distance of that shop.

Shit! It *was* Myers she'd seen. *It had to have been.*

And she'd just lost him!

Hillary Greene reached for the folder in her hand, and opened it out. She selected several pieces of paper, some of them interview statements, others dry forensic reports, and shuffled them in to order.

Danvers watched her, aware of a tight tension in his shoulder blades.

No matter what she said, he didn't believe for a single moment that she could have mishandled a murder investigation. For all that she was still mourning Mel and had lost weight, was obviously fighting off a headache and was exhausted from lack of sleep; it still never occurred to him that she was going to give him anything but the name of the murderer and the evidence to convict.

'Sir, if you'd start by reading these,' Hillary said, 'I'll then give you my conclusions.'

Not, Hillary thought wearily, that he'd need them. Anyone reading the evidence she'd just presented would be able to see at once just where the blame lay.

She leaned back in the chair, and stared blankly at the wall behind Danvers' bent blond head. Mentally she began to compose her letter of resignation.

Janine Mallow was almost at the end of the row of back gates before she found one that wasn't locked. So convinced was she that they must all be barred that she almost fell through the door when it opened for her.

She found herself on a small square of green lawn, in the middle of which was one of those round washing-line contraptions full of toddlers' clothing.

The window facing her was obviously the main living room window of the house, which threw her for a moment, as she was expecting it to be the back kitchen window.

As she headed off to the side of the house, however, where a narrow concrete path led her through to the other side, she quickly realized that the 'back' garden – rather confusingly – was situated at the 'front'. She supposed the architects had designed the row of houses that way for a reason. Perhaps it was something to do with the orientation of the sun. Or, more likely, when the houses had been built, the allotments had been open fields or pastures, and the architects had figured that the residents would rather have the rooms with the views for their main living areas.

Whatever the reason, when Janine stepped through from the narrow side passage, she found herself in a large, spacious, rather pretty front garden.

She followed the path around, glancing quickly into the kitchen window as she passed. But no scandalized mother or curious onlooker gazed back at her, and no one came out to demand what she was doing, so she walked up the neatly edged path, past well-maintained shrubs, and a new-looking shed on to the front gate.

There she paused to glance around, trying to get her bearings. The roof of the big Sainsbury's shop was now clearly visible over to her left. Using that as a guide, she tried to gauge where Gregg's home must be.

With a start she realized it must be one of those in the newer-looking estate just over the road. In fact, one of the low-maintenance gardens she could see about 500 yards ahead of her must be Gregg's.

'Bloody hell,' Janine muttered. All of these houses had a ring-side seat of the rear of DI Peter Gregg's house. So there must be cops stationed all around here on this street, Janine realized, with a lift of her spirits. Nobody guarding Gregg could have failed to check out this rear access. All she had to do was find them and warn them.

And even as she glanced up and down she saw two people parked in a dark-red Mondeo a few hundred yards down the street. One of them was looking up and down the road through binoculars. Yes!

She didn't know of the unfolding drama back in Thame. If she had, she'd have guessed that Evans would have already warned all his operatives at Gregg's place that Myers might be about to try and pull something off, and so the officers in the car would have taken her warning seriously indeed.

She was just about to open the gate, intending to go up to the car and introduce herself, and tell them that she thought she'd spotted Myers in the area, when a slight noise off to her left stopped her.

She froze, with her hand on the gate, for a moment, too terrified to move.

Then she slowly turned her head. She could see nothing. Not a cat moving, not even a couple of sparrows arguing in one of the bushes. But something *had* moved – she was convinced of it. Something fairly heavy, too. And the sound had definitely had a stealthy quality to it.

Janine felt her heart begin to pound, and she felt bile rise up in her throat.

And then she saw a movement in the shed in the far corner of the garden.

The people who owned the house were obviously keen gardeners, and had recently purchased a rather orange-looking, do-it-yourself kit shed from B&Q. And it came complete with a rather large, plastic-sheeted window.

And inside it, Janine was positive she saw something move.

She slowly stepped backwards, retreating down the pavement, keeping one eye on the shed as she did so. When she was almost past the window, she saw a large shadow rise up, and realized a man had been crouching on the shed floor. Which was why he hadn't seen her walk up the path and stand by the gate.

Instinctively she ducked, down, putting her hands out in front of her on to the damp lawn to stop herself from falling on her face. Scuttling without much dignity, she managed to make her way back towards the narrow concrete path by the side of the house.

Although she had the gun in her bag, fitted with the makeshift silencer, when Janine Mallow reached into the bag, it was for her mobile phone that she scrabbled. She wanted, oddly enough, not to call DCI Gawain Evans, but her old boss Hillary Greene.

It was instinctive, this need to talk to Hillary, and she'd already dialled the first four digits of Hillary Greene's office telephone number when she saw the plastic window of the shed move.

As she watched, fascinated, a small knife poked through the heavy plastic window, and began to cut out a small, neat hole.

And in that moment, Janine knew without a shadow of doubt why the man inside the shed was cutting that hole. He was cutting it so that he could poke the barrel of a sniper rifle through it, and rest it on the wooden ledge for support.

He was setting up the shot.

She dropped the mobile back into her bag and stared in fascination.

Like most people, Janine Mallow had felt a deep resentment towards DI Peter Gregg. If he hadn't botched the Myers case, none of the nightmare of the last few months would have happened. She wouldn't have had to bury her husband, or face the thought of childbirth and child-rearing alone. She wouldn't have to be alone in that big house every night, but would have had Mel there, to cook dinner or make jokes about how fat she was getting.

And now here, just a few feet away from her, in that ridiculous cheap little shed, was the man who'd taken her life and future away from her.

All she had to do was walk up and push open the door and … Janine blinked as she saw her hand pressing against the wooden door.

She couldn't remember walking up to the shed – let alone giving her brain the order to push open the door.

Inside, Clive Myers lifted his rifle from the floor and fed it through the cut-out gap in the window. He carefully positioned it, taking the time to get the right balance and feeling the weight of it shift against his shoulder. He wriggled himself against it until it felt right, then put his eye forward, getting ready to settle his socket against the telescopic sight. But before he could do so, he felt himself hesitate.

Something was wrong.

Something was different.

For a moment, he couldn't understand what it was. The street outside was still deserted. There was nobody in the house behind him, for he'd checked that out before choosing this shed as his vantage point. And no cars had parked in the road, indicating a new arrival.

Besides, it wasn't the noise level that had changed, but the level of light. It was *lighter* in here now than it had been a moment ago.

He felt a cold draught of warning wash over him, and began to turn his head to look behind him. His memory was already telling him that there was no mechanism inside the shed for shutting the door on the inside – there was no need for one. But he was sure that he'd pulled the door hard to behind him. And there wasn't much of a breeze outside. Certainly not enough to catch the door and make it open of its own accord.

As he began to turn, he could feel adrenaline surge through his body as his instincts kicked in. And the old survival training had him reaching for his army knife, tucked down at the side of his boot, even as he turned.

He knew that the rifle in his hand was useless now. It would take him several precious seconds to pull it back out of the small plastic hole in the window, then he'd have to turn with it, and pull the trigger. All of which would take far too long. Whoever had found him would have more than enough time to launch a counter attack.

Within less than half a second his body turned and crouched, his weight swivelling on his toes as he turned to face the source of danger. Staring into the brightly lit doorway, he felt his hand touch the hilt of the knife and begin to extract it.

Yes, there was someone there.

A cop. It had to be. He'd noticed the horde of officers trying to protect DI Peter Gregg, of course, and he couldn't think of anybody else who'd have any business inspecting garden sheds in the area.

Barely a second had passed now, since he'd first realized something was wrong.

The knife was already beginning to clear his boot, when his

brain processed what his eyes were seeing, and sent the message screaming through his neural pathways.

A woman.

It was a woman stood there – a woman with long blonde hair and a rounded stomach.

A pregnant woman!

For maybe another half a second, Clive Myers froze. He was trying desperately to match up two vastly disparate things. One part of his mind was in combat mode, a soldier on a mission, facing an unexpected enemy. But the second part of his mind belonged to a normally decent human being, who found himself looking at a pretty blonde pregnant woman.

And he couldn't make the two parts of his dilemma gel into one coherent thought.

And in that moment of confusion, Janine Mallow raised her hand, and saw a lemonade bottle. It made her blink, because, for a moment she had no idea why she was holding an empty lemonade bottle.

But Clive Myers knew. Clive Myers was looking beyond it and seeing the gun in her hand.

And instantly, his dilemma faded.

His hand cleared his boot. He knew he couldn't get up off the floor and tackle her before she could fire. His only chance was to throw the knife.

He felt his arm muscles flex. His eyes widened.

And in that moment, Janine Mallow shot him.

Back at HQ Hillary Greene watched Paul Danvers read the last line on the last page, and close the file.

He looked up at her, puzzled. 'I don't get it,' he surprised her by saying.

'Sir?'

'You've got very little that's of use by way of forensics. You've got no witnesses, and just the two likely suspects. You think it's Martha Hepton?' he asked tentatively.

Hillary blinked. Was it possible he really hadn't seen it?

'Sir, look at the date on the Linda Quirke file again,' she began as her mobile phone shrilled in her pocket. She swore and reached for it absently.

'All the time, it was staring us in the face who did it,' Hillary carried on grimly, 'and Eddie Philpott's stolen watch and ring alone should have handed us the answer on a silver platter, but the lack of … Hello? Look, can this wait …' she began to snap into her mobile phone, then she froze.

Paul Danvers, watching her, saw all the colour suddenly leave her face. '*What?*' she said, expelling the word in a single shocked syllable. Faintly, Danvers could hear what sounded like a hysterical female voice babbling away on the other end of the line.

'Calm down,' Hillary said sharply, swallowing hard. 'Just stop talking for a moment.'

She stood up and walked restlessly towards the door, turning her back to Danvers, her shoulders hunching protectively against him. 'Now, say that again, slowly and quietly,' Hillary murmured into the phone.

Behind her, Paul Danvers got slowly to his feet, not sure why he was doing so. His heart was beating hard, and he had a sudden sense of real foreboding.

'Oh no,' Hillary Greene groaned. Then yelped sharply, '*No!* Don't do that. Don't move. Just stay exactly where you are. Do you know the name of the road?'

She listened, her shoulders shaking now with tension. 'All right. I'll find you. I'll be there, just wait for me. We'll sort it out. I promise. Just don't do anything, don't touch anything, don't *say* anything to anybody if they get there before I do. Just stay right where you are.' Her voice was frantic now. 'Do you understand?'

She listened, then snapped the phone shut. She turned, her eyes focusing on Paul Danvers with difficulty. It was as if she'd forgotten where she was, and what they'd been in the middle of doing.

'Sir,' she said vaguely. 'Sir, I've got to go.'

'What?' Danvers said. 'But the Philpott case. You wanted an arrest warrant? What the hell's going on, Hillary? Are you in trouble?'

'No sir,' she said tonelessly. 'Not me. But I have to go. We'll talk about the Philpott case when I get back.'

Danvers stared at her, nonplussed. 'Hillary, what's happened? I can help. Let me help you,' he pleaded.

Hillary Greene already had her hand on the door. When she turned back to look at him, she smiled grimly.

'I doubt that you can sir,' she said. 'I doubt that anybody can.'

And with that, she turned and ran.

CHAPTER FOURTEEN

Neville Colt slowly turned the handle to the outer porch and felt the door mechanism disengage. Very carefully he pushed the door open, centimetre by centimetre, but felt no resistance. Just as Mervyn Jones had indicated to his boss DCI Evans, the door was open and free of any booby traps.

So far so good.

Next he crouched down in front of the inner door and checked it over thoroughly with a range of gadgets that used everything from electro-magnetic readers and sonic pulsar technology, to a plain and simple picklock. It took him nearly a quarter of an hour, but eventually he was through the two doors and into the hall.

On hands and knees he quickly found the fishing line the two police officers inside the lounge had talked about. Without changing the tension on the wire in any way, he was able to trace it to the lounge door, where it disappeared in the gap at the bottom.

OK. Now for the stairs, he thought grimly. Behind him, two of his men shadowed his every move, placing their feet where he placed his, each clutching a gun. It had been decided that Neville Colt would take the lead and check for booby traps, whilst his back-up came fully armed, in case Clive Myers was indeed upstairs on his bed, and decided to come out shooting.

Neville Colt was a fifty-two-year-old veteran of this game, and his hands were perfectly steady as he crawled on all fours to the first step. Fit and lean though he was, he could still hear his breathing, which sounded loud behind the visor of his helmet. As toughened as technology could make it, he knew that should a cleverly concealed device blow up in his face, his helmet and visor would probably not be able to save his life.

Very carefully, he reached for a little hooked knife on his tool belt, and began to remove the first tack on the stairway carpet. First he had to lift the carpet and see if there were any wires anywhere or signs of recent carpentry. If not, he'd then proceed up the stairs one step at a time, with a magnifying lens attached to his helmet, which would let him see if the rest of the carpet had any signs of tampering. Ideally, he'd go up the stairs removing the carpet as he went, but with a possible suspect on the premises, such time-consuming care had been deemed counter-productive.

Carefully, keeping his breathing steady, he began to remove the second tack.

Hillary Greene turned off at the main roundabout, speeding past the large Sainsbury's store there and taking the next few left turns. In her mind, she was running over Janine's panicked telephone call of just a few minutes ago.

Had she really shot Clive Myers? Was it possible he was not in Thame, where she knew a potentially explosive stand-off was under way, but really here in Kidlington? Word had come down about the bomb threat as she was racing out through the door, the desk sergeant more or less shouting the news to her as she ran past. She hadn't caught all of it of course, but enough to understand what was happening.

She braked hard, spotting the street name Janine had babbled over the telephone, and the driver of the Astra behind her tooted angrily.

Hillary sped a short way up the road, then abruptly slowed down. DI Gregg's minders must be stationed all along this road, and she didn't want to draw attention to herself just yet. So far, she could see no congregation of people at any of the houses, so it was just possible that nobody had heard the shot.

She spotted the two police officers in the car as she idled past, and saw them take note of her number plate. It would only take them a few minutes to run it, and then contact base for instructions. She would have about twenty minutes, if that, in order to assess the situation and decide what to do.

She saw Janine's forlorn blonde figure a moment later, standing just inside the garden gate of one of the houses on her left. She'd spotted Puff the Tragic Wagon, her boss's old Polo Golf the moment it had turned down the street, and was waving frantically.

Now Janine gave a dry sob of relief as Hillary Greene pulled in and clambered out.

'I've killed him,' were her first words as Hillary reached her. Her face was deadly pale, and tear tracks marked her cheeks. She was shaking hard, and Hillary stepped inside the gate and down the path a little way, pulling the younger woman further into the garden. She led her to where a small wall formed an L-shape around the porch entrance, providing them with a low seat.

She took Janine's hands in her own, aghast at how icy they were, and forced her down. 'Sit down. Now, where is he?'

Janine pointed a trembling finger at a new-looking, cheap orange shed in the corner of the garden.

Hillary swallowed hard. 'OK. Stay here, I'll take a quick look,' she ordered.

Janine nodded wordlessly.

Hillary crossed quickly to the shed, took a deep breath, and looked inside, without actually going in.

The first thing she saw was the sniper rifle, its ominously sleek, strangely insubstantial profile snaring her eye. Its barrel was resting through the plastic covering of the window, and its butt rested clumsily on the floor. It was only as her eyes went downwards, following the line of the rifle, that she saw the man on the floor.

She felt a small cry escape her, for her first thought was that the man on the floor couldn't possibly be Clive Myers. It looked nothing like him. Then she got a grip. Who else would be holed up in a shed with a sniper's rifle and a prime view of DI Peter Gregg's back garden?

Still without going inside or touching anything, Hillary knelt down. Now, closer to the ground, she could see that the ex-army man was wearing a wig. And two more things became clearly obvious.

It was Clive Myers after all.

And he was dead.

He lay utterly still, with no signs of breathing, and his open, staring eyes never blinked. Only a small amount of blood seeped into the coarse wooden flooring of the hut, indicating that he'd died quickly. In his right hand lay a wickedly sharp-looking knife, with a bone handle.

Hillary jerked upright and walked back to Janine. There she crouched down in front of her and waited until her ex-sergeant's tear- and fear-filled eyes met hers, and then took a deep breath.

'All right, Janine, I want you to listen to me,' she said clearly. 'I need to know what happened here, and I need to know fast. Don't lie, and keep to the facts. I don't know how long we have before others get here, and we need to get our stories straight. Do you understand?'

Janine gulped and nodded.

In Thame, Neville Colt crawled up the last stair and found himself on a small landing. Three doors led off it – he was guessing a bathroom and two bedrooms.

All three doors were shut.

Great, he thought grimly, and held up a hand, indicating to the two men behind him that he wanted complete silence.

He listened hard, but could hear nothing. Neither a dripping tap nor the creak of a bedspring broke the silence. Well, if Myers was up here, he was lying very still, Colt mused.

The bomb disposal man didn't think that Myers would have heard them coming up the stairs, and nobody watching the house had seen any movements in the windows. Still, the man could be behind one of these doors, and ex-army men tended to have good instincts.

There was going to be no easy way out of this one.

With a sigh, Neville began to crawl on his hands and knees to the first door. And through the magnifying lens attached to his helmet, he saw the first of the three fishing lines. He froze, and held up his hand again, but this time his fingers gave the silent signal for a hidden device.

Behind him, and according to protocol, his men retreated halfway down the stairs and lay flat, giving themselves cover. Not that it would probably be enough to save them if Neville Colt got it wrong.

Lying carefully prone on his stomach now, the bomb disposal man studied the fishing lines, and realized at once that one end of each of them disappeared behind a door.

'Thorough sod, aren't you?' Neville muttered to himself.

He set up a mini camera on two of the doors and set the monitor close to his face. Whilst dealing with his first choice of door, he also needed to keep an eye on the other two.

Just in case Clive Myers decided to peep out and shoot him.

'I was parked by Gregg's place, and this white van passed me,' Janine began, her voice shaking. 'He didn't look like Myers, but I recognized his ears.'

Hillary nodded. 'Good. Go on.'

'I followed him, and he parked just by the allotments that come to the backs of these houses.' She jerked her head backwards, and again Hillary nodded encouragement.

'I thought I'd lost him there, but I tried each of the back garden doors, and found this one was open. I walked around and to the front gate, and sensed a movement in the shed behind me, over in the corner there. I crouched down and moved backwards. Then I saw a knife cutting a hole in the plastic window.'

Hillary glanced nervously up the path, but apart from the odd passing car, there was no sound of voices or approaching feet.

'OK. What did you do next?' she encouraged softly.

'I pushed open the door,' Janine said in a small voice, and Hillary tried not to wince at such crass stupidity.

'He was on the floor, about to look down the rifle sighting. He twisted and turned, so fast. I could see his hand had a knife in it and I shot him,' Janine got it out all in a rush, and in one single breath.

Hillary flinched again.

'You shot him with what?'

'With my gun.'

'You don't have a gun.'

'I ... got one the other night. Off a skell I know.'

Hillary closed her eyes briefly as her heart sank. That, of course, changed everything. 'Where is it now?' she asked tightly.

Janine blinked, then stared down at her hands. 'I don't know,' she wailed.

Hillary nodded. 'Shush! Not so much noise. OK. Wait here.'

She turned and went back to the shed. This time she saw a long, greasy-looking heavy canvas bag that was lying against a wall, and presumably belonged to Myers. And just a few yards in front of it, she saw the gun, an unfamiliar cheap-looking model, probably one of the many unreliable makes that were flooding out of the old Eastern bloc nowadays.

She also saw the blackened end of the lemonade bottle and swallowed hard. Not only had Janine Mallow armed herself, she'd rigged up a crude silencer as well. So it wasn't any wonder the cops down the road hadn't heard the shot. The confines of the shed would have helped muffle the noise as well. Although a second shot fired from it would have been loud enough to be heard, Hillary guessed.

Feeling sick to her stomach, she got up and went back to Mel's widow. Both the presence of the gun and the silencer had premeditation written all over them.

Feeling ill, Hillary forced herself to stay calm. 'You fired just the once?' she asked urgently, and Janine nodded.

'I don't even remember doing it,' Janine said, sounding bewildered. 'He just moved so fast. And the look in his eye – I knew he was going to kill me.'

Something in the way she spoke made the tension drain out of Hillary Greene. She'd always had a good sense of when somebody was lying to her, and she'd have bet her last penny that Janine wasn't doing so now.

So it had been self-defence after all.

But who'd believe it.

'Hillary,' Janine's small voice snapped her back on track. 'I've really killed him, haven't I?'

Hillary licked her dry lips and nodded. 'Yes. But you have to remember, he was ex-army,' she said gruffly. 'He was getting ready to throw the knife at you. Hell, he already had it in his hand when you fired. You had no other choice.' And, when Janine continued to stare at her, a growing horror building in her eyes, Hillary scrambled for something to keep her from going under.

And found it. 'Think of the baby,' Hillary said urgently. 'Mel's baby. If you'd died, he or she would have died too. And that bastard already did for Mel. You couldn't let him do for Mel's child as well, could you?'

Janine Mallow took a deep, shaky breath. 'You're right,' she said.

Hillary managed a wan smile. 'Just hold on to that thought, no matter what,' she advised firmly. For no matter how foolish Janine had been, no matter how bent on revenge or how vigilante her actions might have been, she *had* acted in genuine self-defence.

But the gun was a problem. A huge problem.

'Janine, the skell you got the gun from. Will he keep his mouth shut?' she asked.

Janine stared at her. Hillary felt ice trickle through her veins.

'Janine, listen to me,' she said urgently. 'This is how it has to be. You read about DI Gregg's return in the papers, and you were worried. You went over there to talk to him, and saw a man who looked like Myers pass in a white van. On impulse, you followed him here. You saw him go into this shed with a suspicious-looking canvas bag. You waited, wondering what to do for the best, then saw something curious happening at the window. What you saw made you suspicious and you went inside. There you saw a man looking down a rifle barrel. You panicked and made a sound. He heard you and looked around. You saw a small handgun attached to a lemonade bottle lying on the ground near his feet and you picked it up. But when you straightened from picking it up, the man was crouched down with a knife in his hand, and was either about to throw it at you or come at you with it. Instinctively and without thinking, you fired the gun. Then you dropped it, came out here and called me.'

Hillary paused and took a long, slow breath. 'Can you remember that?'

Janine Mallow felt something warm and wet on her face and realized she was crying again. Absently, she reached up and wiped the tears off her face.

'I think so,' she said unsteadily.

'You should,' Hillary said, squeezing her hands hard. 'It's the exact truth, with just one exception. The gun with the silencer was already here, OK? You saw it, crouched for it, and when you straightened up you were in dire peril of your life. That's the only thing that's different from the truth right?' she asked sharply, and Janine nodded.

'Right.'

'Janine, you mustn't ever, no matter what, tell anyone that you came here with that gun in your bag. *Shit!*'

'What?'

'Your bag. Where is it?'

Janine blinked, then realized it was still slung over her shoulder. She pulled it off and handed it to Hillary. 'What?'

'The gun oil,' Hillary said. 'If you had the gun in your bag, forensics will find traces of it. Janine, do you keep a spare bag in your car?'

'Sure – a fancy one, in the boot.'

'All right. Give me your car keys – I'll have to go and get it and hide this one. Where's your car parked?'

Janine told her as she handed over the keys then watched dully as Hillary Greene disappeared behind the house. She sat on the wall, her stomach aching, feeling bereft and abandoned and – belatedly – badly frightened.

Only now that it was all over did Janine Mallow realize the full horror of her predicament.

'OK, I'm going in,' Neville Colt whispered towards the top of the stairs, and grinned as a thumb appeared briefly in an upwards-pointing 'OK' gesture.

He'd cut the fishing wire a moment previously, and now he belly-flopped to the door and peered underneath the gap. He could just about make out the white porcelain trunk of a toilet, and realized it was the bathroom. He got to his hands and knees and minutely scanned the doorknob.

Then, gently, infinitely slowly, he pushed the door open.

The allotments, she was glad to see, were deserted. Hillary ran quickly along the grass pathways and out on to the road, where she then walked more circumspectly to the T-junction, relieved to see Janine's car parked where she'd said it would be.

She was careful to wait until there was no traffic passing before she opened the boot and saw a blue, soft-leather handbag, wrapped in a clear plastic bag, resting on top of the spare wheel. She removed it and slung it across her shoulder.

As she did so, she heard the unmistakable sound of a dustbin lorry.

Unable to believe her luck, she glanced up and down and noticed for the first tine that the pavements were lined with blue and brown bins.

'Yes!' It was like a gift from fate.

She hurriedly walked up to the nearest bin and emptied the contents of Janine's bag into one bin, careful to remove any identifying papers first. Then she frantically ripped out the silk lining on the bag and stuffed it into another bin further down, before finally putting the bag itself into yet a third bin.

Perhaps the precaution was overkill, but Hillary was in no mood to take chances.

Then, hiding the blue leather bag as best she could under her coat, she ran across the allotments and back to Janine.

She was breathless by the time she got there, but at least Mel's widow was still alone.

'All right. Let's go over the story again,' Hillary said. 'Now, when you parked the car, did anybody notice you get out? Any old lady walking a dog, or a mother pushing a toddler's chair?'

'No.'

'Anybody on the allotments?'

'Yes, the old man who was hoeing.'

Hillary drew her breath in sharply. 'Did he get a good look at you?'

Janine nodded miserably.

'Then he probably saw the bag you were carrying,' Hillary responded grimly. 'Your old one was black, this is blue. Let's just hope he wasn't very observant.' She thought it unlikely the man would remember. From bitter experience she knew just how unobservant witnesses could be. 'Anyone else?'

'No. There was a middle-aged woman going into one of the sheds, but I saw her, she didn't see me.'

'OK, so it's just the one witness. He's old, and was presumably a fair few feet away when he saw you?'

'A good fifty yards, I'd say, boss,' Janine said, automatically using her old title for Hillary.

'OK. So we've got eyewitness covered, and we've got some of the forensics sorted. Just a sec.' She scooted back to the doorway of the shed, and glanced inside.

What she saw made her heart plunge. Clive Myers' hands were bare of any gloves – which meant that he should have left his fingerprints on the handgun.

Most people in her situation would have been tempted to take the gun and wrap Myers' fingers around it, but Hillary knew better. No matter how much you tried, it was hard to make a dead, unresponsive hand curve around a complicated piece of kit like a handgun in the same way as a living person's would.

Instead, Hillary stood on tiptoe and peered down into the long greasy canvas bag lying on the floor. Inside, she could see what looked as though it could be a beige-coloured glove, tossed carelessly down.

She longed to go and check, but daren't. Forensics would know at once if she'd gone inside, and she intended to tell them that she hadn't. It would make their story more believable. The less messing around with the scene she did, the better.

She went back to Janine. 'It makes sense for Myers to have been wearing gloves, right up until the time he set up the rifle,' Hillary said, explaining her thoughts. 'Then he'd have needed the tactile advantage of bare hands. That will explain his lack of prints on the handgun, and the presence of yours. Will your skell have had the sense to wipe the gun clean of his prints?'

'I gave the gun a good clean when I got it, boss,' Janine muttered.

Then she drew in a deep, shaky breath. 'I can't go to gaol,' she whispered. 'You know what a cop's life will be like in gaol.'

Hillary paled. 'You won't go to gaol,' she said, clutching Janine's hand compulsively. 'Nobody is going to want to jam you up. Myers is in there with a rifle, and was obviously about to try and kill DI Gregg. Ballistics will prove that it was the same gun that killed Mel. You acted in self-defence. OK, you shouldn't have been here, and you should have told someone the moment you saw Myers cut that hole in the window, but even that won't be enough to do you serious harm. And you can bet your life that the PR machine will go into overdrive to make sure that the media depicts you as the heroine of the hour – the pregnant widow of a murdered hero saving DI Gregg from the same killer. Nobody's going to be looking too hard for evidence to contradict our story.'

Which was true. Up to a point. But the investigation was bound to be painstaking, and Janine's part in it was bound to raise some serious issues. All it would take would be one unknown witness to come forward, or an unlucky piece of evidence to come to light and they'd both be in hot water.

'Remember, everyone's going to be on our side,' Hillary said, not sure whether she was trying to reassure Janine or herself.

Janine nodded and swallowed hard.

Hillary watched her closely. 'Listen to me, Janine. They'll be coming soon. They'll separate us, and grill us closely. You know how it is – the urge to confess everything will be immense. But once you do, once you deviate from the story, once you tell them you came here armed, it's all over. They'll have no choice but take it to trial. You might be lucky with the jury or you might not. But, like you said, you can't go to gaol. So stick to the story, no matter what. You have to ride it out, no matter how hard it gets. Do you understand that?'

Janine nodded. Then her eyes widened and she drew in her breath sharply, her arms hugging her middle.

'What?' Hillary asked sharply.

'My stomach's killing me,' Janine said. 'It's been playing me up all day.'

The words hit Hillary like a hammer blow, and for one sickening moment, she felt the world tilt suddenly around her. She took a staggering step backwards. Then, white-faced, she fumbled for her mobile and dialled 999.

In Thame, Neville Colt stared down at a small cassette recorder on the bathroom floor. The fishing line had been attached to it. But he had no desire to switch it on and listen to Clive Myers' message.

Instead he left the room as it was, backed out and had a quick whispered conversation with the two men on the stairs. Then he went back to the next door, cut the fishing line, and went in.

It was a small bedroom, feminine in appearance, with posters of a pop group fixed on the walls. Again, there was a cassette recorder.

Grimly now, almost sure of what he'd find, Neville Colt went to the last door. This must be the master bedroom. This would be where Clive Myers, if he was at home, was lying in wait.

He cut the fishing line, turned his head to nod at the two armed men behind him, checked the door handle, then opened the door from his prone position and lay flat as the two men vaulted over him and went in.

Neville quickly followed when they gave the all clear. The room was empty. Inside, the now expected cassette player was placed on the floor by the bed.

Neville got to his feet. It was time to go down and check the lounge door and let those two poor sods sweating it out downstairs get out and back to their families.

'Yes, I need an ambulance,' Hillary Greene said to the female voice that answered her call. She cited her rank and gave the address. 'I have a pregnant woman in difficulties,' she added curtly.

On being told one would be there within five minutes, Hillary thanked the voice and hung up.

'Why'd you do that?' Janine asked, genuinely puzzled.

Hillary looked at her helplessly. Did she really not realize how ominous a 'stomach ache' from a pregnant woman sounded? Obviously she didn't. And remembering Janine's problems with hypertension, and not wanting to scare her even further, Hillary forced herself to smile craftily. Silently, she tapped a finger to her temple.

'Think about it, Janine. If you get carted off to hospital, they can hardly question you right away, can they? It'll give you some breathing space and give *me* time to get my version in first. Hopefully, if you can convince the docs that you need to be kept in overnight, by the time they get around to questioning you most of the hard work will already have been done.'

Janine nodded, impressed. Trust Hillary to think of everything. 'Look, boss, thanks for all this. I know you're going out on a limb for me. Well, I know it's really for Mel, but well, you know. I *am* grateful. I know you well enough to know this can't be sitting right with you either. So thanks.'

Hillary swallowed a hard lump in her throat and nodded. Then she stared dialling another number.

Janine watched her, fascinated. She began to feel oddly unfocused and vague. In fact, she felt as if she could just curl up and go to sleep, and recognized the symptoms of shock. Suddenly she yawned hugely.

'I need to speak to Chief Superintendent Donleavy,' Hillary Greene said into the phone.

'I'm afraid he's in a meeting,' the calm voice of his secretary informed her.

'It's urgent,' Hillary insisted. 'This is DI Greene. Please interrupt the meeting and tell him I need him to come to the phone at once. It's crucial that he does so.'

Donleavy's secretary knew a crisis when she heard one. And, like most good secretaries, she also knew who those individuals were whom her boss trusted, and would want to speak to at such a time, and who were those that he wouldn't. 'Just one moment.'

Hillary watched Janine anxiously, her eyes on the blonde

woman's legs. No blood was running down them, so surely a miscarriage couldn't be imminent, could it? She didn't know what she'd do if her old friend's unborn child should be lost now.

In the distance she could hear a siren. No doubt the police officers watching Gregg's house would be thrown into a flap, wondering if it could be a diversion.

'DI Greene?' Donleavy's voice in her ear distracted her thoughts.

'Sir. We have a problem,' she said, with massive understatement.

In Thame, DCI Evans slapped the backs of Mervyn Jones and Ray Potter as they jogged past him.

'Well done lads,' Evans said, grinning.

'Guv.' Both men nodded. They knew they'd have to give statements back at the nick before they could even think of going home, and Evans, understanding their need, let them go without much more than a cursory nod.

He looked back at the house and waited for Neville Colt to join him. Briefly, as he climbed out of his heavy protective clothing, the bomb disposal man gave him a run down of what he'd found.

'So no explosives at all?' Evans asked, surprised.

'None. Only these in each of the rooms upstairs.' Neville held out one of the cassette recorders. Evans stared at it as though it was a live cobra, making no move to handle it.

'It's OK,' Colt said, with a grin. 'I've gone over it. It's perfectly safe. By the way, my lads will be at the house most of the night, just making sure there's nothing nasty hidden away in there. But my guess is there never were any explosives in there.'

DCI Evans nodded. He picked up the cassette recorder and depressed the PLAY button. And nearly dropped it, as a loud recorded BOOM echoed around the street.

Two of the bomb disposal men stopped and looked at them

curiously. Evans, shaken and sick to his stomach, could only shake his head as Neville Colt burst into laughter. But then, the bomb squad, Evans knew, were famous for their weird sense of humour.

CHAPTER FIFTEEN

It felt strange being interviewed in her own nick. Granted, they were not downstairs in an interview room, and she hadn't, obviously, asked to have a solicitor present. But even so, Hillary felt a distinct sense of irony as she took a seat in front of Marcus Donleavy's desk. The chief superintendent sighed, and rubbed a hand across his forehead.

It was nearly eight o'clock at night, and it had been a long day. Next to Hillary sat DCI Gawain Evans and Marcus's secretary who, having been asked to work late, was now taking notes. A machine recorded all that was being said. A record somewhat belying Marcus Donleavy's opening words.

'This is, of course, an unofficial interview, Hillary. That will take place some time tomorrow afternoon, I imagine, with an independent review board. Right now, this is simply a fact-finding operation. Are we all agreed?'

Hillary smiled wryly. Everybody in the room knew that this debriefing was bound to be the starting point for any inquiry, and set the tone for the whole procedure. But both DCI Evans and Hillary were willing to play along. After all, it suited them both.

'First of all, Hillary, have you heard from the Radcliffe concerning Inspector Mallow's condition?'

Hillary cleared her throat carefully. 'She's still under observation sir. Her gynaecologist isn't happy about her level of hypertension, and she's been given a course of drugs to help prevent miscarriage. But they want to keep her in overnight, and they're still not saying if she can go home tomorrow. From what I can gather, I think it unlikely. She's had a severe shock, after all, and even without the complications of pregnancy, DI Mallow needs time to recover.'

Donleavy gave a crooked grin. Now the gauntlet had been thrown down, and any officer assigned to interview Janine Mallow was well and truly warned. If she should have a miscarriage at any point, guilt had just been apportioned, before the first word had been spoken. As had been Hillary's intention all along, of course. And it all but guaranteed that any questioning of her ex-sergeant would be gentle.

Beside Hillary Greene, DCI Evans caught Donleavy's eye and carefully looked away. Like Donleavy, he understood what was happening here, and was beginning to understand just why DI Hillary Greene's stock was so high at Thames Valley.

He hadn't really got to know the woman during the Mallow investigation, and he was beginning to realize that it was very much his loss.

'Quite. Perhaps, DI Greene, you could give your report now?' Donleavy said quietly.

Hillary spoke slowly and carefully for nearly half an hour as she described the events of that afternoon, beginning with the desperate plea for help from Janine that she'd taken in Paul Danvers' room and ending with the arrival of Donleavy on the scene. After she'd finished, the chief superintendent asked her a few clarifying questions, and then dismissed her.

'Go home and get some rest,' he ordered briefly. 'I'll see that you're not bothered again tonight.'

Hillary nodded gratefully, turned and left. Both men watched her straight-backed, calm exit, then Donleavy sighed, and turned off the tape recorder. He dismissed his secretary with gratitude and asked her if she could stay on even longer and transcribe the notes. She, of course, agreed and left quietly.

Evans had apprised them all of the events in Thame. He'd been in the car heading back to HQ when news had broken of the events in a small orange shed back in Kidlington, which had so unexpectedly solved and closed his case. Now, the senior officers looked at one another thoughtfully.

'Well, it all seems straightforward enough,' Evans began cautiously. 'Any news from forensics yet?'

'Only early prelims,' Donleavy said. 'But there's nothing to contradict DI Greene's version of events.'

Yet.

The unspoken word lay ominously between them.

Evans sighed and stretched. He'd be glad to get back to London, and he certainly didn't envy Donleavy the months ahead. Even if an independent inquiry finally cleared Janine Mallow of any major wrongdoing, the press was still going to have a field day. And if, as both men privately thought, there was just a little bit more to the Myers' affair than met the eye, then things could get very nasty, very quickly.

'Well,' Evans said, 'I need to stand down the team. And they're still mopping up in Thame. I'd better show my face back there.'

Both men rose and solemnly shook hands.

The next morning Hillary came in early. And, as expected, the moment she stepped into the lobby all conversation stopped, leaving a heavy silence. Then the desk sergeant called out a cheerful greeting. Hillary smiled at him wanly and nodded.

Hillary knew as she climbed the stairs that everybody would have heard what had happened, and formed an opinion by now. And she had a very good idea what the majority of her fellow officers were thinking.

In the main office she endured a similar drop in noise level as she walked through the door. Then Sam Waterstone, at his desk by the door, was the first to talk to her, his voice loud and meant to be heard.

'Hello, Hill. A good result yesterday. Well done.'

Hillary nodded. 'Thanks, Sam. It's not the way I would have wanted it, but I'm not complaining.'

Her words broke the spell, and by the time she'd got to her desk she'd had her back metaphorically slapped by all those she passed, and their unstinting support gave her a boost.

Not surprisingly, she'd hardly slept a wink.

She slung her bag on to her desk, and set to work. And the first thing on her agenda was to get an arrest warrant in the Eddie Philpott case before she could be waylaid by the review board. She reached for the telephone, glad to find her favourite judge had just got in to his office, and got the paperwork under way.

Keith Barrington was next in; he shot Hillary a quick glance as he settled himself at his desk. Like everyone else, he was dying to ask her for a first-hand account of yesterday's events, but didn't have the nerve. Gemma and, to Hillary's surprise, Frank Ross came in together, Ross giving her a quick, assessing look.

'So the blonde bombshell offed Myers then,' he said bluntly. 'Good for her. And at least you had the guts to stick by her,' he added grudgingly.

It was, Hillary thought with a wince, what everyone else was thinking but not saying.

'Lovely to see you too, Frank,' she said drily, earning a few smiles and sniggers from the rest of the room. 'Since you've decided to put in a full day's work for once, you can nip down to the county court and get this.'

She waved the arrest warrant documents at him. He sighed and reached for them. He'd just started to rise when Hillary saw him pause and begin to smile. And since a smiling Frank Ross was always guaranteed to be a cause for alarm, Hillary too rose and turned around. Superintendent Brian Vane was crossing the room towards her. His face was tight with some kind of suppressed emotion, and Hillary felt her spine stiffen.

DCI Danvers also spotted him and quickly emerged from his cubicle to follow his immediate superior to Hillary's desk.

Gemma felt the room become tense and quiet and felt her

own nerves stretch. She glanced quickly at her boss, wondering whether Hillary knew what it was all about, but her DI's face was as tight and grim as Vane's own.

'So, DI Greene,' Brian Vane's opening words, quiet though they were, carried clearly. 'You chose to ignore all my warnings and get involved in DCI Evans's operation?'

Hillary sighed slightly. 'You're mistaken sir,' she said levelly. 'I've had nothing to do with Mel's case.'

'Don't give me that!' Vane responded. 'I distinctly remember telling you not to encourage DI Janine Mallow's unfortunate and insubordinate determination to interfere in the investigation into her husband's murder.'

'Yes sir,' Hillary remained cool. 'And I did my best to—'

'Did you or did you not tell her to do a house-to-house of the main road, looking for reluctant witnesses to Superintendent Mallow's shooting?'

Hillary tensed. Shit. Who had told him that? She caught Frank Ross smirking, and shot him a quick, keen look that everyone in the room caught.

The silence suddenly became electric.

'Janine needed to do something, sir, she was going mad being inactive. And since she was suffering with hypertension, which could have threatened her pregnancy, I thought some harmless activity—'

'That's enough!' Vane said. He hadn't yet raised his voice, but it trembled with either triumph or anger – Hillary couldn't tell which. 'When you received that call for help from DI Mallow yesterday, it was your duty to report it instantly to your superior officer. You had no authority to go to the scene or interfere. Is that clear?'

'Yes sir.'

'A fact I'm sure the inquiry will also be keen to underline,' Vane emphasized, making it clear that he'd make damn sure of it.

'I'm sure they will sir,' Hillary agreed meekly.

Vane's eyes narrowed suspiciously, as a belated sense of self-preservation rippled over him.

When he'd heard about what had happened yesterday, he'd been overjoyed. It had dismayed him to learn that DI Hillary Greene was going to be assigned so closely to him, and he'd been searching ever since for ways to get her shuffled off sideways. With yesterday's débâcle, he'd thought the opportunity had at last been handed to him on a platter. She'd broken so many rules there was no way she was going to get off with anything less than a severe disciplinary warning. Maybe more. Consequently, he'd been looking forward to this confrontation all morning. Now though, he felt the first shimmer of unease. Somehow it was all getting away from him, yet even though he couldn't tell how, he knew that Hillary Greene was to blame.

'I'll be talking to the Chief Constable later, DI Greene,' he said. 'I'm warning you now, I take an extremely serious view of your conduct.'

'Yes sir.'

Brian Vane glanced around and became aware of a hostile wave of eyes watching him. He nodded briefly at Danvers, firmed his lips closely together and began to walk away.

Hillary let him get almost halfway across the room before turning to Paul and saying in a clear voice. 'Sir, I'm sending Frank to the courts for the arrest warrant. Can I bring in my chief suspect in the Philpott case?'

Danvers blinked, caught by surprise, and opened his mouth to tell her that he needed to be briefed first, since he had no idea what she was on about. But then he realized that he could do no such thing – he simply could not let her down with the whole room watching and listening.

'Of course, DI Greene. You're confident of the outcome?' he asked, needing some sort of reassurance from her none the less.

Hillary smiled her gratitude at him, knowing full well that she now owed him one. 'Yes sir. I think a full confession is likely,' she said confidently.

'Good work, DI Greene,' Paul said warmly, and Brian Vane's back stiffened as he continued through the silent room and out of the door.

'Silly bastard,' Frank Ross said furiously, glaring at Vane's back. He knew, as Hillary knew, that Vane had just seriously blown it.

Ross's apparent condemnation broke the silence, and somebody began to laugh.

Danvers retreated back to his office and sat shakily down in his seat. Only now was the enormity of what he'd just done beginning to sink in. He'd given Hillary the authority to arrest someone for murder without having the least idea of who it was, or why Hillary thought him or her guilty. More than that, he'd just helped her in whatever power play she was conducting against Vane.

And all of that with possible disciplinary charges hovering over her. It had not been smart – and he wouldn't have done it for anybody else. He only hoped Hillary knew just what the hell she was doing.

It was only then that DCI Paul Danvers began to realize just how deeply his feelings for Hillary Greene was affecting his judgement. And knew that something would have to be done about it.

'Gemma, you're with me,' Hillary said crisply to her sergeant, who nodded calmly and reached for her bag.

Outside, they took Gemma's car, with the sergeant driving. It wasn't until they were pulling out of the car park that Gemma realized she had no idea where they were going.

'Which way, Guv?'

'The Knott,' Hillary said briskly.

Gemma drove, her hands feeling tense on the wheel. Like everyone else, she was overflowing with adrenaline, and felt twitchy. 'That was some scene back there,' she remarked, deciding now to take the bull by the horns.

Hillary, who was staring morosely out of the window, turned

and looked at her, almost uncomprehendingly. Gemma swallowed hard. Damn, her boss had some balls. She'd just taken on a Detective Superintendent, and seemed practically not to have noticed. 'With Vane,' she added. 'Guv, was it wise to make an enemy of him like that?' she added nervously.

Hillary grunted. 'Vane always was my enemy,' she said darkly. 'And there's nothing I can do about it, so there's no point wasting any effort soft-soaping him.'

Gemma drew in a sharp breath. 'So the scuttlebutt's right,' she said, making Hillary turn her head sharply.

'What scuttlebutt?' she asked, and listened as Gemma told her that the whole station was wondering why she and the super were at loggerheads.

'That nick's worse than living on bloody Coronation Street,' Hillary grumbled.

'But won't Vane have the perfect excuse to get rid of you now, Guv?' Gemma asked nervously. For better or worse, Hillary Greene was the key to her own promotional prospects, and should Hillary fall from grace, any kudos Gemma had gained from working with her would quickly fade away.

Hillary glanced across at her and grinned. 'Don't worry,' she said softly. 'Let me tell you a few facts of life, Sergeant. Nearly everybody at that HQ loved Mel Mallow. And all of them have been choking down outrage and bile for months at having his killer swanning around and sticking up two fingers at us. Now Mel's wife has killed him, and everybody back there is now doing a mental jive in celebration, even if they can't openly show it in front of the brass. Are you with me so far?'

Gemma nodded. She knew from overhearing the uniforms in the car park that Hillary was right. Everyone had been gleeful over Janine Mallow's shooting of Clive Myers, and considered it righteous. Especially since word had come back from Wales about the discovery of Gary Firth's body. Added to that, ballistics had been working all night, and just an hour ago had confirmed that the rifle found in the shed had been the same weapon that had been used in the killing of Detective Superintendent Phillip Mallow.

'Right,' she said.

'And, by association, everyone is on my side for sticking by her, and putting my arse on the line as well. Right?' Hillary said, without any indication of either pleasure or pride in what she'd done.

Gemma glanced at her warily. 'Right.'

'And now Vane has just publicly given me a rollicking, practically admitting that he's going to do everything he can to see me go down for it. Yes?'

'Right again.'

'So what do you think people are doing now, back at HQ?'

Gemma sighed. 'Guv, the fact that the rank and file are on your side won't help you when Vane starts talking to the chief constable,' she warned.

Hillary sighed patiently. 'You're still not getting it. Think like the top brass. They have a potential PR and media nightmare looming. All they can do is ride it and try to direct it. So Janine Mallow is going to be the heroine of the hour. She prevented Clive Myers from claiming his third victim, a serving police officer. Right now, she's in hospital, bravely fighting to keep her baby. What do you think's going to happen to anyone who tries to rock the boat?'

Gemma grinned.

'Oh.'

Hillary smiled grimly. 'Yes. Oh. The chief constable is not going to take too kindly to Vane stirring up an ants' nest right now. Not with reporters skulking about, hot for a story. He's going to be told to tow the line and shut up.'

Gemma let out her breath in a slow whoosh.

'Why do you think Frank called him a stupid bastard?' Hillary asked, beginning to smile. 'Let's face it, he was hardly likely to be sticking up for me, was he?'

Gemma laughed.

Then frowned.

'Guv?'

'What?'

'Who are we about to arrest? For Philpott's murder I mean?'

'The obvious suspect,' replied Hillary. 'Nine times out of ten, Sergeant, it's always the obvious suspect who did it.'

Gemma frowned. 'Oh. Right.'

Half an hour later Donleavy entered the observation room and nodded to a nervous-looking Paul Danvers. Both men turned to face the one-way mirror. Inside interview room number three, Hillary Greene and Gemma Fordham sat facing Rachel Warner.

'She's the daughter of the victim, I understand?' Donleavy said calmly.

'Yes sir. She's also dying of cancer.'

Donleavy sighed heavily. Like Danvers, he hoped Hillary knew what she was doing. A successful conclusion to her latest murder case would do her the world of good right now. But another disaster could bury her.

'The time is 10.20.' Gemma Fordham began to go over the ritual for the tape, intoning the names and ranks of those present, stating that Rachel Warner had waived the right to a solicitor, and adding that she could change her mind and have a solicitor present at any time. When she'd finished, there was a brief, almost sad silence.

Hillary slowly leaned forward and smiled at Rachel wearily. 'I'm sorry, Mrs Warner,' she said softly. 'I know this must be an ordeal for you. Do you need a doctor present? We have one on call at the station.'

'No, I'm fine for the moment.'

'If you feel you want to have medical attention at any time, you only have to say,' Hillary urged her seriously.

Rachel Warner looked at her and shrugged, as if to say, 'What's the point?' It was then that Hillary knew this was probably going to be the shortest interview of her career.

'Mrs Warner, I believe that you killed your father, Edward Philpott, on Monday last, the sixth of October. I believe you hit him on the back of his head with his spade, whilst he was working in his garden. Is this true?'

Rachel Warner looked at Hillary curiously. She felt tired, and for the first time in many, many weeks, faintly curious. It was as if dying had sucked all the minor, irritating emotions out of her.

'How did you know?' she asked curiously.

Hillary smiled briefly. 'The watch.'

Rachel frowned. 'My watch?'

'No. Your father's watch,' Hillary corrected. 'Well, yours too of course. The first day we talked, you told me you were afraid you were going to be late taking your children to school. Do you remember?'

'That's right, I was,' Rachel said. 'But we weren't late at all.'

'No. Your watch was slow, and needed batteries. Remember?'

'Yes. I still haven't got around to it.' Rachel stared down at the watch on her wrist, looking faintly puzzled.

'That morning, when you took the watch and ring from your father's body to make it look like a robbery, you automatically checked the time on your father's watch. What you didn't know was that that morning your father had put on his watch by half an hour in order not to be late for a meeting. That's why you thought you'd be late for school.'

'Oh.'

'What did you do with his watch and ring by the way?' Hillary asked casually.

'I threw them in the river. When I went for my walk after dropping the kids off.'

'Where exactly?'

'Off the little red-brick bridge, just before Jackson's meadow.'

Hillary nodded. The police divers would find it.

'I see.'

Rachel looked at Gemma, then at Hillary. 'Don't you want to know why I did it?' she asked, and for the first time since

Hillary and Gemma had appeared on her doorstep to take her in, she showed signs of tension.

Hillary rubbed a tired hand across her head and sighed heavily. 'I'm sorry Rachel. But we already know why.'

Gemma shifted on her seat beside Hillary.

Like the two men silently watching, Gemma had felt an enormous sense of relief when Rachel Warner had admitted to killing her father. It showed Hillary had got it right, yet again. And after telling them where to find her father's watch and ring, there would be physical evidence as well.

But Gemma had no idea why Rachel had killed her father, and she couldn't for the life of her think why she should have. In fact, it made no sense to her, even now. Surely Rachel had needed her father to take care of her kids, who now faced an incredibly uncertain future?

'It was because of Linda Quirke, wasn't it?' Hillary Greene said softly, and Gemma looked up quickly.

Rachel Warner was staring, appalled at Hillary. 'Please don't,' she said, her eyes filling with tears. Hillary made a small sound, quickly pulled a pack of tissues from her purse and handed them over.

'I'm sorry,' she said, yet again. 'I'll make it as quick as I can, but it has to be done. You do see that, don't you?'

Rachel gulped and buried her face in a tissue.

'I tell you what, let me ask the questions and you simply say yes or no. How about that?' Hillary asked softly. Strictly speaking, this interview was breaking a few rules, but since Hillary knew the case would never come to trial – Rachel would be dead before that could happen – she knew that the CPS wouldn't have any cause to complain about sloppy interview techniques.

'What put me on to it was the timing of your mother leaving your father. She left within two months of Linda Quirke going missing,' Hillary began. 'She suspected your father of having something to do with that, didn't she?'

Rachel's eyes peered fearfully over the top of the tissue. 'Yes,' she whispered. 'I heard them arguing one night, when they thought I was in bed.'

'But you never believed it,' Hillary said gently.

'No, of course not! I loved my father.'

'But, all these years later, when you were diagnosed with a terminal illness, you couldn't help but begin to wonder,' Hillary said gently.

Rachel gave a reluctant nod.

'And your circumstances couldn't be worse, could they?' Hillary carried on, and with genuine sympathy. 'Your husband was dead, and you'd been living in your father's house for several years. And after you were gone, your father would almost certainly be granted custody of your children.'

'Yes,' Rachel whispered, staring at Hillary with all the fascination of a rabbit for a snake.

'And to make matter's worse, your daughter, Julie, was the same age as Linda was, when she went missing.'

Rachel nodded and gulped.

'Why didn't you just have a word with the child welfare people, Rachel?' Hillary asked with some reluctance. 'If you'd explained your fears, maybe you could have come to some other arrangement. You didn't have to kill him.'

'Oh, I couldn't,' Rachel said passionately. 'I couldn't tell the world that I thought my dad was some sort of pervert. A child killer! How would my poor Mark and Julie have felt, growing up with the world thinking their granddad was some foul thing?'

Hillary took a long slow breath.

'So you decided the only thing you could do was kill him?'

'Yes. It happened just like you said. I made sure the kids were in the front room, then went out into the garden. I just waited until he had his back to me and then I hit him. I'm not sure how I got the strength. Then I took the watch and ring, took the kids to school, dumped his things in the river and called you. I never thought you'd figure it out,' she added artlessly. Then she gave an exhausted smiled. 'But really, it doesn't matter, does it? That you have, I mean?'

No, Hillary thought sadly. *I don't suppose it does, at that.*

It was a very sombre group of people that went back to Hillary's desk. Donleavy congratulated her, very publicly, for another job well done, and went back to his room. Ever the politician, he'd wanted to be seen by everyone not to be tarred with the same brush as Vane.

Danvers sat half on and half off her desk and swung a leg thoughtfully. 'She won't stand trial, of course,' he said.

'No,' Hillary agreed. Normally, at this point, she'd suggest a celebratory drink at her local pub, but nobody was in any mood for self-congratulation.

'So do you think he did it?' Barrington asked. 'Edward Philpott, I mean. Did he kill Linda Quirke?'

'We'll probably never know,' Hillary answered. 'But there's bound to be a renewed investigation into the Quirke case. Who knows, the wife might have got it wrong? Personally, I think she probably used Linda Quirke as an excuse to get out of an unhappy marriage.'

'What makes you think that?' Gemma asked, aware that many ears were tuned in as others wondered the same thing.

'Think about it,' Hillary said. 'If you thought your old man had had something to do with a young girl's disappearance, would you then leave your two young children behind in that same man's care?'

Danvers blinked. 'Not unless he terrified her into it.'

Hillary shrugged. 'Like I said. We'll probably never know. Rachel Warner had a horrible fear that he *was* guilty and in the end, that's what counted.'

Gemma shook her head. 'Shit. I never thought the time would come when I'd feel sorry for a killer.'

'She was on strong medication,' Barrington put in tentatively. 'That could have affected her judgement.'

Hillary slowly leaned back in her chair.

'You look like hell,' Danvers said firmly. 'Why don't you take the rest of the day off? I can organize the divers and do the paperwork.'

Hillary nodded. 'Thanks. I think I will.'

That afternoon, she lay on her narrow bunk, staring up at the ceiling of the boat.

She supposed she should feel depressed, but for some reason she didn't. Her murder case had been solved, but bringing in a dying woman desperate to save her children was hardly designed to make anyone feel good.

Janine Mallow had yet to be questioned by anyone, but if she should break, both she and probably Hillary could end up serving time. As they would, if forensics threw their story a curve, or if Janine's skell talked, or if any witnesses turned up.

And with Vane hovering in the wings, with nothing to lose if he could manage to stick the knife into her, she should be feeling as miserable as sin.

So why wasn't she?

Although she was no psychologist, it didn't take Hillary long to understand why, for the first time in months, she was suddenly starting to feel better.

It was because, at last, the guilt she'd felt over Mel was lifting. She'd stood by whilst he died right beside her, then stood by again while a stranger investigated his case. But now, in saving Janine, albeit at the potential cost to her own career and freedom, she'd redeemed herself.

It would have been no good saving Janine if she hadn't had to risk something in order to do it. But now she could forgive herself at last.

And with that thought, Hillary Greene rolled over on her bed, closed her eyes and fell deeply asleep.

226